WILLIAM A. ALCOTT
THE YOUNG MAN'S GUIDE

WILLIAM A. ALCOTT
THE YOUNG MAN'S GUIDE

# THE YOUNG MAN'S GUIDE

## BY WILLIAM A. ALCOTT

# CONTENTS

# CHAPTER I.

On the Formation of Character. - SECTION I. *Importance of aiming high, in the formation of character.*

To those who have carefully examined the introduction and table of contents, I am now prepared to give the following general direction; *Fix upon a high standard of character.* To be *thought* well of, is not sufficient. The point you are to aim at, is, the greatest possible degree of usefulness.

Some may think there is danger of setting *too high* a standard of action. I have heard teachers contend that a child will learn to write much faster by having an *inferior copy*, than by imitating one which is comparatively perfect; 'because,' say they, 'a pupil is liable to be discouraged if you give him a *perfect* copy; but if it is only a little in advance of his own, he will take courage from the belief that he shall soon be able to equal it.' I am fully convinced, however, that this is not so. The *more* perfect the copy you place before the child, provided it be *written*, and not *engraved*, the better. For it must always be *possible* in the nature of things, for the child to imitate it; and what is not absolutely impossible, every child may reasonably be expected to aspire after, on the principle, that whatever man *has done*, man *may* do.

So in human conduct, generally; whatever is possible should be aimed at. Did my limits permit, I might show that it is a part of the divine economy to place before his rational creatures a perfect standard of action, and to make it their duty to come up to it.

He who only aims at *little*, will *accomplish* but little. *Expect* great things, and *attempt* great things. A neglect of this rule produces more of the difference in the character, conduct, and success of men, than is commonly supposed. Some start in life without any leading object at all; some with a low one; and some aim high:—and just in proportion to the elevation at which they aim, will be their progress and success. It is an old proverb that he who aims at the sun, will not reach it, to be sure, but his arrow will fly higher than if he aims at an object on a level with himself. Exactly so is it, in the formation of character, except in one point. To reach the sun with a arrow is an impossibility, but a youth may aim high without attempting impossibilities.

Let me repeat the assurance that, as a general rule, *you may be whatever you will resolve to be.* Determine that you will be useful in the world, and you *shall* be. Young men seem to me utterly unconscious of what they are capable of being and doing. Their efforts are often few and feeble, because they are not awake to a full conviction that any thing great or distinguished is in their power.

But whence came en Alexander, a Cæsar, a Charles XII, or a Napoleon? Or whence the better order of spirits,—a Paul, an Alfred, a Luther, a Howard, a Penn, a Washington? Were not these men once like yourselves? What but self exertion, aided by the blessing of Heaven, rendered these men so conspicuous for usefulness? Rely upon it,—what these men once *were*, you *may be*. Or at the least, you may make a nearer approach to them, than you are ready to believe. Resolution is almost omnipotent. Those little words, *try*, and *begin*, are sometimes great in their results. 'I can't,' never accomplished any thing;—'I will try,' has achieved wonders.

This position might be proved and illustrated by innumerable facts; but one must suffice.

I

A young man who had wasted his patrimony by profligacy, whilst standing, one day, on the brow of a precipice from which he had determined to throw himself, formed the sudden resolution to regain what he had lost. The purpose thus formed was kept; and though he began by shoveling a load of coals into a cellar, for which he only received twelve and a half cents, yet he proceeded from one step to another till he more than recovered his lost possessions, and died worth sixty thousand pounds sterling.

You will derive much advantage from a careful perusal of the lives of eminent individuals, especially of those who were *good* as well as great. You will derive comparatively little benefit from reading the lives of those scourges of their race who have drenched the earth in blood, except so far as it tends to show you what an immense blessing they *might* have been to the world, had they devoted to the work of human improvement those mighty energies which were employed in human destruction. Could the physical and intellectual energy of Napoleon, the order and method of Alfred, the industry, frugality, and wisdom of Franklin and Washington, and the excellence and untiring perseverance of Paul, and Penn, and Howard, be united in each individual of the rising generation, who can set limits to the good, which they might, and inevitably would accomplish! Is it too much to hope that some happier age will witness the reality? Is it not even probable that the rising generation may afford many such examples?

SECTION II. *On Motives to action.* - Not a few young men either have no fixed principles, no governing motive at all, or they are influenced by those which are low and unworthy. It is painful to say this, but it is too true. On such, I would press the importance of the following considerations.

Among the motives to action which I would present, the first is a regard to *your own happiness*. To this you are by no means indifferent at present. Nay, the attainment of happiness is your primary object. You seek it in every desire, word, and action. But you sometimes mistake the road that leads to it, either for the want of a friendly hand to guide you, or because you refuse to be guided. Or what is most common, you grasp at a smaller good, which is near, and apparently certain, and in so doing cut yourselves off from the enjoyment of a good which is often infinitely greater, though more remote.

Let me urge, in the second place, a regard for the family to which you belong. It is true you can never fully know, unless the bitterness of ingratitude should teach you, the extent of the duty you owe to your relatives; and especially to your parents. You *cannot* know—at least till you are parents yourselves,—how their hearts are bound up in yours. But if you do not *in some measure* know it, till this late period, you are not fit to be parents.

In the third place, it is due to society, particularly to the neighborhood or sphere in which you move, and to the *associations* to which you may belong, that you strive to attain a very great elevation of character. Here, too, I am well aware that it is impossible, at your age, to perceive fully, how much you have it in your power to contribute, if you will, to the happiness of those around you; and here again let me refer you to the advice and guidance of aged friends.

But, fourthly, it is due to the nation and age to which you belong, that you fix upon a high standard of character. This work is intended for American youth. *American!* did I say? This word, alone, ought to call forth all your energies, and if there be a slumbering faculty within you, arouse it to action. Never, since the creation, were the youth of any age or country so imperiously called upon to exert themselves, as those whom I now address. Never before were there so many important interests at stake. Never were such immense results depending upon a generation of men, as upon that which is now approaching the stage of action. These rising millions are destined, according to all human probability, to form by far the greatest nation that ever constituted an entire community of freemen, since the world began. To form the character of these millions involves a greater amount of responsibility, individual and collective, than any other work to which humanity has ever been called. And the reasons are, it seems to me, obvious.

Now it is for you, my young friends, to determine whether these weighty responsibilities shall be fulfilled. It is for you to decide whether this *greatest* of free nations shall, at the same time, be the *best*. And as every nation is made up of individuals, you are each, in reality, called upon daily, to settle this question: 'Shall the United States, possessing the most ample means of instruction within the reach of nearly all her citizens, the happiest government, the healthiest of climates, the greatest abundance of the best and most wholesome nutriment, with every other possible means for developing all the powers of human nature, be peopled with the most vigorous, powerful, and happy race of human beings which the world has ever known?'

There is another motive to which I beg leave, for one moment, to direct your attention. You are bound to fix on a high standard of action, from the desire of obeying the will of God. *He* it is who has cast your lot in a country which—all things considered—is the happiest below the sun. *He* it is who has given you such a wonderful capacity for happiness, and instituted the delightful relations of parent and child, and brother and sister, and friend and neighbor. I might add, *He* it is, too, who has given you the name *American*,—a name which alone furnishes a passport to many civilized lands, and like a good countenance, or a becoming dress, prepossesses every body in your favor.

But what young man is there, I may be asked, who is not influenced more or less, by all the motives which have been enumerated? Who is there that does not seek his own happiness? Who does not desire to please his parents and other relatives, his friends and his neighbors? Who does not wish to be distinguished for his attachment to country and to liberty? Nay, who has not even some regard, in his conduct, to the will of God?

I grant that many young men, probably the most of those into whose hands this book will be likely to fall, are influenced, more or less, by all these considerations. All pursue their own happiness, no doubt. By far the majority of the young have, also, a general respect for the good opinion of others, and the laws of the Creator.

Still, do not thousands and tens of thousands mistake, as I have already intimated, in regard to what really promotes their own happiness? Is there any certainty that the greatest happiness of a *creature* can be secured without consulting the will of the Creator? And do not those young persons greatly err, who suppose that they can secure a full amount, even of earthly blessings, without conforming, with the utmost strictness, to those rules for conduct, which the Bible and the Book of Nature, so plainly make known?

Too many young men expect happiness from wealth. This is their great object of study and action, by night and by day. Not that they suppose there is an inherent value in the wealth itself, but only that it will secure the means of procuring the *happiness* they so ardently desire. But the farther they go, in the pursuit of wealth, for the sake of happiness, especially if successful in their plans and business, the more they forget their original purpose, and seek wealth for the *sake* of wealth. To *get rich*, is their principal motive to action.

So it is in regard to the exclusive pursuit of sensual pleasure, or civil distinction. The farther we go, the more we lose our original character, and the more we become devoted to the objects of pursuit, and incapable of being roused by other motives.

The laws of God, whether we find them in the constitution of the universe around us, or go higher and seek them in the revealed word, are founded on a thorough knowledge of human nature, and all its tendencies. Do you study natural science—the laws which govern matter, animate and inanimate? What is the lesson which it constantly inculcates, but that it is man's highest interest not to violate or attempt to violate the rules which Infinite Wisdom has adopted; and that every violation of his laws brings punishment along with it? Do you study the laws of God, as revealed in the Bible? And do not they, too, aim to inculcate the necessity of constant and endless obedience to his will, at the same time that their rejection is accompanied by the severest penalties which heaven and earth can inflict? What, in short, is the obvious design of the Creator, wherever and whenever any traces of his character and purposes can be discovered? What, indeed, but to show us that it is our most obvious duty and interest to love and obey Him?

The young man whose highest motives are to seek his own happiness, and please his friends and neighbors, and the world around him, does much. This should never be denied. He merits much—not in the eye of God, for of this I have nothing to say in this volume—but from his fellow men. And although he may have never performed a single action from a desire to obey God, and make his fellow men really *better*, as well as happier, he may still have been exceedingly useful, compared with a large proportion of mankind.

But suppose a young man possesses a character of this stamp—and such there are. How is he ennobled, how is the dignity of his nature advanced, how is he elevated from the rank of a mere companion of creatures,—earthly creatures, too,—to that of a meet companion and fit associate for the inhabitants of the celestial world, and the Father of all; when to these traits, so excellent and amiable in themselves, is joined the pure and exalted desire to pursue his studies and his employments, his pleasures and his pastimes—in a word, every thing—even the most trifling concern which is *worth* doing, exactly as God would wish to have it done; and make the *means* of so doing, his great and daily study?

This, then, brings us to the highest of human motives to action, the love of God. Thou shalt love the Lord thy God supremely, and thou shalt love thy neighbor as thyself, are the two great commands which bind the human family together. When our love to God is evinced by pure love to man, and it is our constant prayer, 'Lord what wilt thou have me to *do*;' then we come under the influence of motives which are worthy of creatures destined to immortality. When it is our meat and drink, from a sacred regard to the Father of our spirits, and of all things in the universe, material and immaterial, to make every thought, word and action, do good—have a bearing upon the welfare of one or more, and the more the better—of our race, then alone do we come up to the dignity of our nature, and, by Divine aid, place ourselves in the situation for which the God of nature and of grace designed us.

I have thus treated, at greater length than I had at first intended, of the importance of having an *elevated aim*, and of the *motives to action*. On the *means* by which young men are to attain this elevation, it is the purpose of this little work to dwell plainly and fully. These *means* might be classed in three great divisions; viz. *physical, mental,* and *moral.* Whatever relates to the health, belongs to the first division; whatever to the improvement of the mind, the second; and the formation of good manners and virtuous habits, constitutes the third. But although an arrangement of this sort might have been more logical, it would probably have been less interesting to the reader. The means of religious improvement, appropriately so called, require a volume of themselves.

SECTION III. *Industry.* - Nothing is more essential to usefulness and happiness in life, than habits of industry. 'This we commanded you,' says St. Paul, 'that if any would not work, neither should he eat.' Now this would be the sober dictate of good sense, had the apostle never spoken. It is just as true now as it was 2,000 years ago, that no person possessing a sound mind in a healthy body, has a right to live in this world without labor. If he claims an existence on any other condition, let him betake himself to some other planet.

There are many kinds of labor. Some which are no less useful than others, are almost exclusively mental. You may make your own selection from a very wide range of employments, all, perhaps, equally important to society. *But something you must do.* Even if you happen to inherit an ample fortune, your health and happiness demand that you should labor. To live in idleness, even if you have the means, is not only injurious to yourself, but a species of fraud upon the community, and the children,—if children you ever have,—who have a claim upon you for what you can earn and do.

Let me prevail with you then, when I urge you to set out in life fully determined to depend chiefly on yourself, for pecuniary support; and to be in this respect, independent. In a country where the general rule is that a person shall rise,—if he rise at all,—by his own merit, such a resolution is indispensable. It is usually idle to be looking out for support from some other quarter. Suppose you should obtain a place of office or trust through the friendship, favor, or affection of others; what then? Why, you hold your post at uncertainties. It may be taken from you at almost any hour. But if you depend on yourself alone, in this respect, your mountain stands strong, and cannot very easily be moved.

He who lives upon any thing except his own labor, is incessantly surrounded by rivals. He is in daily danger of being out-bidden; his very bread depends upon caprice, and he lives in a state of never ceasing fear. His is not, indeed, the dog's life, '*hunger* and idleness,' but it is worse; for it is 'idleness with *slavery*;' the latter being just the price of the former.

Slaves, are often well *fed* and decently *clothed*; but they dare not *speak.* They dare not be suspected even to *think* differently from their master, despise his acts as much as they may;—let him be tyrant, drunkard, fool, or all three at once, they must either be silent, or lose his approbation. Though possessing a thousand times his knowledge, they yield to his assumption of superior understanding; though knowing it is they who, in fact, do all that he is paid for doing, it is destruction to them to *seem as if they thought* any portion of the service belonged to themselves.

You smile, perhaps, and ask what all this tirade against slavery means. But remember, there is slavery of several kinds. There is *mental* slavery as well as bodily; and the former is not confined to any particular division of the United States.

Begin, too, with a determination to labor through life. There are many who suppose that when they have secured to themselves a competence, they shall sit with folded arms, in an easy chair, the rest of their days, and enjoy it. But they may be assured that this will never do. The very fact of a person's having spent the early and middle part of life in active usefulness, creates a necessity, to the body and mind, of its continuance. By this is not meant that men should labor as *hard* in old age, even in proportion to their strength, as in early life. Youth requires a great variety and amount of action, maturity not so much, and age still less. Yet so much as age does, in fact, demand, is more necessary than to those who are younger. Children are so tenacious of life, that they do not *appear* to *suffer immediately*, if exercise is neglected; though a day of reckoning must finally come.

Hence we see the reason why those who retire from business towards the close of life, so often become diseased, in body and mind; and instead of enjoying life, or making those around them happy, become a source of misery to themselves and others.

Most people have a general belief in the importance of industrious habits; and yet not a few make strange work in endeavoring to form them. Some attempt to do it by compulsion; others by flattery. Some think it is to be accomplished by set lessons, in spite of example; others by example alone.

A certain father who was deeply convinced of the importance of forming his sons to habits of industry, used to employ them whole days in removing and replacing heaps of stones. This was well intended, and arose from regarding industry as a high accomplishment; but there is some danger of defeating our own purpose in this way, and of producing *disgust*. Besides this, labor enough can usually be obtained which is obviously profitable.

All persons, without exception, ought to labor more or less, every day in the open air. Of the truth of this opinion, the public are beginning to be sensible; and hence we hear much said, lately, about manual labor schools. Those who, from particular circumstances, cannot labor in the open air, should substitute in its place some active mechanical employment, together with suitable calisthenic or gymnastic exercises.

It is a great misfortune of the present day, that almost every one is, by his own estimate, *raised above his real state of life*. Nearly every person you meet with is aiming at a situation in which he shall be exempted from the drudgery of laboring with his hands.

Now we cannot all become '*lords*' and '*gentlemen*,' if we would. There must be a large part of us, after all, to make and mend clothes and houses, and carry on trade and commerce, and, in spite of all that we can do, the far greater part of us must actually *work* at something; otherwise we fall under the sentence; 'He who will not *work* shall not *eat*.' Yet, so strong is the propensity to be *thought* 'gentlemen;' so general is this desire amongst the youth of this proud money making nation, that thousands upon thousands of them are, at this moment, in a state which may end in starvation; not so much because they are too *lazy* to earn their bread, as because they are too *proud*!

And what are the *consequences?* A lazy youth becomes a burden to those parents, whom he ought to comfort, if not support. Always aspiring to something higher than he can reach, his life is a life of disappointment and shame. If marriage *befall* him, it is a real affliction, involving others as well as himself. His lot is a thousand times worse than that of the common laborer. Nineteen times out of twenty a premature death awaits him: and, alas! how numerous are the cases in which that death is most miserable, not to say ignominious!

SECTION IV. *On Economy.* - There is a false, as well as a true economy. I have seen an individual who, with a view to economy, was in the habit of splitting his wafers. Sometimes a thick wafer can be split into two, which will answer a very good purpose; but at others, both parts fall to pieces. Let the success be ever so complete, however, all who reflect for a moment on the value of time, must see it to be a losing process.

I knew a laboring man who would hire a horse, and spend the greater part of a day, in going six or eight miles and purchasing half a dozen bushels of grain, at sixpence less a bushel than he must have given near home. Thus to gain fifty cents, he subjected himself to an expense, in time and money, of one hundred and fifty. These are very common examples of defective economy; and of that 'withholding' which the Scripture says 'tends to poverty.'

Economy in time is economy of money—for it needs not Franklin to tell us that time is equivalent to money. Besides, I never knew a person who was economical of the one, who was not equally so of the other. Economy of time will, therefore, be an important branch of study.

But the study is rather difficult. For though every young man of common sense knows that an hour is *sixty minutes*, very few seem to know that sixty minutes make an hour. On this account many waste fragments of time,—of one, two, three or five minutes each—without hesitation, and apparently without regret;—never thinking that fifteen or twenty such fragments are equal to a full hour. 'Take care of the pence, the pounds will take care of themselves,' is not more true, than that hours will take care of themselves, if you will only secure the minutes.[1]

In order to form economical habits, several important points must be secured. You must have for every *purpose* and *thing* a *time*, and *place*; and every thing must be done *at the time*, and all things put *in their place.*

1. *Every thing must be done at the time.* Whether you attempt little or much, let every hour have its employment, in business, study, social conversation, or diversion; and unless it be on extraordinary occasions, you must not suffer your plan to be broken. It is in this way that many men who perform an incredible amount of business, have abundant leisure. And it is for want of doing business systematically that many who effect but little, never find much leisure. They spend their lives in literally 'doing nothing.'

An eminent prime minister of Holland was asked how he could perform such a vast amount of business, as it was known he did, and yet have so much leisure. 'I do every thing at the time;' was the reply.

Some of you will say you have no room for any plan of your own; that your whole time is at the will of your master, or employer. But this is not so. There are few persons who are so entirely devoted to others as not to have minutes, if not hours, every day, which they can call their own. Now here it is that character is tried and proved. He alone who is wise in small matters, will be wise in large ones. Whether your unoccupied moments amount in a day to half an hour, or an hour, or two hours, have something to do in each of them. If it be social conversation, the moment your hour arrives, engage in it at once; if study, engage at once in that. The very fact that you have but a very few minutes at your command, will create an interest in your employment during that time.

Perhaps no persons read to better purpose than those who have but very little leisure. Some of the very best minds have been formed in this manner. To repeat their names would be to mention a host of self educated men, in this and in other countries. To show what can be done, I will mention one fact which fell under my own observation. A young man, about fifteen years of age, unaccustomed to study, and with a mind wholly undisciplined, read Rollin's Ancient History through in about three months, or a fourth of a year; and few persons were ever more closely confined to a laborious employment than he was during the whole time. Now to read four such works as Rollin in a year, is by no means a matter to be despised.

2. *Every thing should have its place.* Going into a shop, the other day, where a large number of persons were employed, I observed the following motto, in large letters, pasted on the side of the room; 'Put every thing in its proper place.' I found the owner of the shop to be a man of order and economy.

An old gentleman of my acquaintance, who always had a place for every thing, made it a rule, if any thing was out of its place, and none of his children could find it, to blame the whole of them. This was an unreasonable measure, but produced its intended effect. His whole family follow his example; they have a place for every thing, and they put every thing in its place.

Unless both the foregoing rules are observed, true economy does not and cannot exist. But without economy, life is of little comparative value to ourselves or others. This trait of character is *generally* claimed, but more *rarely* possessed.

SECTION V. *Indolence.* - One of the greatest obstacles in the road to excellence, is indolence. I have known young men who would reason finely on the value of time, and the necessity of rising early and improving every moment of it. Yet I have also known these same *aspiring* young men to lie dozing, an hour or two in the morning, after the wants of nature had been reasonably, and more than reasonably gratified. You can no more rouse them, with all their fine arguments, than you can a log. There they lie, completely enchained by indolence.

I have known others continually complain of the shortness of time; that they had no time for business, no time for study, &c. Yet they would lavish hours in yawning at a public house, or hesitating whether they had better go to the theatre or stay; or whether they had better get up, or indulge in 'a little more slumber.' Such people wear the most galling chains, and as long as they continue to wear them there is no reasoning with them.

An indolent person is scarcely human; he is half quadruped, and of the most stupid species too. He may have good intentions of discharging a duty, while that duty is at a distance; but let it approach, let him view the time of action as near, and down go his hands in languor. He *wills*, perhaps; but he *un*wills in the next breath.

What is to be done with such a man, especially if he is a young one? He is absolutely good for nothing. Business tires him; reading fatigues him; the public service interferes with his pleasures, or restrains his freedom. His life must be passed on a bed of down. If he is employed, moments are as hours to him—if he is amused, hours are as moments. In general, his whole time eludes him, he lets it glide unheeded, like water under a bridge. Ask him what he has done with his morning,—he cannot tell you; for he has lived without reflection, and almost without knowing whether he has lived at all.

The indolent man sleeps as long as it is possible for him to sleep, dresses slowly, amuses himself in conversation with the first person that calls upon him, and loiters about till dinner. Or if he engages in any employment, however important, he leaves it the moment an opportunity of talking occurs. At length dinner is served up; and after lounging at the table a long time, the evening will probably be spent as unprofitably as the morning: and this it may be, is no unfair specimen of his whole life. And is not such a wretch, for it is improper to call him a man—good for nothing? What is he good for? How can any rational being be willing to spend the precious gift of life in a manner so worthless, and so much beneath the dignity of human nature? When he is about stepping into the grave, how can he review the past with any degree of satisfaction? What is his history, whether recorded here or there,—in golden letters, or on the plainest slab—but, 'he was born' and 'he died!'

SECTION VI. *Early Rising and Rest.* - Dr. Rush mentions a patient of his who thought himself wonderfully abstinent because he drank no spirituous or fermented liquors, *except a bottle of wine or so*, after dinner!

In like manner some call it early to retire at *ten or eleven o'clock*. Others think *ten very late*. Dr. Good, an English writer on medicine, in treating of the appropriate means of preventing the gout in those who are predisposed to it, after giving directions in regard to diet, drink, exercise, &c., recommends an early hour of retiring to rest. 'By all means,' says he, 'you should go to bed by eleven.'

To half the population of New England such a direction would seem strange; but by the inhabitants of cities and large towns, who already begin to ape the customs and fashions of the old world, the caution is well understood. People who are in the habit of making and attending parties which commence at 9 or 10 o'clock in the evening, can hardly be expected to rise with the sun.

We hear much said about the benefit of the morning air. Many wise men have supposed the common opinion on this subject to be erroneous; and that the mistake has arisen from the fact that being refreshed and invigorated by rest, the change is *within* instead of *without*; that our physical frames and mental faculties are more healthy than they were the previous evening, rather than that the surrounding atmosphere has altered.

Whether the morning air is *more* healthy or not, it is certainly healthy enough. Besides, there are so many reasons for early rising that if I can persuade the reader to go to bed early, I shall have little fear of his lying late in the morning.

1st. He who rises early and plans his work, and early sets himself about it, generally finds his business go well with him the whole day. He has taken time by the foretop; and will be sure to go before, or *drive* his business; while his more tardy neighbor 'suffers his business to drive him.' There is something striking in the feeling produced by beginning a day's work thus seasonably. It gives an impulse to a man's thoughts, speech, and actions, which usually lasts through the day. This is not a mere whim, but sober fact; as can be attested by thousands. The person who rises late, usually pleads (for mankind are very ingenious in defence of what falls in with their own inclinations,) that he does as much in the progress of the day, as those who rise early. This may, in a few instances, be true; but in general, facts show the reverse. The motions of the early riser will be more lively and vigorous all day. He may, indeed, become dull late in the evening, but he ought to be so.

Sir Matthew Hale said that after spending a Sunday well, the rest of the week was usually prosperous. This is doubtless to be accounted for—in part at least—on the above principle.

2. In the warm season, the morning is the most agreeable time for labor. Many farmers and mechanics in the country perform a good half day's work before the people of the city scarcely know that the sun shines.[2]

3. To lie snoring late in the morning, assimilates us to the most beastly of animals. Burgh, an ingenious English writer, justly observes; 'There is no time spent more stupidly than that which some luxurious people pass in a morning between sleeping and waking, after nature has been fully gratified. He who is awake may be doing something: he who is asleep, is receiving the refreshment necessary to fit him for action: but the hours spent in dozing and slumbering can hardly be called existence.'

The late Dr. Smith, of Yale College, in his lectures, used to urge on his hearers never to take '*the second nap*.' He said that if this rule were steadily and universally followed by persons in health,—there would be no dozing or oversleeping. If, for once, they should awake from the first nap before nature was sufficiently restored, the next night would restore the proper balance. In laying this down as a rule, Dr. Smith would, of course, except those instances in which we are awakened by accident.

4. It has been remarked by experienced physicians that they have seldom, if ever, known a person of great age, who was not an early riser. In enumerating the causes of longevity, Rush and Sinclair both include early rising.

5. It is a trite but just maxim that one hour's sleep before midnight is worth two afterward. Why it is so, would perhaps be difficult to say. The power of habit is great, and as the majority of children are trained to go to bed early, perhaps this will in part account for the fact. So when the usual hour for meal arrives, a given amount of food eaten at the time, is digested in a more healthy and regular manner than if eaten one, or two, or three hours afterwards. Again, nature certainly intended man should exercise during the day, and sleep in the night. I do not say the *whole* night; because in the winter and in high northern latitudes, this would be devoting an unreasonable portion of time to sleep. It would hardly do to sleep three or four months. But in all countries, and in all climates, we should try to sleep half our hours before midnight.

6. The person who, instead of going to bed at nine, sits up till eleven, and then sleeps during two hours of daylight the following morning, is grossly negligent of economy. For, suppose he makes this

his constant practice, during his whole *business* life, say fifty years. The extra oil or tallow which he would consume would not be estimated at less than one cent an evening; which, in fifty years would be $182.50. Not a very large sum to be sure; but, to every *young* man, worth saving; since, to a community of 1,000 young men, the amount would be no less than $182,500. Then the loss in health and strength would be far greater, though it is obvious that it cannot so easily be computed.

7. Once more. If an hour's sleep before midnight is worth more than an hour in the morning, then an hour in the morning is of course worth less than an hour before midnight, and a person must sleep a greater number of hours in the morning to obtain an equal amount of rest. A person retiring at eleven and rising at eight, would probably get no more rest, possibly less, than a person who should sleep from nine to five;—a period one hour shorter. But if so, he actually loses an hour of time a day. And you well know, if Franklin had not told you so, that *time is money.*

Now, if we estimate the value of this time at ten cents an hour for one person in four, of the population of the United States—and this is probably a fair estimate—the loss to an individual in a year, or 313 working days, would be $31.30; and in 50 years $1,565. A sum sufficient to buy a good farm in many parts of the country. The loss to a population equal to that of the United States, would, in fifty years, be no less than five thousand and eighty-six millions of dollars!

But this is not the whole loss. The time of the young and old is beyond all price for the purposes of mental and moral improvement. Especially is this true of the precious golden hours of the morning. Think, then, of the immense waste in a year! At twelve hours a day, more than a million of years of valuable time are wasted annually in the United States.

I have hitherto made my estimates on the supposition that we do not sleep too much, in the aggregate, and that the only loss sustained arises from the *manner of procuring it.* But suppose, once more, we sleep an hour too much daily. This involves a waste just twice as great as that which we have already estimated.

Do you startle at these estimates! It is proper that many of you should. You have misspent time enough. Awake your 'drowsy souls,' and shake off your stupid habits. Think of Napoleon breaking up the boundaries of kingdoms, and dethroning kings, and to accomplish these results, going through with an amount of mental and bodily labor that few constitutions would be equal to, with only *four hours of sleep in the twenty-four.* Think of Brougham too, who *works* as many hours, perhaps, as any man in England, and has as much influence, and yet sleeps as few; i.e., only four. A hundred persons might be named, and the list would include some of the greatest benefactors of their race, who never think of sleeping more than *six* hours a day. And yet many of you are scarcely contented with eight!

Would you conquer as Bonaparte did—not states, provinces, and empires,—but would you aspire to the high honor of conquering yourselves, and of extending your conquests intellectually and morally, you must take the necessary steps. The path is a plain one; requiring nothing but a little moral courage. 'What man has done, man may do.' I know you do not and ought not to aspire to conquer kingdoms, or to become prime ministers; but you ought to aspire to get the victory over yourselves:— a victory as much more noble than those of Napoleon, and Cæsar, and Alexander, as intellectual and moral influence are superior to mere brute force.

SECTION VII. *On Duty to Parents.* - It was the opinion of a very eminent and observing man, that those who are obedient to parents, are more healthy, long lived, and happy than those who are disobedient. And he reasons very fairly on the subject.

Now I do not know whether the promise annexed to the fifth command, (whatever might have been intended, as addressed to the Jews,) has any special reference to happiness in this life. I only know that in general, those who are obedient to parents are apt to be virtuous in other respects; for the virtues as well as the vices usually go in companies. But that virtue in general tends to long life and happiness, nobody will entertain a doubt.

I am sorry, however, to find that the young, when they approach adult years, are apt to regard authority as irksome. It should not be so. So long as they remain under the parental roof, they ought to feel it a pleasure to conform to the wishes of the parents in all the arraignments of the family, if not absolutely unreasonable. And even in the latter case, it is my own opinion—and one which has not been hastily formed, either—that it would be better to submit, with cheerfulness; and for three reasons.

1st. For the sake of your own reputation; which will always be *endangered* by disobedience, however unjust the parental claim may be.

2d. From a love of your parents, and a sense of what you owe them for their kind care; together with a conviction that perfect rectitude is not to be expected. You will find error, more or less, every where around you—even in yourselves; why should you expect perfection in your parents?

3d. Because it is better to *suffer* wrong than to *do* wrong. Perhaps there is nothing which so improves human character, as suffering wrongfully; although the world may be slow to admit the principle. More than this; God himself has said a great deal about *obedience to parents.*

If real evils multiply so that a young man finds he cannot remain in his father's house, without suffering not only in his feelings, but permanently in his temper and disposition, I will not say that it is never best to leave it. I do not believe, however, there is *often* any such necessity. Of those who leave their paternal home on this plea, I believe nine hundred and ninety-nine in a thousand might profitably remain, if they would; and that a very large number would find the fault in themselves—in their own temper, disposition or mistaken views—rather than in their parents.

And what is to be *gained* by going away? Unfortunately this is a question too seldom asked by restless, or headstrong youths; and when asked and answered, it is usually found that their unhappy experience proves the answer to have been incorrect. I have seldom known a youth turn out well who left his parents or his guardian or master. On this subject, Franklin, I know, is often triumphantly referred to; but for one such instance as that, I hazard nothing in saying there are hundreds of a contrary character. Within the circle of my own observation, young men who leave in this manner, have wished themselves back again a thousand times.

But be this as it may, so long as you remain in the family, if you are 70 years of age, by all means yield to authority implicitly, and if possible, cheerfully. Avoid, at least, altercation and reproaches. If things do not go well, fix your eye upon some great example of suffering wrongfully, and endeavor to profit by it.

There is no sight more attractive than that of a well ordered family; one in which every child, whether five years old or fifty, submits cheerfully to those rules and regulations which parental authority has thought fit to impose. It is, to use a strong expression, an image of heaven. But, exactly in the same proportion, a family of the contrary character resembles the regions below.

Nor is this all. It is an ancient maxim,—and however despised by some of the moderns, none can be more true,—that he only is fit to command who has first learned to obey. Obedience, is, in fact, the great lesson of human life. We first learn to yield our will to the dictates of parental love and wisdom. Through them we learn to yield submissively to the great laws of the Creator, as established in the material world. We learn to avoid, if possible, the flame, the hail, the severity of the cold, the lightning, the tornado, and the earthquake; and we do not choose to fall from a precipice, to have a heavy body fall on us, to receive vitriol or arsenic into our stomachs, (at least in health) or to remain a very long time, immersed in water, or buried in the earth. We submit also to the government under which we live. All these are lessons of obedience. But the Christian goes farther; and it is his purpose to obey not only all these laws, but any additional ones he may find imposed, whether they pertain to material or immaterial existences.

In short, he who would put himself in the most easy position, in the sphere allotted him by the Author of Nature, must learn *to obey*,—often implicitly and unconditionally. At least he must know how to obey: and the earlier this knowledge is acquired, and corresponding habits established, the better and happier will he find his condition, and the more quiet his conscience.

SECTION VIII. *Faithfulness.* - Hardly any thing pleases me more in a young man, than faithfulness to those for whom he is employed, whether parents, guardians, masters, or others.

There appears to be a strange misapprehension, in the minds of many, in regard to this point. There are few who will not admit, in theory, whatever may be their practice, that they ought to be faithful to their parents. And by far the majority of the young doubtless perceive the propriety of being faithful to their masters; so long at least, as they are present. I will even go farther and admit that the number of young men—sons, wards, apprentices, and servants—who would willingly be so far unfaithful as to do any thing positively wrong because those who are set over them happen to be absent, is by no means considerable.

But by faithfulness to our employers, I mean something more than the mere doing of things because we are *obliged* to do them, or because we *must*. I wish to see young men feel an interest in the well being and success of their employers; and take as good care of their concerns and property, whether they are present or absent, as if they were their own. The youth who would be more industrious, persevering, prudent, economical, and attentive in business, if the profits were his own, than he now is, does not in my opinion come up to the mark at which he should aim.

The great apology for what I call unfaithfulness to employers, is, 'What shall I get by it?' that is, by being faithful. I have seen many a young man who would labor at the employment regularly assigned him, during a certain number of hours, or till a certain job was completed, after which he seemed unwilling to lift a finger, except for his own amusement, gratification, or emolument. A few minutes' labor might repair a breach in a wall or corn crib, and save the owner many dollars' worth of property, but it is passed by! By putting a few deranged parcels of goods in their proper place, or writing down some small item of account, which would save his employer much loss of time or money, or both, a faithful clerk might often do a great service. Would he not do it, if the loss was to be his own? Why not then do it for his employer?

Those who neglect things, or perform them lazily or carelessly, because they imagine they shall get nothing for it, would do well to read the following story of a devoted and faithful domestic; which I suppose to be a fact. It needs no comment.

A Mahratta Prince, in passing through a certain apartment, one day, discovered one of his servants asleep with his master's slippers clasped so tightly to his breast, that he was unable to disengage them. Struck with the fact, and concluding at once, that a person who was so jealously careful of a trifle, could not fail to be faithful when entrusted with a thing of more importance, he appointed him a member of his body-guards. The result proved that the prince was not mistaken. Rising in office, step by step, the young man soon became the most distinguished military commander in Mahratta; and his fame ultimately spread through all India.

SECTION IX. *On Forming Temperate Habits.* - 'Be temperate in all things,' is an excellent rule, and of very high authority.

*Drunkenness* and *Gluttony* are vices so degrading, that advice is, I must confess, nearly lost on those who are capable of indulging in them. If any youth, unhappily initiated in these odious and debasing vices, should happen to see what I am now writing, I beg him to read the command of God, to the Israelites, Deut. xxi. The father and mother are to take the bad son 'and bring him to the elders of the city; and they shall say to the elders, this our son will not obey our voice: he is a *glutton* and a *drunkard.* And all the men of the city shall stone him with stones, that he die.' This will give him some idea of the odiousness of his crime, at least in the sight of Heaven.

But indulgence *far short* of gross drunkenness and gluttony is to be deprecated; and the more so, because it is too often looked upon as being no crime at all. Nay, there are many persons, who boast of a refined taste in matters connected with eating and drinking, who are so far from being ashamed of employing their thoughts on the subject, that it is their boast that they do it.

Gregory, one of the Christian fathers, says: 'It is not the *quantity* or the *quality* of the meat, or drink, but the *love of it*, that is condemned:' that is to say, the indulgence beyond the absolute demands of nature; the hankering after it; the neglect of some duty or other for the sake of the enjoyments of the table. I believe, however, there *may* be error, both in *quantity* and *quality*.

This *love* of what are called 'good eating and drinking,' if very unamiable in grown persons, is perfectly hateful in a *youth*; and, if he *indulge* in the propensity, he is already half ruined. To warn you against acts of fraud, robbery, and violence, is not here my design. Neither am I speaking against acts which the jailor and the hangman punish, nor against those moral offences which all men condemn, but against indulgences, which, by men in general, are deemed not only *harmless*, but *meritorious*; but which observation has taught me to regard as destructive to human happiness; and against which all ought to be cautioned, even in their boyish days.

Such indulgences are, in the first place, very *expensive*. The materials are costly, and the preparation still more so. What a monstrous thing, that, in order to satisfy the appetite of one person there must be one or two others *at work constantly*.[3] More fuel, culinary implements, kitchen room: what! all these merely to tickle the palate of four or five people, and especially people who can hardly pay their bills! And, then, the *loss of time*—the time spent in pleasing the palate!

"A young man," says an English writer, "some years ago, offered himself to me, as an *amanuensis*, for which he appeared to be perfectly qualified. The terms were settled, and I requested him to sit down, and begin; but looking out of the window, whence he could see the church clock, he said, somewhat hastily, 'I *cannot* stop *now* sir, I must go to *dinner*.' 'Oh!' said I, 'you *must* go to dinner, must you! Let the dinner, which you *must* wait upon to-day, have your constant services, then; for you and I shall never agree.'

"He had told me that he was in *great distress* for want of employment; and yet, when relief was there before his eyes, he could forego it for the sake of getting at his eating and drinking three or four hours sooner than was necessary."

This anecdote is good, so far as it shows the folly of an unwillingness to deny ourselves in small matters, in any circumstances. And yet punctuality, even at meals, is not to be despised.

*Water-drinkers* are universally *laughed at*: but, it has always seemed to me, that they are amongst the most welcome of guests, and that, too, though the host be by no means of a niggardly turn. The truth is, they give *no trouble*; they occasion *no anxiety* to please them; they are sure not to make their sittings *inconveniently long*; and, above all, their example teaches *moderation* to the rest of the company.

Your notorious 'lovers of good cheer' are, on the contrary, not to be invited without *due reflection*. To entertain one of them is a serious business; and as people are not apt voluntarily to undertake such pieces of business, the well-known 'lovers of good eating and drinking' are left, very generally, to enjoy it by themselves, and at their own expense.

But, all other considerations aside, *health*, one of the most valuable of earthly possessions, and without which all the rest are worth nothing, bids us not only to refrain from *excess* in eating and drinking, but to stop short of what might be indulged in without any *apparent* impropriety.

The words of Ecclesiasticus ought to be often read by young people. 'Eat modestly that which is set before thee, and *devour* not, lest thou be *hated*. When thou sittest amongst many, reach not thine hand out first of all. *How little is sufficient for a man well taught! A wholesome sleep* cometh of a temperate belly. Such a man *riseth up in the morning*, and is *well at ease with himself*. Be not too hasty of meats; for excess of meats bringeth sickness, and choleric disease cometh of gluttony. By surfeit have many perished, and he that *dieteth himself prolongeth his life*. Show not thy valiantness in wine; for wine hath destroyed many.'

How true are these words! How well worthy of a constant place in our memories! Yet, what pains have been taken to apologize for a life contrary to these precepts! And, what punishment can be too great, what mark of infamy sufficiently signal, for those pernicious villains of talent, who have employed that talent in the composition of *Bacchanalian songs*; that is to say, pieces of fine and captivating writing in praise of one of the most odious and destructive vices in the black catalogue of human depravity!

'Who,' says the eccentric, but laborious Cobbett, 'what man, ever performed a greater quantity of labor than I have performed? Now, in a great measure, I owe my capability to perform this labor to my disregard of dainties. I ate, during one whole year, one mutton chop every day. Being once in town, with one son (then a little boy) and a clerk, while my family was in the country, I had, for several weeks, nothing but legs of mutton. The first day, a leg of mutton boiled or *roasted*; second, *cold*; third, *hashed*; then, leg of mutton *boiled*; and so on.

'When I have been by myself, or nearly so, I have *always* proceeded thus: given directions for having *every day the same thing*, or alternately as above, and every day exactly at the same hour, so as to prevent the necessity of any *talk* about the matter. I am certain that, upon an average, I have not, during my life, spent more than *thirty-five minutes a day at table*, including all the meals of the day. I like, and I take care to have, good and clean victuals; but, if wholesome and clean, that is enough. If I find it, by chance, *too coarse* for my appetite, I put the food aside, or let somebody do it; and leave the appetite to gather keenness.'

Now I have no special desire to recommend *mutton chops* to my readers, nor to hold out the example of the individual whose language I have quoted, as worthy of general imitation. There is one lesson to be learned, however. Cobbett's never tiring industry is well known. And if we can rely on his own statements in regard to his manner of eating, we see another proof that what are called 'dainties,' and even many things which are often supposed to be necessaries, are very far from being indispensable to health or happiness.

I am even utterly *opposed* to the rapid eating of which he speaks. In New England especially, the danger is on the other side. 'Were it not from respect to others, I never would wish for more than eight minutes to eat my dinner in,' said a merchant to me one day. Now *I* can *swallow* a meal at any time, in *five* minutes; but this is not *eating*. If it is, the teeth were made—as well as the saliva—almost in vain. No! this *swallowing* down a meal in five or even ten minutes, so common among the active, enterprising, and industrious people of this country, is neither healthy, nor decent, nor economical. And instead of spending only *thirty-five minutes* a day in eating; every man, woman, and child ought, as a matter of duty, to spend about *twice* the time in that way. This would give the teeth and salivary glands an opportunity to come up to the work which God in nature assigned them. We may indeed cheat them for a time, but not with impunity, for a day of reckoning will come; and some of our rapid eaters will find their bill (in stomach or liver complaints, or gout or rheumatism) rather large. They will probably lose more time in this way, than they can possibly save by eating rapidly.

The idea of preventing conversation about what we eat is also idle, though Dr. Franklin and many other wise men, thought otherwise. Some of our students in *commons* and elsewhere, suppose themselves highly meritorious because they have adopted the plan of appointing one of their number to read to the company, while the rest are eating. But they are sadly mistaken. Nothing is gained by the practice. On the contrary, much is lost by it. The bow cannot always remain bent, without injury. Neither can the mind always be kept 'toned' to a high pitch. *Mind* and *body* must and will have their relaxations.

I am not an advocate for *wasting time* or for *eating more* than is necessary. Nay, I even believe, on the contrary, with most *medical* men, that we generally eat about twice as much as nature requires. But I do say, and with emphasis, that food must be *masticated.*

Before I dismiss the subject of temperance, let me beseech you to resolve to free yourselves from slavery to *tea* and *coffee.* Experience has taught me, that they are *injurious to health.* Even my habits of sobriety, moderate eating, and early rising, were not, until I left off using them, sufficient to give me that complete health which I have since had.

I do not undertake to prescribe for others exactly; but, I do say, that to pour down regularly, every day, a quart or two of *warm liquid,* whether under the name of tea, coffee, soup, grog, or any thing else, is greatly injurious to health. However, at present, what I have to represent to *you, is the great deduction which they make, from your power of being useful,* and also from your *power to husband your income,* whatever it may be, and from whatever source arising. These things *cost* something; and wo to him who forgets, or never knows, till he pays it, how large a bill they make—in the course of a year.

How much to be desired is it, that mankind would return once more, to the use of no other drink than that pure beverage which nature prepared for the sole drink of man! So long as we are in health, we need no other; nay, we have no right to any other. It is the testimony of all, or almost all whose testimony is worth having, that water is the best known drink. But if water is *better* than all others, *all others are,* of course, *worse than water.*

As to food and drink *generally,* let me say in conclusion, that *simplicity* is the grand point to aim at. Water, we have seen, is the sole drink of man; but there is a great variety of food provided for his sustenance. He is allowed to select from this immense variety, those kinds, which the experience of mankind generally, combined and compared with his own, show to be *most useful.* He can *live* on almost any thing. Still there is a *choice* to be observed, and so far as his circumstances permit, he is in duty bound to exercise that choice. God has said by his servant Paul; 'Whether ye eat or drink, or whatsoever ye do,' &c.

What we believe to be most useful to us, though at first disagreeable, we may soon learn to prefer. Our habits, then, should be early formed. We should always remember these two rules, however. 1st. The fewer different articles of food used at any one meal, the better; however excellent in their nature those may be which are left untasted. 2. Never eat a moment longer than the food, if well masticated, actually *revives* and *refreshes* you. The moment it makes you feel heavy or dull, or palls upon the taste, *you have passed the line of safety.*

SECTION X. *On Suppers.* - *Suppers,* properly so called, are confined, in a considerable degree, to cities; and I was at first in doubt whether I should do as much good by giving my voice against them, as I should of mischief by spreading through the country the knowledge of a wretched practice. But farther reflection has convinced me that I ought to offer my sentiments on this subject.

By suppers, I mean a fourth meal, just before going to bed. Individuals who have eaten quite as many times during the day as nature requires, and who take their tea, and perhaps a little bread and butter, at six, must go at nine or ten, they think, and eat another hearty meal. Some make it the most luxurious repast of the day.

Now many of our plain country people do not know that such a practice exists. They often eat too much, it is true, at *their* third meal, but their active habits and pure air enable them to digest it better than their city brethren could. Besides, their third meal never comes so late, by several hours, as the suppers of cities and towns.

Our English ancestors, 200 years ago, on both sides of the Atlantic, dined at eleven, took tea early, and had no suppers. So it was with the Jews of old, one of the healthiest nations that ever lived beyond the Mediterranean. They knew nothing of our modern dinners at three or four, and suppers at nine, ten, or eleven.

But not to 'take something late at night with the rest,' would at present be regarded as 'vulgar,' and who could endure it? Here, I confess, I tremble for some of my readers, whose lot it is to be cast in the city, lest they should, in this single instance, hesitate to 'take advice.' But I will hope for better things.

If you would give your stomach a season of repose, as well as the rest of your system; if you would sleep soundly, and either dream not at all, or have your dreams pleasant ones; if you would rise in the morning with your head clear, and free from pain, and your mouth clean and sweet, instead of being parched, and foul; if you would unite your voice—in spirit at least—with the voices of praise to the Creator, which ascend every where unless it be from the dwellings of creatures that should be men,—if, in one word, you would lengthen your lives several years, and increase the enjoyment of the last thirty years 33 per cent. without diminishing that of the first forty, then I beg of you to abstain from *suppers*!

I am acquainted with one individual, who partly from a conviction of the injury to himself, and partly from a general detestation of the practice, not only abstains from every thing of the kind, but from long observation of its effects, goes to the other extreme, and seldom takes even a *third* meal. And I know of no evil which arises from it. On the contrary, I believe that, for him, no course could be better. Be that as it may, adult individuals should never eat more than three times a day, nor should they ever partake of any food, solid or liquid, within three or four hours of the period of retiring to rest.

But if eating ordinary suppers is pernicious, what shall we say of the practice which some indulge who aspire to be pillars in church or state, with others of pretensions less lofty, of going to certain eating houses, at a very late hour, and spending a considerable portion of the night—not in eating, merely, but in quaffing poisonous draughts, and spreading noxious fumes, and uttering language and songs which better become the inmates of Pandemonium, than those of the counting-house, the college, or the chapel! If there be within the limits of any of our cities or towns, scenes which answer to this horrid picture, let 'it not be told in Gath, or published in the streets of Askelon,' lest the fiends of the pit should rejoice;—lest the demons of darkness should triumph.

SECTION XI. *On Dress.* - The object of dress is fourfold: 1st. It is designed as a covering; 2d. As a means of warmth; 3d. As a defence; 4th. To improve our appearance.

These purposes of dress should all be considered; and in the order here presented. That dress, which best answers all these purposes combined, both as respects the material and the *form* or *fashion*, is unquestionably the best and most appropriate. It is certainly true that the impressions which a person's first appearance makes upon the minds of those around him are deep and permanent, and the subject should receive a measure of our attention, on this account. It is only a slight tax which we pay for the benefits of living in civilized society. When, however, we sacrifice every thing else to appearance, we commit a very great error. We make that first in point of importance, which ought to be fourth.

Let your dress be as cheap as may be without shabbiness, and endeavor to be neither first nor last in a fashion. Think more about the cleanliness, than the gloss or texture of your clothes. Be always as clean as your occupation will permit; but never for one moment believe that any human being, who has good sense, will love or respect you *merely* on account of a fine or costly coat.

Extravagance in the haunting of *play-houses*, in *horses*, in every thing else, is to be avoided, but in young men, extravagance in *dress* particularly. This sort of extravagance, this waste of money on the decoration of the body, arises solely from vanity, and from vanity of the most contemptible sort. It arises from the notion, that all the people in the street, for instance, will be *looking at you*, as soon as you walk out; and that they will, in a greater or less degree, think the better of you on account of your fine dress.

Never was a notion more false. Many sensible people, that happen to see you, will think nothing at all about you: those who are filled with the same vain notion as you are, will perceive your attempt to impose on them, and despise it. Rich people will wholly disregard you, and you will be envied and hated by those who have the same vanity that you have, without the means of gratifying it.

Dress should be suited, in some measure, to our condition. A surgeon or physician need not dress exactly like a carpenter; but, there is no reason why any body should dress in a very *expensive* manner. It is a great mistake to suppose, that they derive any *advantage* from exterior decoration.

For after all, men are estimated by other *men* according to their capacity and willingness to be in some way or other *useful*; and, though, with the foolish and vain part of *women*, fine clothes frequently do something, yet the greater part of the sex are much too penetrating to draw their conclusions solely from the outside appearance. They look deeper, and find other criterions whereby to judge. Even if fine clothes should obtain you a wife, will they bring you, in that wife, *frugality, good sense*, and that kind of attachment which is likely to be lasting?

Natural beauty of person is quite another thing: this always has, it always will and must have, some weight even with men, and great weight with women. But, this does not need to be set off by expensive clothes. Female eyes are, in such cases, discerning; they can discover beauty though surrounded by rags: and, take this as a secret worth half a fortune to you, that women, however vain they may be themselves, *despise vanity in men.*

SECTION XII. *Bashfulness and Modesty.* - Dr. Young says, 'The man that blushes is not quite a brute.' This is undoubtedly true; yet nothing is more clear, as Addison has shown us, than that a person may be both bashful and impudent.

I know the world commend the former quality, and condemn the latter; but I deem them both evils. Perhaps the latter is the greater of the two. The proper medium is true modesty. This is always commendable.

We are compelled to take the world, in a great measure, as it is. We can hardly expect men to come and buy our wares, unless we advertise or expose them for sale. So if we would commend ourselves to the notice of our fellow men, we must set ourselves up,—not for something which we are not;—but for what, upon a careful examination, we find reason to think we are. Many a good and valuable man has gone through *this* life, without being properly estimated; from the vain belief that true merit could not always escape unnoticed. This belief, after all, is little else but a species of fatalism.

By setting ourselves up, I do not mean puffing and pretending, or putting on airs of haughtiness or arrogance; or any affectation whatever. But there are those—and some of them are persons of good sense, in many respects, who can scarcely answer properly, when addressed, or look the person with whom they are conversing in the face; and who often render themselves ridiculous *for fear they shall be so.* I have seen a man of respectable talents, who, in conversation never raised his eyes higher than the tassels of his friend's boots; and another who could never converse without turning half or three quarters round, so as to present his shoulder or the backside of his head, instead of a plain, honest face.

I have known young men *injured* by bashfulness. It is vain to say that it should not be so. The world is not what it should be, in many respects; *and I must insist* that it is our duty, to take it as it is, in order to make it better, or even in order to live in it with comfort. He that *thinks* he *shall* not, most surely *will* not, please. A man of sense, and knowledge of the world, will assert his own rights, and pursue his own purposes as steadily and uninterruptedly as the most impudent man living; but then there is at the same time an air of modesty in all he does; while an overbearing or impudent *manner* of doing the same things, would undoubtedly have given offence. Hence a certain wise man has said; 'He who knows the world will not be too bashful; and he who knows himself will never be impudent.'

Perpetual embarrassment in company or in conversation, is sometimes even construed into meanness. Avoid,—if you can do it, without too great a sacrifice—every appearance of deserving a charge so weighty.

SECTION XIII. *Politeness and Good-Breeding.* - Awkwardness is scarcely more tolerable than bashfulness. It must proceed from one of two things; either from not having kept good company, or from not having derived any benefit from it. Many very worthy people have certain odd tricks, and ill habits, that excite a prejudice against them, which it is not easy to overcome. Hence the importance of *good-breeding*.

Now there are not a few who despise all these *little things* of life, as they call them; and yet much of their lives is taken up with them, small as they are. And since these self same little things cannot be dispensed with, is it not better that they should be done in the easiest, and at the same time the pleasantest manner possible?

There is no habit more difficult to attain, and few so necessary to possess, as perfect good-breeding. It is equally inconsistent with a stiff formality, an impertinent forwardness, and an awkward bashfulness. True Christian education would seem to include it; and yet unfortunately, Christians are not always polite.

Is it not surprising that we may sometimes observe, in mere men of the world, that kind of carriage which should naturally be expected from an individual thoroughly imbued with the spirit of Christianity, while his very neighbors, who are professing Christians, appear, by their conduct, to be destitute of such a spirit? Which, then, in practice (I mean so far as this fact is concerned) are the best Christians? But I know what will be the answer; and I know that these things ought not so to be.

No good reason can be given why a Christian should not be as well-bred as his neighbor. It is difficult to conceive how a person can follow the rules given in the Sermon on the Mount, without being, and showing himself to be, well-bred. I have even known men who were no friends to the bible, to declare it as their unequivocal belief that he whose life should conform to the principles of that sermon, could not avoid being *truly polite*.

There are not a few who *confound* good-breeding with affectation, just as they confound a reasonable attention to dress with foppery. This calling things by wrong names is very common, how much soever it may be lamented.

*Good-breeding*, or true politeness, is the art of showing men, by external signs, the internal regard we have for them. It arises from good sense, improved by good company. Good-breeding is never to be learned, though it may be *improved*, by the study of books; and therefore they who attempt it, appear stiff and pedantic. The really well-bred, as they become so by use and observation, are not liable to affectation. You see good-breeding in all they do, without seeing the art of it. Like other habits, it is acquired by practice.

An engaging manner and genteel address may be out of our power, although it is a misfortune that it should be so. But it is in the power of every body to be kind, condescending, and affable. It is in the power of every person who has any thing to say to a fellow being, to say it with kind feelings, and with a sincere desire to please; and this, whenever it is done, will atone for much awkwardness in the manner of expression. Forced complaisance is foppery; and affected easiness is ridiculous.

Good-breeding is, and ought to be, an amiable and persuasive thing; it beautifies the actions and even the looks of men. But the *grimace* of good-breeding is not less *odious*.

In short, good-breeding is a forgetting of ourselves so far as to seek what may be agreeable to others, but in so artless and delicate a manner as will scarcely allow them to *perceive* that we are so employed; and the regarding of ourselves, not as the centre of motion on which every thing else is to revolve, but only as one of the wheels or parts, in a vast machine, embracing other wheels and parts of equal, and perhaps more than equal importance. It is hence utterly opposed to selfishness, vanity, or pride. Nor is it proportioned to the supposed riches and rank of him whose favor and patronage you would gladly cultivate; but extends to all. It knows how to contradict with respect; and to please, without adulation.

The following are a few plain directions for attaining the character of a well-bred man.

1. Never weary your company by talking too long, or too frequently.

2. Always look people in the face when you address them, and generally when they are speaking to you.

3. Attend to a person who is addressing you. Inattention marks a trifling mind, and is a most unpardonable piece of rudeness. It is even an *affront*; for it is the same thing as saying that his remarks are not *worth* your attention.

4. Do not interrupt the person who is speaking by saying *yes*, or *no*, or *hem*, at every sentence; it is the most useless thing that can be. An occasional assent, either by word or action, may be well enough; but even a nod of assent is sometimes repeated till it becomes disgusting.

5. Remember that every person in a company likes to be the *hero* of that company. Never, therefore, engross the whole conversation to yourself.

6. Learn to sit or stand still, while another is speaking to you. You will not of course be so rude as to dig in the earth with your feet, or take your penknife from your pocket and pair your nails; but there are a great many other little movements which are scarcely less clownish.

7. Never anticipate for another, or *help him out*, as it is called. This is quite a rude affair, and should ever be avoided. Let him conclude his story for himself. It is time enough for you to make corrections or additions afterward, if you deem his account defective. It is also a piece of impoliteness to interrupt another in his remarks.

8. Say as little of *yourself* and *your friends* as possible.

9. Make it a rule never to accuse, without due consideration, any body or association of men.

10. Never try to appear more wise or learned than the rest of the company. Not that you should *affect* ignorance; but endeavor to remain within your own proper sphere.

SECTION XIV. *Personal Habits.* - I have elsewhere spoken of the importance of early rising. Let me merely request you, in this place, to form a *habit* of this kind, from which no ordinary circumstances shall suffer you to depart. Your first object after rising and devotion, should be to take a survey of the business which lies before you during the day, making of course a suitable allowance for exigencies. I have seldom known a man in business thrive—and men of business we all ought to be, whatever may be our occupation—who did not rise early in the morning, and plan his work for the day. Some of those who have been most successful, made it a point to have this done before daylight. Indeed, I was intimately acquainted with one man who laid out the business of the day, attended family worship, and breakfasted before sunrise; and this too, at all seasons of the year.

Morning gowns and slippers are very useful things, it is said. But the reasons given for their utility are equally in favor of *always* wearing them. 'They are loose and comfortable.' Very well: Should not our dress always be loose? 'They save *other clothes.*' Then why not wear them all day long? The truth, after all, is, that they are *fashionable*, and as we usually give the *true* reason for a thing *last*, this is probably the principal reason why they are so much in use. I am pretty well convinced, however, that they are of little real use to him who is determined to eat his bread 'in the sweat of his face,' according to the Divine appointment.

Looking-glasses are useful in their place, but like many other conveniences of life, by no means indispensable; and so much abused, that a man of sense would almost be tempted, for the sake of example, to lay them aside. Of all wasted time, none is more *foolishly* wasted than that which is employed in *unnecessary* looking at one's own pretty face.

This may seem a matter of small consequence; but nothing can be of small importance to which we are obliged to attend *every day.* If we dressed or shaved but once a year, or once a month, the case would be altered; but this is a piece of work that must be done once every day; and, as it may cost only about *five minutes* of time, and may be, and frequently is, made to cost *thirty*, or even *fifty minutes*; and, as only fifteen minutes make about a fiftieth part of the hours of our average daylight; this being the case, it is a matter of real importance.

SIR JOHN SINCLAIR asked a friend whether he meant to have a son of his (then a little boy) taught Latin? 'No,' said he, 'but I mean to do something a great deal better for him.' 'What is that?' said Sir John. 'Why,' said the other, 'I mean to teach him *to shave with cold water, and without a glass.*'

My readers may smile, but I can assure them that Sir John is not alone. There are many others who have adopted this practice, and found it highly beneficial. One individual, who had tried it for years, has the following spirited remarks on the subject.

'Only think of the inconvenience attending the common practice! There must be *hot water*, to have this there must be *a fire*, and, in some cases, a fire for that purpose alone; to have these, there must be a *servant*, or you must light a fire yourself. For the want of these, the job is put off until a later hour: this causes a stripping and another dressing bout: or, you go in a slovenly state all that day, and the next day the thing must be done, or cleanliness must be abandoned altogether. If you are on a journey, you must wait the pleasure of the servants at the inn before you can dress and set out in the morning; the pleasant time for travelling is gone before you can move from the spot: instead of being at the end of your day's journey in good time, you are benighted, and have to endure all the great inconveniences attendant on tardy movements. And all this from the apparently insignificant affair of shaving. How many a piece of important business has failed from a short delay! And how many thousand of such delays daily proceed from this unworthy cause!'

These remarks are especially important to those persons in boarding-houses and elsewhere, for whom hot water, if they use it, must be expressly prepared.

Let me urge you never to say I cannot go, or do such a thing, till I am shaved or dressed. Take care always to BE *shaved and dressed*, and then you will always be ready to act. But to this end the habit must be formed in early life, and pertinaciously adhered to.

There are those who can truly say that to the habit of adhering to the principles which have been laid down, they owe much of their success in life; that however sober, discreet, and abstinent they might have been, they never could have accomplished much without it. We should suppose by reasoning beforehand, that the *army* could not be very favorable to steady habits of this or any other kind; yet the following is the testimony of one who had made the trial.

'To the habit of early rising and husbanding my time well, more than to any other thing, I owed my very extraordinary promotion in the army. I was *always ready*. If I had to mount guard at *ten*, I was ready at *nine*: never did any man, or any thing, wait one moment for me. Being, at an age *under twenty years*, raised from corporal to sergeant major *at once*, over the heads of thirty sergeants, I should naturally have been an object of envy and hatred; but this habit of early rising really subdued these passions.

'Before my promotion, a clerk was wanted to make out the morning report of the regiment. I rendered the clerk unnecessary; and, long before any other man was dressed for the parade, my work for the morning was all done, and I myself was on the parade ground, walking, in fine weather, for an hour perhaps.

'My custom was this: to get up, in summer, at daylight, and in winter at four o'clock; shave, dress, even to the putting of my sword-belt over my shoulder, and having my sword lying on the table before me, ready to hang by my side. Then I ate a bit of cheese, or pork, and bread. Then I prepared my report, which was filled up as fast as the companies brought me in the materials. After this, I had an hour or two to read, before the time came for any duty out of doors, unless when the regiment, or part of it, went out to exercise in the morning. When this was the case, and the matter was left to me, I always had it on the ground in such time as that the bayonets glistened in the *rising sun*; a sight which gave me delight, of which I often think, but which I should in vain endeavor to describe.

'If the *officers* were to go out, eight or ten o'clock was the hour. Sweating men in the heat of the day, or breaking in upon the time for cooking their dinner, puts all things out of order, and all men out of humor. When I was commander, the men had a long day of leisure before them: they could ramble into the town or into the woods; go to get raspberries, to catch birds, to catch fish, or to pursue any other recreation, and such of them as chose, and were qualified, to work at their trades. So that here, arising solely from the early habits of one very young man, were pleasant and happy days given to hundreds.'

For my own part, I confess that only a few years since, I should have laughed heartily at some of these views, especially the cold water system of shaving. But a friend whom I esteemed, and who shaved with cold water, said so much in its favor that I ventured to make the trial; and I can truly say that I would not return to my former slavery to hot water, if I had a servant who had nothing else to do but furnish it. I cannot indeed say with a recent writer (I think in the Journal of Health) that cold water is a great deal *better* than warm; but I can and do say that it makes little if any difference with me which I use; though on going out into the cold air immediately afterward, the skin is more likely to chap after the use of warm water than cold. Besides I think the use of warm water more likely to produce eruptions on the skin.—Sometimes, though not generally, I shave, like Sir John Sinclair, without a glass; but I would never be enslaved to one, convenient as it is.

SECTION XV. *Bathing and Cleanliness.* - Cleanliness of the body has, some how or other, such a connection with mental and moral purity, (whether as cause or effect—or both—I will not undertake now to determine) that I am unwilling to omit the present opportunity of urging its importance. There are those who are so attentive to this subject as to wash their whole bodies in water, either cold or warm, every day of the year; and never to wear the same clothes, during the day, that they have slept in the previous night. Now this habit may by some be called whimsical; but I think it deserves a *better name*. I consider this extreme, if it ought to be called an extreme, as vastly more safe than the common extreme of *neglect*.

Is it not shameful—*would* it not be, were human duty properly understood—to pass months, and even years, without washing the whole body once? There are thousands and tens of thousands of both sexes, who are exceedingly nice, even to fastidiousness, about externals;—who, like those mentioned in the gospel, keep clean the 'outside of the cup and the platter,'—but alas! how is it within? Not a few of us,—living, as we do, in a land where soap and water are abundant and cheap—would blush, if the whole story were told.

This chapter, if extended so far as to embrace the whole subject of cleanliness of person, dress, and apartments, and cold and warm bathing, would alone fill a volume; a volume too, which, if well prepared, would be of great value, especially to all young men. But my present limits do not permit of any thing farther. In regard to *cold bathing,* however, allow me to refer you to two articles in the third volume of the Annals of Education, pages 315 and 344, which contain the best directions I can give on this subject.

SECTION XVI. *On Little Things.* - There are many things which, viewed without any reference to prevailing habits, manners, and customs, appear utterly unworthy of attention; and yet, after all, much of our happiness will be found to depend upon them. We are to remember that we live—not alone, on the earth—but among a *multitude*, each of whom claims, and is entitled to his own estimate of things. Now it often happens that what we deem a *little* thing, another, who views the subject differently, will regard as a matter of importance.

Among the items to which I refer, are many of the customary salutations and civilities of life; and the modes of *dress*. Now it is perfectly obvious that many common phrases which are used at meeting and separating, during the ordinary interviews and concerns of life, as well as in correspondence, are in themselves wholly unmeaning. But viewed as an introduction to things of more importance, these little words and phrases at the opening of a conversation, and as the language of hourly and daily salutation, are certainly useful. They are indications of good and friendly feeling; and without them we should not, and could not, secure the confidence of some of those among whom we are obliged to live. They would regard us as not only unsocial, but selfish; and not only selfish, but proud or misanthropic.

On account of meeting with much that disgusts us, many are tempted to avoid society generally. The frivolous conversation, and still more frivolous conduct, which they meet with, they regard as a waste of time, and perhaps even deem it a duty to resign themselves to solitude. This, however, is a great mistake. Those who have been most useful to mankind acted very differently. They mingled with the world, in hopes to do something towards reforming it. The greatest of philosophers, as well as of Christians;—even the FOUNDER of Christianity himself—sat down, and not only sat down, but ate and drank in the society of those with whose manners, and especially whose vices, he could have had no possible sympathy.

Zimmerman, who has generally been regarded as an apostle of solitude, taught that men ought not to 'reside in deserts, or sleep, like owls, in the hollow trunks of trees.' 'I sincerely exhort my disciples,' says he, 'not to absent themselves morosely from public places, nor to avoid the social throng; which cannot fail to afford to judicious, rational, and feeling minds, many subjects both of amusement and instruction. It is true, that we cannot relish the pleasures and taste the advantages of society, without being able to give a patient hearing to the tongue of folly, to excuse error, and to bear with infirmity.'

In like manner, we are not to disregard wholly, our dress. It is true that the shape of a hat, or the cut of a coat may not add to the strength of the mind, or the soundness of the morals; but it is also true that people form an opinion often from our exterior appearance; and will continue to do so: and first impressions are very difficult to be overcome. If we regard our own usefulness, therefore, we shall not consider the fashion or character of our dress as a little thing in its results. I have said elsewhere that we ought neither to be the first nor the last in a fashion.

We should remember, also, that the *world*, in its various parts and aspects, is made up of little things. So true is this, that I have sometimes been very fond of the paradoxical remark, that 'little things are great things;' that is, in their *results*. For who does not know that throughout the physical world, the mightiest results are brought about by the silent working of small causes? It is not the tornado, or the deluge, or even the occasional storm of rain, that renews and animates nature, so much as the gentle breeze, the soft refreshing shower, and the still softer and gentler dews of heaven.

So in human life, generally, they are the little things often, that produce the mightier results. It is he who takes care of pence and farthings, not he who neglects them, that thrives. It is he alone who guards his lips against the first improper word,—trifling as it may seem—that is secure against future profanity. He who indulges one little draught of alcoholic drink, is in danger of ending a tippler; he who gives loose to one impure thought, of ending the victim of lust and sensuality. Nor is it one single gross, or as it were accidental act, viewed as insulated from the rest—however injurious it may be—that injures the body, or debases the mind, so much as the frequent repetition of those smaller errors, whose habitual occurrence goes to establish the predominating choice of the mind, or affection of the soul.

Avoid then, the pernicious, the fatal error, that *little* things are of no consequence: little sums of money, little fragments of time, little or trifling words, little or apparently unimportant actions. On this subject I cannot help adopting—and feeling its force too,—the language of a friend of temperance in regard to those who think themselves perfectly secure from danger, and are believers in the harmlessness of *little* things. 'I tremble,' said he, 'for the man that does not tremble for himself.'

SECTION XVII. *Of Anger, and the means of restraining it.* - There is doubtless much difference of native temperament. One person is easily excited, another, more slowly. But there is a greater difference still, resulting from our habits.

If we find ourselves easily led into anger, we should be extremely careful how we indulge the first steps that lead towards it. Those who naturally possess a mild temper may, with considerable safety, do and say many things which others cannot. Thus we often say of a person who has met with a misfortune, 'It is good enough for him;' or of a criminal who has just been condemned to suffer punishment, 'No matter; he deserves it.' Or perhaps we go farther, and on finding him acquitted, say, 'He ought to have been hanged, and even hanging was too good for him.'

Now all these things, in the mouths of the irritable, lead the way to an indulgence of anger, however unperceived may be the transition. It is on this principle that the saying of St. John is so strikingly true; 'He that hateth his brother is a murderer;' that is, he that indulges hatred has the seeds within him, not only of out-breaking anger, but of murder.

It is on this account that I regret the common course taken with children in relation to certain smaller tribes of the animal creation. They are allowed not only to destroy them,—(which is doubtless often a duty,) but to destroy them in *anger*; to indulge a permanent hatred towards them; and to think this hatred creditable and scriptural. When such feelings lead us to destroy even the most troublesome or disgusting reptiles or insects *in anger*, we have so far prepared the way for the indulgence of anger towards our fellow creatures, whenever their conduct shall excite our displeasure.

We can hence see why he who has a violent temper should always speak in a low voice, and study mildness and sweetness in his tones. For loud, impassioned, and boisterous tones certainly excite impassioned feelings. So do all the *actions* which indicate anger. Thus Dr. Darwin has said that any individual, by using the language and actions of an angry person, towards an imaginary object of displeasure, and accompanying them by threats, and blows, with a doubled or clinched fist, may easily work himself into a rage. Of the justice of this opinion I am fully convinced, from actual and repeated experiments.

If we find ourselves apt to be angry, we should endeavor to avoid the road which leads to it. The first thing to be done, is to govern our voice. On this point, the story of the Quaker and the merchant may not be uninstructive.

A merchant in London had a dispute with a Quaker gentleman about the settlement of an account. The merchant was determined to bring the action *into court*,—a course of proceeding to which the Quaker was wholly opposed;—he therefore used every argument in his power to convince the merchant of his error; but all to no purpose.

Desirous of making a final effort, however, the Quaker called at the house of the merchant, one morning, and inquired of the servant if his master was at home. The merchant hearing the inquiry from the top of the stairs, and knowing the voice, called out, loudly, 'Tell that rascal I am not at home.' The Quaker, looking up towards him, said calmly; 'Well, friend, may God put thee in a better mind.'

The merchant was struck with the meekness of the reply, and after thinking more deliberately of the matter, became convinced that the Quaker was right, and he in the wrong. He requested to see him, and after acknowledging his error, said, 'I have one question to ask you. How were you able to bear my abuse with so much patience?'

'Friend,' replied the Quaker, 'I will tell thee. I was naturally as hot and violent as thou art. But I knew that to indulge my temper was sinful, and also very foolish. I observed that men in a passion always spoke very loud; and I thought if I could control my voice, I should keep down my passions. I therefore made it a rule never to let it rise above a certain key; and by a careful observance of this rule, I have, with the blessing of God, entirely mastered my natural temper.'

When you are tempted by the conduct of those around you, to be angry, endeavor to consider the matter for a few moments. If your temper be so impetuous that you find this highly difficult, you may adopt some plan or device for gaining time. Some recommend counting twenty or thirty, deliberately. The following anecdote of the celebrated Zimmerman is exactly in point, and may afford useful hints for instruction.

Owing in part to a diseased state of body, Zimmerman was sometimes irritable. One day, a Russian princess and several other ladies entered his apartment to inquire after his health; when, in a fit of petulance, he rose, and requested them to leave the room. The prince entered some time afterward, when Zimmerman had begun to repent of his rashness, and after some intervening conversation, advised him, whenever he felt a disposition to treat his friends so uncivilly again, to repeat, *mentally*, the Lord's prayer. This advice was followed, and with success. Not long afterward the same prince came to him for advice in regard to the best manner of controlling the violence of those transports of affection towards his young and amiable consort, in which young and happy lovers are so apt to indulge. 'My dear friend,' said Zimmerman, 'there is no expedient which can surpass your own. Whenever you feel yourself overborne by passion, you have only to repeat the Lord's prayer, and you will be able to reduce it to a steady and permanent flame.'

By adopting Zimmerman's rule, we shall, as I have already observed, gain time for reflection, than which nothing more is needed. For if the cause of anger be a report, for example, of injury done to us by an absent person, either in words or deeds, how do we know the report is true? Or it may be only partly true; and how do we know, till we consider the matter well, whether it is worth our anger at all? Or if at all, perhaps it deserves but a little of it. It may be, too, that the person who said or did the thing reported, did it by mistake, or is already sorry for it. At all events, nothing can be gained by haste; much *may* be by delay.

If a passionate person give you ill language, you ought rather to pity than be angry with him, for anger is a species of disease. And to correct one evil, will you make another? If his being angry is an evil, will it mend the matter to make *another* evil, by indulging in passion yourself? Will it cure his disease, to throw yourself into the same distemper? But if not, then how foolish is it to indulge improper feelings at all!

On the same principles, and for the same reasons, you should avoid returning railing for railing; or reviling for reproach. It only kindles the more heat. Besides, you will often find silence, or at least very gentle words, as in the case of the Quaker just mentioned, the best return for reproaches which could be devised. I say the best 'return;' but I would not be understood as justifying any species of *revenge*. The kind of *return* here spoken of is precisely that treatment which will be most likely to cure the distemper in the other, by making him see, and be sorry for, his passion.

If the views taken in this section be true, it is easy to see the consummate folly of all violence, whether between individuals or collective bodies, whether it be by *striking, duelling,* or *war.* For if an individual or a nation has done wrong, will it annihilate that wrong to counteract it by *another* wrong? Is it not obvious that it only makes two evils, where but one existed before? And can two *wrongs* ever make one *right* action? Which is the most rational, when the choice is in our power, to add to one existing evil, another of similar or greater magnitude; or to keep quiet, and let the world have but one cup of misery instead of two?

Besides, the language of Scripture is *every where* full and decided on this point. 'Recompense to no man evil for evil,' and 'wo to him by whom the offence cometh,' though found but once or twice in just so many words, are in fact, some of the more prominent doctrines of the New Testament; and I very much doubt whether you can read many pages, in succession, in any part of the bible, without finding this great principle enforced. The daily example of the Saviour, and the apostles and early Christians, is a full confirmation of it, in practice.

# CHAPTER II.

On the Management of Business. - SECTION I. *On commencing Business.*

Young men are usually in haste to commence business for themselves. This is an evil, and one which appears to me to be increasing. Let me caution my readers to be on their guard against it.

The evils of running in debt will be adverted to elsewhere. I mention the subject in this place, because the earlier you commence business, the greater the necessity of resorting to credit. You may, indeed, in some employments, begin on a very small scale; but this is attended with serious disadvantages, especially at the present day, when you must meet with so much competition. Perhaps a few may be furnished with capital by their friends, or by inheritance. In the latter case they may as well *use* their money, if they receive it; but I have already endeavored to show that it is generally for the interest of young men to rely upon their own exertions. It is extremely difficult for a person who has ever relied on others, to act with the same energy as those who have been thrown upon their own resources.[4] To learn the art of inheriting property or receiving large gifts, and of acting with the same energy as if left wholly to our own resources, must be reserved, I believe, for future and wiser generations of our race.

I repeat it, therefore, every person had better defer going into business for himself, until he can stand entirely on his own footing. Is it asked how he can have funds from his own resources, before he has actually *commenced* business for himself? Why the thing is perfectly easy. He has only to labor a few years in the service of another. True it is, he may receive but moderate wages during this time; but on the other hand, he will be subjected to little or no risk.

Let 1,000 young men, at the age of 30 years, enter into business with a given amount of capital, all acquired by their own hard earnings, and let them pursue their business 30 years faithfully; that is, till they are 60 years of age. Let 1,000 others commence at the age of 20, with three times the amount of capital possessed by the former, but at the same time either inherited, or loaned by their friends, and let them pursue their calling till *they* are 60 years of age; or for a period of 40 years. We will suppose the natural talents, capacity for doing business, and expenditures—in fact every thing,—the same, in both cases. Now it requires no gift of prophecy to foretell, with certainty, that at 60 years of age a far greater proportion of the 1,000, who began at 30 and depended solely on their own exertions, will be men of wealth, than of those who began at 20 with three times their capital. The reason of these results is found in the very nature of things, as I have shown both above, and in my remarks on industry.

But these views are borne out by facts. Go into any city in the United States, and learn the history of the men who are engaged in active and profitable business, and are thriving in the world, and my word for it, you will find the far greater part began life with nothing, and have had no resources whatever but their own head and hands. And in no city is this fact more strikingly verified than in Boston. On the other hand, if you make a list of those who fail in business from year to year, and learn their history, you will find that a very large proportion of them relied on inheritances, credit, or some kind of foreign aid in early life;—and not a few begun very young.

There is no doctrine in this volume, which will be more unpopular with its readers, than this. Not a few will, I fear, utterly disbelieve it. They look at the exterior appearance of some young friend, a little older than themselves, who has been *lifted* into business and gone on a year or two, and all appears fair and encouraging. They long to imitate him. Point them to a dozen others who have gone only a little farther, and have made shipwreck, and it weighs nothing or next to nothing with them. They suspect mismanagement, (which doubtless sometimes exists) and think *they* shall act more wisely.

In almost every considerable shop in this country may be found young men who have nearly served out their time as apprentices, or perhaps have gone a little farther, even, and worked a year or two as journeymen. They have been industrious and frugal, and have saved a few hundred dollars. This, on the known principles of human nature, has created a strong desire to make additions; and the desire has increased in a greater ratio than the sum. They are good workmen, perhaps, or if not, they generally think so; and those who have the least merit, generally have the most confidence in themselves. But if there be one who *has* merit, there is usually in the neighborhood some hawk-eyed money dealer, who knows that he cannot better invest his funds than in the hands of active young men. This man will search him out, and offer to set him up in business; and his friends, pleased to have him noticed, give security for payment. Thus flattered, he commonly begins; and after long patience and perseverance, he may, by chance, succeed. But a much greater number are unsuccessful, and a few drown their cares and perplexities in the poisoned bowl, or in debauchery;—perhaps both—thus destroying their minds and souls; or, it may be, abruptly putting an end to their own existence.

Young men are apt to reason thus with themselves. 'I am now arrived at an age when others have commenced business and succeeded. It is true I may not succeed; but I know of no reason why my prospects are not as good as those of A, B, and C, to say the least. I am certainly as good a workman, and know as well how to manage, and attend to my own concerns, without intermeddling with those of others. It is true my friends advise me to work as a journeyman a few years longer; but it is a hard way of living. Besides, what shall I learn all this while, that I do not already know? They say I shall be improving in the *practical* part of my business, if not in the *theory* of it. But shall I not improve while I work for myself? Suppose I make blunders. Have not others done the same? If I fall, I must get up again. Perhaps it will teach me not to stumble again. The fact is, old people never think the young know or can do any thing till they are forty years old. I am determined to make an effort. A good opportunity offers, and such a one may never again occur. I am confident I shall succeed.'

How often have I heard this train of reasoning pursued! But if it were correct, how happens it that those facts exist which have just been mentioned? More than this; why do almost all men assert gratuitously after they have spent twenty years in their avocation, that although they thought themselves wise when they began their profession, they were exceedingly ignorant? Who ever met with a man that did not feel this ignorance more sensibly after twenty years of experience, than when he first commenced?

This self flattery and self confidence—this ambition to be men of business and begin to figure in the world,—is not confined to any particular occupation or profession of men, but is found in all. Nor is it confined to those whose object in life is *pecuniary* emolument. It is perhaps equally common among those who seek their happiness in ameliorating the condition of mankind by legislating for them, settling their quarrels, soothing their passions, or curing the maladies of their souls and bodies.

Perhaps the evil is not more glaring in any class of the community than in the medical profession. There is a strong temptation to this, in the facility with which licenses and diplomas may be obtained. Any young man who has common sense, if he can read and write tolerably, may in some of the States, become a knight of the lancet in three years, and follow another employment a considerable part of the time besides. He has only to devote some of his *extra* hours to the study of anatomy, surgery, and medicine, recite occasionally to a practitioner, as ignorant, almost, as himself; hear one series of medical lectures; and procure certificates that he has studied medicine 'three years,' including the time of the lectures; and he will be licensed, almost of course. Then he sallies forth to commit depredations on society at discretion; and how many he kills is unknown. 'I take it for granted, however,' said a President of a College, three years ago, who understood this matter pretty well, 'that every half-educated young physician, who succeeds at last in getting a *reputable* share of practice, must have rid the world, rather prematurely, of some dozen or twenty individuals, at the least, in order to qualify himself for the profession.'

The evil is scarcely more tolerable, as regards young ministers, except that the community in general have better means of knowing when they are imposed upon by ignorance or quackery in this matter, than in most other professions. The principal book for a student of theology is in the hands of every individual, and he is taught to read and understand it. The great evil which arises to students of divinity themselves from entering their profession too early, is the loss of health. Neither the minds nor the bodies of young men are equal to the responsibilities of this, or indeed of any other profession or occupation, at 20, and rarely at 25. Nothing is more evident than that young men, generally, are losers in the end, both in a pecuniary point of view and in regard to health, by commencing business before 30 years of age. But this I have already attempted to show.

As regards candidates for the ministry, several eminent divines are beginning to inculcate the opinion, with great earnestness, that to enter fully upon the active duties of this laborious vocation before the age I have mentioned, is injurious to themselves and to the cause they wish to promote— the cause of God. And I hope their voices will be raised louder and louder on this topic, till the note of remonstrance reaches the most distant villages of our country.

It has often occurred to me that every modest young man, whatever may be his destination, *might* learn wisdom from consulting the history of the YOUNG MAN OF NAZARETH as well as of the illustrious reformer who prepared the way for him.[5] *Our* young men, since newspapers have become so common, are apt to think themselves thoroughly versed in law, politics, divinity, &c.; and are not backward to exhibit their talents. But who is abler at disputation than HE who at twelve years of age proved a match for the learned doctors of law at Jerusalem? Did he, whose mind was so mature at twelve, enter upon the duties of *his* ministry (a task more arduous than has ever fallen to the lot of any *human* being) at 18 or 20 years of age? But why not, when he had so much to do?—Or did he wait till he was in his 30th year?

The great question with every young man should not be, When can I get such assistance as will enable me to commence business;—but, Am I well *qualified* to commence? Perfect in his profession, absolutely so, no man ever will be; but a measure of perfection which is rarely if ever attained under 30 years of age, is most certainly demanded. To learn the simplest handicraft employment in some countries, a person must serve an apprenticeship of at least *seven years*. Here, in America, half that time is thought by many young men an intolerable burden, and they long to throw it off. They wish for what they call a better order of things. The consequences of this feeling, and a growing spirit of insubordination, are every year becoming more and more deplorable.

SECTION II. *Importance of Integrity.* - Every one will admit the importance of integrity in all his dealings, for however dishonest he may be himself, he cannot avoid perceiving the necessity of integrity in others. No society could exist were it not for the measure of this virtue which remains. Without a degree of *confidence*, in transacting business with each other, even the savage life would be a thousand times more savage than it now is. Without it, a gang of thieves or robbers could not long hold together.

But while all admit the sterling importance of strict integrity, how few practise it! Let me prevail when I entreat the young not to hazard either their reputation or peace of mind for the uncertain advantages to be derived from unfair dealing. It is *madness*, especially in one who is just beginning the world. It would be so, if by a single unfair act he could get a fortune; leaving the loss of the soul out of the question. For if a trader, for example, is once generally known to be guilty of fraud, or even of taking exorbitant profits, there is an end to his reputation. Bad as the world is, there is some respect paid to integrity, and wo be to him who forgets it.

If a person habitually allows himself in a single act not sanctioned by the great and golden rule of loving others as we do ourselves, he has entered a road whose everlasting progress is downward. Fraudulent in *one* point, he will soon be so in another—and another; and so on to the end of the chapter, if there be any end to it. At least no one who has gone a step in the downward road, can assure himself that this will not be the dreadful result.

An honest bargain is that only in which the fair market price or value of a commodity is mutually allowed, so far as this is known. The market price is usually, the equitable price of a thing. It will be the object of every honest man to render, in all cases, an equivalent for what he receives. Where the market price cannot be known, each of the parties to an honest contract will endeavor to come as near it as possible; keeping in mind the rule of doing to others as they would desire others to do to them in similar circumstances. Every bargain not formed on these principles is, in its results, unjust; and if intentional, is fraudulent.

There are a great many varieties of this species of fraud.

1. *Concealing the market price.* How many do this; and thus buy for less, and sell for more than a fair valuation! Why so many practise this kind of fraud, and insist at the same time that it is no fraud at all, is absolutely inconceivable, except on the supposition that they are blinded by avarice. For they perfectly know that their customers would not deal with them at any other than market prices, except from sheer ignorance; and that the advantage which they gain, is gained by misapprehension of the real value of the commodities. But can an honest man take this advantage? Would he take it of a child? Or if he did, would not persons of common sense despise him for it?

But why not as well take advantage of a child as of a man? Because, it may be answered, the child does not know the worth of what he buys or sells; but the man does, or might. But in the case specified, it is evident he *does not* know it, if he did he would not make the bargain. And for proof that such conduct is downright fraud, the person who commits it, has only to ask himself whether he would be willing others should take a similar advantage of *his* ignorance. 'I do as I agree,' is often the best excuse such men can make, when reasoned with on the injustice of their conduct, without deciding the question, whether their agreement is founded on a desire to do right.

2. Others *misrepresent the market price*. This is done in various ways. They heard somebody say the price in market was so or so; or such a one bought at such or such a price, or another sold at such a price: all of which prices, purchases, and sales are *known positively* to be different from those which generally prevail. Many contrive to satisfy their consciences in this way, who would by no means venture at once upon plain and palpable lying.

3. The selling of goods or property which is *unsound and defective*, under direct professions that it is sound and good, is another variety of this species of fraud. It is sometimes done by direct lying, and sometimes by indefinite and hypocritical insinuations. Agents, and retailers often assert their wares to be good, because those of whom they have received them *declare* them to be such. These declarations are often believed, because the seller appears or professes to believe them; while in truth, he may not give them the least credit.

One of the grossest impositions of this kind—common as it is—is practised upon the public in advertising and selling nostrums as safe and valuable medicines. These are ushered into newspapers with a long train of pompous declarations, almost always false, and *always* delusive. The silly purchaser buys and uses the medicine chiefly or solely because it is sold by a respectable man, under the sanction of advertisements to which that respectable man lends his countenance. Were good men to decline this wretched employment, the medicines would probably soon fall into absolute discredit; and health and limbs and life would, in many instances, be preserved from unnecessary destruction.

4. Another species of fraud consists in *concealing the defects* of what we sell. This is the general art and villany of that class of men, commonly called *jockeys*; a class which, in reality, embraces some who would startle at the thought of being such;—and whole multitudes who would receive the appellation with disdain.

The common subterfuge of the jockey is, that he gives no false accounts; that the purchaser has eyes of his own, and must judge of the goods for himself. No defence can be more lame and wretched; and hardly any more impudent.

No purchaser can possibly discover many of the defects in commodities; he is therefore obliged to depend on the seller for information concerning them. All this the seller well knows, and if an honest man, will give the information. Now as no purchaser would buy the articles, if he knew their defects, except at a reduced price, whenever the seller does not give this information, and the purchaser is *taken in*, it is by downright villany, whatever some may pretend to the contrary. Nor will the common plea, that if they buy a bad article, they have a right to sell it again as well as they can, ever justify the wretched practice of selling defective goods, at the full value of those which are more perfect.

5. A fraud, still meaner, is practised, when we endeavor to *lower the value of such commodities as we wish to buy.* 'It is naught, it is naught, says the buyer, but when he hath gone his way he boasteth,' is as applicable to our times, as to those of Solomon. The ignorant, the modest, and the necessitous—persons who should be the last to suffer from fraud,—are, in this way, often made victims. A decisive tone and confident airs, in men better dressed, and who are sometimes supposed to know better than themselves, easily bear down persons so circumstanced, and persuade them to sell their commodities for less than they are really worth.

Young shopkeepers are often the dupes of this species of treatment. Partly with a view to secure the future custom of the stranger, and partly in consequence of his statements that he can buy a similar article elsewhere at a much lower price, (when perhaps the quality of the other is vastly inferior) they not unfrequently sell goods at a positive sacrifice—and what do they gain by it? The pleasure of being laughed at by the purchaser, as soon as he is out of sight, for suffering themselves to be *beaten down*, as the phrase is; and of having him boast of his bargain, and trumpet abroad, without a blush, the value of the articles which he had just been decrying!

6. I mention the use of *false weights and measures* last, not because it is a less heinous fraud, but because I hope it is less frequently practised than many others. But it is a lamentable truth that weights and measures are *sometimes* used when they are *known* to be false; and quite often when they are *suspected* to be so. More frequently still, they are used when they have been permitted to become defective through inattention. They are often formed of perishable materials. To meet this there are in most of our communities, officers appointed to be sealers of weights and measures. When the latter are made of substances known to be liable to decay or wear, the proprietor is unpardonable if he does not have them frequently and thoroughly examined.

I have only adverted to some of the more common kinds of fraud; such as the young are daily, and often hourly exposed to, and against which it is especially important, not only to their own reputation, but to their success in business, that they should be on their guard. I will just *enumerate* a few others, for my limits preclude the possibility of any thing more than a bare enumeration.

1. Suffering borrowed articles to be injured by our negligence. 2. Detaining them in our possession longer than the lender had reason to expect. 3. Employing them for purposes not contemplated by the lender. 4. The returning of an article of inferior value, although in *appearance* like that which was borrowed. 5. Passing suspected bank bills, or depreciated counterfeit or clipped coin. Some persons are so conscientious on this point, that they will sell a clipped piece for *old metal*, rather than pass it. But such rigid honesty is rather rare. 6. The use of pocket money, by the young, in a manner different from that which was known to be contemplated by the parent, or master who furnished it. 7. The employment of time in a different manner from what was intended; the mutilating, by hacking, breaking, soiling, or in any other manner wantonly injuring buildings, fences, and other property, public or private;—and especially crops and fruit trees. 8. Contracting debts, though ever so small, without the almost certain prospect of being able to pay them. 9. Neglecting to pay them at the time expected. 10. Paying in something of less value than we ought. 11. Breaches of trust. 12. Breaking of promises. 13. Overtrading by means of borrowed capital.

SECTION III. *Method in Business.* - There is one class of men who are of inestimable value to society—and the more so from their scarcity;—I mean *men of business.* It is true you could hardly offer a greater insult to most persons than to say they are not of this class; but you cannot have been very observing not to have learned, that they who most deserve the charge will think themselves the most insulted by it.

Nothing contributes more to despatch, as well as safety and success in business, than method and regularity. Let a person set down in his memorandum book, every morning, the several articles of business that ought to be done during the day; and beginning with the first person he is to call upon, or the first place he is to go to, finish that affair, if possible, before he begins another; and so on with the rest.

A man of business, who observes this method, will hardly ever find himself hurried or disconcerted by forgetfulness. And he who sets down all his transactions in writing, and keeps his accounts, and the whole state of his affairs, in a distinct and accurate order, so that at any time, by looking into his books, he can see in what condition his concerns are, and whether he is in a thriving or declining way;—such a one, I say, deserves properly the character of a man of business; and has a pretty fair prospect of success in his plans.[6] But such exactness seldom suits the man of pleasure. He has other things in his head.

The way to transact a great deal of business in a little time, and to do it well, is to observe three rules. 1. Speak to the point. 2. Use no more words than are necessary, fully to express your meaning. 3. Study beforehand, and set down in writing afterwards, a sketch of the transaction.

To enable a person to *speak* to the point, he must have acquired, as one essential pre-requisite, the art of *thinking* to the point. To effect these objects, or rather *this* object, as they constitute in reality but *one*, is the legitimate end of the study of grammar; of the importance of which I am to speak elsewhere. This branch is almost equally indispensable in following the other two rules; but here, a thorough knowledge of numbers, as well as of language, will be demanded.

SECTION IV. *Application to Business.* - There is one piece of prudence, above all others, absolutely necessary to those who expect to raise themselves in the world by an employment of any kind; I mean a constant, unwearied application to the main pursuit. By means of persevering diligence, joined to frugality, we see many people in the lowest and most laborious stations in life, raise themselves to such circumstances as will allow them, in their old age, that relief from *excessive* anxiety and toil which are necessary to make the decline of life easy and comfortable.

Burgh mentions a merchant, who, at first setting out, opened and shut his shop every day for several weeks together, without selling goods to the value of two cents; who by the force of application for a course of years, rose, at last, to a handsome fortune. But I have known many who had a variety of opportunities for settling themselves comfortably in the world, yet, for want of steadiness to carry any scheme to perfection, they sunk from one degree of wretchedness to another for many years together, without the least hopes of ever getting above distress and pinching want.

There is hardly an employment in life so trifling that it will not afford a subsistence, if constantly and faithfully followed. Indeed, it is by indefatigable diligence alone, that a fortune can be acquired in any business whatever. An estate procured by what is commonly called a lucky hit, is a rare instance; and he who expects to have his fortune made in that way, is about as rational as he who should neglect all probable means of earning, in hopes that he should some time or other find a treasure.

There is no such thing as continuing in the same condition without an income of some kind or other. If a man does not bestir himself, poverty must, sooner or later, overtake him. If he continues to expend for the necessary charges of life, and will not take the pains to gain something to supply the place of what he deals out, his funds must at length come to an end; and the misery of poverty fall upon him at an age when he is less able to grapple with it.

No employment that is really useful to mankind deserves to be regarded as mean. This has been a stumbling stone to many young men. Because they could not pursue a course which they deemed sufficiently respectable, they neglected business altogether until so late in life that they were ashamed to make a beginning. A most fatal mistake. Pin making is a minute affair, but will any one call the employment a mean one? If *so*, it is one which the whole civilized world encourage, and to which they are under lasting obligation daily. Any useful business ought to be reputable, which is reputably followed.

The character of a drone is always, especially among the human species, one of the most contemptible. In proportion to a person's activity for his own good and that of his fellow creatures, he is to be regarded as a more or less valuable member of society. If all the idle people in the United States were to be buried in one year, the loss would be trifling in comparison with the loss of only a *very few* industrious people. Each moment of time ought to be put to proper use, either in business, in improving the mind, in the innocent and necessary relaxations and entertainments of life, or in the care of the moral and religious part of our nature. Each moment of time is, in the language of theology, a monument of Divine mercy.

SECTION V. *Proper Time of Doing Business.* - There are times and seasons for every lawful purpose of life, and a very material part of prudence is to judge rightly, and make the best of them. If you have to deal, for example, with a phlegmatic gloomy man, take him, if you can, over his bottle. This advice may seem, at first view, to give countenance to a species of fraud: but is it so? These hypochondriacal people have their fits and starts, and if you do not take them when they are in an agreeable state of mind, you are very likely to find them quite as much below par, as the bottle raises them above. But if you deal with them in this condition, they are no more *themselves* than in the former case. I therefore think the advice correct. It is on the same principles, and in the same belief, that I would advise you, when you deal with a covetous man, to propose your business to him immediately after he has been receiving, rather than expending money. So if you have to do with a drunkard, call on him in the morning; for then, if ever, his head is clear.

Again; if you know a person to be unhappy in his family, meet him abroad if possible, rather than at his own house. A statesman will not be likely to give you a favorable reception immediately after being disappointed in some of his schemes. Some people are always sour and ill humored from the hour of rising till they have dined.

And as in persons, so in things, the *time* is a matter of great consequence; an eye to the rise and fall of goods; the favorable season of importing and exporting;—these are some of the things which require the attention of those who expect any considerable share of success.

It is not certain but some dishonest person, under shelter of the rule, in this chapter, may gratify a wish to take unfair advantages of those with whom he deals. But I hope otherwise; for I should be sorry to give countenance, for one moment, to such conduct. My whole purpose (in this place) is to give direction to the young for securing their own rights; not for taking away the rights of others. The man who loves his neighbor as himself, will not surely put a wrong construction on what I have written. I would fain hope that there is no departure here or elsewhere, in the book, from sound christian morality; for it is the bible, on which I wish to see all moral rules based.

SECTION VI. *Buying upon Trust.* - 'Owe no man any thing,' is an apostolic injunction; and happy is he who has it in his power to obey. In my own opinion, most young men possess this power, did they perceive the importance of using it by *commencing* right. It is not so difficult a thing always to purchase with ready money, as many people imagine. The great difficulty is to moderate our desires and diminish our wants within bounds proportioned to our income. We can expend much, or live on little; and this, too, without descending to absolute penury. It is truly surprising to observe how people in similar rank, condition, and circumstances, contrive to *expend* so very differently. I have known instances of young men who would thrive on an income which would not more than half support their neighbors in circumstances evidently similar.

Study therefore to live within your income. To this end you must *calculate.* But here you will be obliged to learn much from personal experience, dear as her school is, unless you are willing to learn from that of others. If, for example, your income is $600 a year, and you sit down at the commencement of the year and calculate on expending $400, and saving the remainder, you will be very liable to fail in your calculation. But if you call in the experience of wiser heads who have travelled the road of life before you, they will tell you that after you have made every reasonable allowance for necessary expenses during the year, and believe yourself able to lay up $200, you will not, once in ten times, be able to save more than *two thirds* of that sum—and this, too, without any sickness or casualty.

It is an important point *never to buy what you do not want.* Many people buy an article merely because it is cheap, and they can have credit. It is true they imagine they shall want it at some future time, or can sell it again to advantage. But they would not buy at present, if it cost them cash, from their pockets. The mischief is that when the day of payment is distant, the cost seems more trifling than it really is. Franklin's advice is in point; 'Buy what thou hast no need of, and ere long thou shalt sell thy necessaries;'—and such persons would do well to remember it.

The difference between credit and ready money is very great. Innumerable things are not bought at all with ready money, which would be bought in case of trust; so much easier, is it, to *order* a thing than to *pay* for it. A future day, a day of payment must come, to be sure; but that is little thought of at the time. But if the money were to be drawn out the moment the thing was received or offered, these questions would arise; Can I not do without it? Is it indispensable? And if I do not buy it, shall I suffer a loss or injury greater in amount than the cost of the thing? If these questions were put, every time we make a purchase, we should seldom hear of those suicides which disgrace this country, and the old world still more.

I am aware that it will be said, and very truly, that the concerns of merchants, the purchasing of great estates, and various other large transactions, cannot be carried on in this manner; but these are rare exceptions to the rule. And even in these cases, there might be much less of bills and bonds, and all the sources of litigation, than there now is. But in the every day business of life, in transactions with the butcher, the baker, the tailor, the shoemaker, what excuse can there be for pleading the example of the merchant, who carries on his work by ships and exchanges?

A certain young man, on being requested to keep an account of all he received and expended, answered that his business was not to keep account books: that he was sure not to make a mistake as to his income; and that as to his expenditure, the purse that held his money, would be an infallible guide, for he never bought any thing that he did not immediately pay for. I do not mean to recommend to young men not to keep written accounts, for as the world is, I deem it indispensable.

Few, it is believed, will deny that they generally pay, for the same article, a fourth part more, in the case of trust, than in that of ready money. Suppose now, the baker, butcher, tailor, and shoemaker, receive from you $400 a year. Now, if you multiply the $100 you lose, by not paying ready money, by 20, you will find that at the end of twenty years, you have a loss of $2,000, besides the accumulated interest.

The fathers of the English *church*, forbade selling on trust at a higher price than for ready money, which was the same thing in effect as to *forbid trust*; and this was doubtless one of the great objects those wise and pious men had in view; for they were fathers in legislation and morals, as well as in religion. But we of the present age, seem to have grown wiser than they, and not only make a difference in the price, regulated by the difference in the mode of payment, but no one is expected to do otherwise. We are not only allowed to charge something for the *use* of the money, but something additional for the *risk* of the loss which may frequently arise,—and most frequently does arise—from the misfortunes of those to whom we thus assign our goods on trust.

The man, therefore, who purchases on trust, not only pays for being credited, but he also pays his share of what the tradesman loses by his general practice of selling upon trust; and after all, he is not so good a customer as the man who purchases cheaply with ready money. His *name*, indeed, is in the tradesman's book, but with that name the tradesman cannot buy a fresh supply of goods.

Infinite, almost, are the ways in which people lose by this sort of dealing. Domestics sometimes go and order things not wanted at all; at other times more than is wanted. All this would be obviated by purchasing with ready money; for whether through the hands of the party himself, or those of some other person, there would always be an actual counting out of the money. Somebody would see the thing bought, and the money paid. And as the master would give the steward or housekeeper a purse of money at the time, *he* would see the money too, would set a proper value upon it, and would just desire to know upon what it had been expended.

Every man, who purchases for ready money, will naturally make the amount of the purchase as low as possible, in proportion to his means. This care and frugality will make an addition to his means; and therefore, at the end of his life, he will have a great deal more to spend, and still be as rich as if he had been trusted all his days. In addition to this, he will eat, and drink, and sleep *in peace*, and avoid all the endless papers, and writings, and receipts, and bills, and disputes, and lawsuits, inseparable from the credit system.

This is by no means intended as a lesson of *stinginess*, nor is it any part of my purpose to inculcate the plan of *heaping up* money. But purchasing with ready money really gives you more money to purchase with; you can afford to have a greater quantity and variety of enjoyments. In the town, it will tend to hasten your pace along the streets, for the temptation at the windows is answered in a moment by clapping your hand upon your pocket; and the question; 'Do I really want it?' is sure to recur immediately; because the touch of the money will put the thought into your mind.

Now supposing you to have a fortune, even beyond your actual wants, would not the money which you might save in this way, be very well applied in acts of real benevolence? Can you walk or ride a mile, in the city or country, or go to half a dozen houses; or in fact can you open your eyes without seeing some human being, born in the same country with yourself, and who, on that account alone, has some claim upon your good wishes and your charity? Can you, if you would, avoid seeing one person, if no more, to whom even a small portion of your annual savings would convey gladness of heart? Your own feelings will suggest the answer.

SECTION VII. *Of entrusting Business to others.* - 'If you wish to have your business done, go; if not, send.' This is an old maxim; and one which is no less true than old. Every young man, on setting out in the world, should make it a rule, never to trust any thing *of consequence* to another, which he can, without too much difficulty, perform himself.

1. Because, let a person have my interest ever so much at heart, I am sure I regard it *more* myself.

2. Nothing is more difficult than to know, in all cases, the characters of those we confide in. How can we expect to understand the characters of others, when we scarcely know our own? Which of us can know, positively, that he shall never be guilty of another vice or weakness, or yield to another temptation, and thus forfeit public confidence? Who, then, will needlessly trust another, when he can hardly be sure of himself?

3. No substitute we can employ, can *understand* our business as well as ourselves.

4. We can change our measures according to changing circumstances; which gives us those opportunities of doing things in the best way, of which another will not feel justified in availing himself.

As for dependants of every kind, it should ever be remembered that their master's interest sometimes possesses only the second place in their hearts. Self-love, with such, will be the ruling principle of action; and no fidelity whatever will prevent a person from bestowing a good deal of thought upon his own concerns. But this must, of necessity, break in more or less upon his diligence in consulting the interest of his employers. How men of business can venture, as they sometimes do, to trust concerns of great importance, for half of every week in the year, (which is half the whole year) to dependants, and thus expect others to take care of their business, when they will not be at the trouble of minding it themselves, is to me inconceivable! Nor does the detection, from time to time, of fraud in such persons, seem at all to diminish this practice.

There is a maxim among business people, 'never to do that for themselves which they can pay another for doing.' This, though true to a certain extent, is liable to abuse. If every body, without discrimination, could be *safely* trusted, the maxim might be *more* just; since nothing is more obvious than that laborers are often at hand, whose time can be bought for a much less sum of money than you would yourself earn in the meantime. I have often known people make or mend little pieces of furniture, implements of their occupations, &c. to save expense, when they could have earned, at their labor during the same time, twice the sum necessary to pay a trusty and excellent workman for doing it.

But, as I have already observed, persons are not always at hand, in whom you can confide; so that the certainty of having a thing done right, is worth much more than the loss of a little time. Besides, God has never said *how much* we must do in this world. We are indeed to do all we can, and at the same time do it well; but *how much that is*, we must judge. He is not necessarily the most useful man who does even the greatest amount of good;—but he who does the most good, attended with the least evil.

But we should remember that what *others* do, is not done by *ourselves*. Still, an individual may often do many little things without any hindrance to his main object. For example, I would not thank a person to make or mend my pen, or shave me; because I can write as much, or perform as much business of any kind, in a week or month—probably more—if I stop to mend my pens, shave myself daily, make fires, saw and split wood, &c. as if I do not. And the same is true of a thousand other things.

SECTION VIII. *Over Trading.* - I have already classed this among the frauds into which business men are in danger of falling; and I cannot but think its character will be pretty well established by what follows.

Over trading is an error into which many industrious, and active young men are apt to run, from a desire of getting rich more rapidly than they are able to do with a smaller business. And yet profusion itself is not more dangerous. Indeed, I question whether idleness brings more people to ruin than over trading.

This subject is intimately connected with *credit*, for it is the credit system that gives such facilities to over trading. But of the evils of credit I have treated fully elsewhere I will only add, under this head, a few remarks on one particular species of trading. I refer to the conduct of many persons, with large capitals, who, for the sake of adding to a heap already too large, monopolize the market,—or trade for a profit which they know dealers of smaller fortunes cannot possibly live by. If such men really think that raising themselves on the ruin of others, in this manner, is justifiable, and that riches obtained in this manner are fairly earned, they must certainly have either neglected to inform themselves, or stifled the remonstrances of conscience, and bid defiance to the laws of God.

SECTION IX. *Making Contracts beforehand.* - In making bargains—with workmen, for example— always do it beforehand, and never suffer the matter to be deferred by their saying they will leave it to your discretion.

There are several reasons why this ought to be done. 1st. It prevents any difficulty afterward; and does no harm, even when the intentions of both parties are perfectly good. 2d. If you are dealing with a knave, it prevents him from accomplishing any evil designs he may have upon you. 3d. Young people are apt to be deceived by appearances, both from a credulity common to their youth and inexperience, and because neither the young nor the old have any certain method of knowing human character by externals. The most open hearted are the most liable to be imposed upon by the designing.

It will be well to have all your business—of course all contracts—as far as may be practicable, in writing. And it would be well if men of business would make it a constant rule, whenever and wherever it is possible, to draw up a minute or memorial of every transaction, subscribed by both, with a clause signifying that in case of any difference, they would submit the matter to arbitration.

Nothing is more common than for a designing person to put off the individual he wishes to take advantage of, by saying; *We shan't disagree. I'll do what's right about it; I won't wrong you, &c.* And then when accounts come to be settled, and the party who thinks himself aggrieved, says that he made the bargain with the expectation of having such and such advantages allowed him, *No*, says the sharper, *I never told you any such thing.*

It is on this account that you cannot be too exact in making contracts; nor is there indeed any safety in dealing with deceitful and avaricious people, after you have taken all the precaution in your power.

SECTION X. *How to know with whom to deal.* - There are two maxims in common life that seem to clash with each other, most pointedly. The first is, 'Use every precaution with a stranger, that you would wish you had done, should he turn out to be a villain;' and secondly, 'Treat every man as an honest man, until he proves to be otherwise.'

Now there is good advice in both these maxims. By this I mean that they may both be observed, to a certain extent, without interfering with each other. You may be cautious about hastily becoming acquainted with a stranger, and yet so far as you have any concern with him, treat him like an honest man. No *reasonable* person will complain if you do not unbosom yourself to him at once. And if he is unreasonable, you will not *wish* for an intimate acquaintance with him.

My present purpose is to offer a few hints, with a view to assist you in judging of the characters of those with whom it may be your lot to deal. Remember, however, that like all things human, they are imperfect. All I can say is that they are the best I can offer.

There is something in knavery that will hardly bear the inspection of a piercing eye; and you may, more generally, observe in a sharper an unsteady and confused look. If a person is persuaded of the uncommon sagacity of one before whom he is to appear, he will hardly succeed in mustering impudence and artifice enough to bear him through without faltering. It will, therefore, be a good way to try one whom you have reason to suspect of a design upon you, by fixing your eyes upon his, and bringing up a supposition of your having to do with one whose integrity you suspected; stating what you would do in such a case. If the person you are talking with be really what you expect, he will hardly be able to keep his countenance.

It will be a safe rule,—though doubtless there are exceptions to it,—to take mankind to be more or less avaricious. Yet a great love of money is a great enemy to honesty. The aged are, in this respect, more dangerous than the young. It will be your wisdom ever to be cautious of *aged* avarice; and especially of those who, in an affected and forced manner, bring in religion, and talk much of *duty* on all occasions; of all smooth and fawning people; of those who are very talkative, and who, in dealing with you, endeavor to draw off your attention from the point in hand by incoherent or random expressions.

I have already advised you how to proceed with those of whom you have good reason to be suspicious. But by all means avoid entertaining unnecessary suspicions of your fellow beings; for it will usually render both you and them the more miserable. It is often owing to a consciousness of a designing temper, in ourselves, that we are led to suspect others.

If you hear a person boasting of having got a remarkably good bargain, you may generally conclude him by no means too honest; for almost always where one gains much in a bargain, the other loses. I know well that cases occur where both parties are gainers, but not greatly so. And when you hear a man triumph in gaining by another's loss, you may easily judge of his character.

Let me warn you against the sanguine promisers. Of these there are two sorts. The first are those who from a foolish custom of fawning upon all those whom they meet with in company, have acquired a habit of promising great favors which they have no idea of performing. The second are a sort of warm hearted people, who while they lavish their promises have some thoughts of performing them; but when the time comes, and the sanguine fit is worn off, the trouble or expense appears in another light; the promiser cools, and the expectant is disappointed.

Be cautious of dealing with an avaricious and cruel man, for if it should happen by an unlucky turn of trade that you should come into the power of such a person, you have nothing to expect but the utmost rigor of the law.

In negotiating, there are a number of circumstances to be considered; the neglect of any of which may defeat your whole scheme. These will be mentioned in the next section.

SECTION XI. *How to take Men as they are.* - Such a knowledge of human character as will enable us to treat mankind according to their dispositions, circumstances, and modes of thinking, so as to secure their aid in all our *laudable* purposes, is absolutely indispensable. And while all men boast of their knowledge of human nature, and would rather be thought ignorant of almost every thing else than this, how obvious it is that there is nothing in regard to which there exists so much ignorance!

A miser is by no means a proper person to apply to for a favor that will *cost* him any thing. But if he chance to be a man of principle, he *may* make an excellent partner in trade, or arbitrator in a dispute about property; for he will have patience to investigate little things, and to stand about trifles, which a generous man would scorn. Still, as an honest man, and above all as a Christian, I doubt whether it would be quite right thus to derive advantage from the vices of another. In employing the miser, you give scope to his particular vice.

A passionate man will fly into a rage at the most trifling affront, but he will generally forget it nearly as soon, and be glad to do any thing in his power to make up with you. It is not therefore so dangerous to disoblige *him*, as the gloomy, sullen mortal, who will wait seven years for an opportunity to do you mischief.

A cool, slow man, who is somewhat advanced in age, is generally the best person to advise with. For despatch of business, however, make use of the young, the warm, and the sanguine. Some men are of no character at all; but always take a tinge from the last company they were in. Their advice, as well as their assistance, is usually good for nothing.

It is in vain to think of finding any thing very valuable in the mind of a covetous man. Avarice is generally the vice of abject spirits. Men who have a very great talent at making money, commonly have no other; for the man who began with nothing, and has accumulated wealth, has been too busy to think of improving his mind; or indeed, to think of any thing else but property.

A boaster is always to be suspected. His is a natural infirmity, which makes him forget what he is about, and run into a thousand extravagances that have no connection with the truth. With those who have a tolerable knowledge of the world, all his assertions, professions of friendship, promises, and threatenings, go for nothing. Trust him with a secret, and he will surely discover it, either through vanity or levity.

A meek tempered man is not quite the proper person for you; his *modesty* will be easily *confounded.*—The talkative man will be apt to forget himself, and blunder out something that will give you trouble.

A man's ruling passion is the key by which you may come at his character, and pretty nearly guess how he will act in any given circumstances, unless he is a wit or a fool; *they* act chiefly from caprice.

There are likewise connections between the different *parts* of men's characters, which it will be useful for you to study. For example, if you find a man to be hasty and passionate, you may generally take it for granted he is open and artless, and so on. Like other general rules, however, this admits of many exceptions.

A bully is usually a coward. When, therefore, you unluckily have to deal with such a man, the best way is to make up to him boldly, and answer him with firmness. If you show the least sign of submission, he will take advantage of it to use you ill.

There are six sorts of people, at whose hands you need not expect much kindness. The *sordid and narrow minded*, think of nobody but themselves. The *lazy* will not take the trouble to oblige you. The *busy* have not time to think of you. The overgrown *rich man*, is above regarding any one, how much soever he may stand in need of assistance. The *poor and unhappy* often have not the ability. The good natured *simpleton*, however willing, is *incapable* of serving you.[7]

The *age* of the person you are to deal with is also to be considered. *Young* people are easily drawn into any scheme, merely from its being new, especially if it falls in with their love of pleasure; but they are almost as easily discouraged from it by the next person they meet with. They are not good counsellors, for they are apt to be precipitate and thoughtless; but are very fit for action, where you prescribe them a track from which they know they must not vary. Old age, on the contrary, is slow but sure; very cautious; opposed to new schemes and ways of life; inclining, generally, to covetousness; fitter to *consult* with you, than to *act* for you; not so easily won by fair speeches or long reasonings; tenacious of old opinions, customs, and formalities; apt to be displeased with those, especially younger people, who pretend to question their judgment; fond of deference, and of being listened to. Young people, in their anger, mean less than they say; old people more. You may make up for an injury with most young men; the old are generally more slow in forgiving.

The fittest character to be concerned with in business, is, that in which are united an inviolable integrity, founded upon rational principles of virtue and religion, a cool but determined temper, a friendly heart, a ready hand, long experience and extensive knowledge of the world; with a solid reputation of many years' standing, and easy circumstances.

SECTION XII. *Of desiring the good opinion of others.* - A young man is not far from ruin, when he can say, without blushing, *I don't care what others think of me.* To be insensible to public opinion, or to the estimation in which we are held by others, by no means indicates a good and generous spirit.

But to have a due regard to public opinion is one thing, and to make that opinion the principal rule of action, quite another. There is no greater weakness than that of letting our happiness depend *too much* upon the opinion of others. Other people lie under such disadvantages for coming at our true characters, and are so often misled by prejudice for or against us, that if our own conscience condemns us, their approbation can give us little consolation. On the other hand, if we are sure we acted from honest motives, and with a reference to proper ends, it is of little consequence if the world should happen to find fault. Mankind, for the most part, are so much governed by fancy, that what will win their hearts to-day, will disgust them to-morrow; and he who undertakes to please every body at all times, places, and circumstances, will never be in want of employment.

A wise man, when he hears of reflections made upon him, will consider whether they are *just*. If they are, he will correct the faults in question, with as much cheerfulness as if they had been suggested by his dearest friend.

I have sometimes thought that, in this view, enemies were the best of friends. Those who are merely friends in name, are often unwilling to tell us a great many things which it is of the highest importance that we should know. But our enemies, from spite, envy, or some other cause, mention them; and we ought on the whole to rejoice that they do, and to make the most of their remarks.

SECTION XIII. *Intermeddling with the affairs of others.* - There are some persons who never appear to be *happy*, if left to themselves and their own reflections. All their enjoyment seems to come from without; none from within. They are ever for having something to do with the affairs of others. Not a single petty quarrel can take place, in the neighborhood, but they suffer their feelings to be enlisted, and allow themselves to "take sides" with one of the parties. Those who possess such a disposition are among the most miserable of their race.

An old writer says that 'Every one should mind his own business; for he who is perpetually concerning himself about the good or ill fortune of others, will never be at rest.' And he says truly.

46

It is not denied that some men are professionally bound to attend to the concerns of others. But this is not the case supposed. The bulk of mankind will be happier, and do more for others, by letting them alone; at least by avoiding any of that sort of meddling which may be construed into officiousness.

Some of the worst meddlers in human society are those who have been denominated *match-makers*. A better name for them, however, would be match-*breakers*, for if they do not actually break more matches than they make, they usually cause a great deal of misery to those whom they are instrumental in bringing prematurely together.

Many people who, in other respects, pass for excellent, do not hesitate to take sides on almost all occasions, whether they know much about the real merits of the case or not. Others judge, at once, of every one of whom they hear any thing evil, and in the same premature manner.

All these and a thousand other kinds of 'meddling' do much evil. The tendency is to keep men like Ishmael, with their hands against every man, and every man's hands against theirs.

SECTION XIV. *On Keeping Secrets.* - It is sometimes said that in a good state of society there would be no necessity of *keeping* secrets, for no individual would have any thing to conceal. This *may* be true; but if so, society is far—very far—from being as perfect as it ought to be. At present we shall find no intelligent circle, except it were the society of the glorified above, which does not require occasional secrecy. But if there are secrets to be kept, somebody must keep them.

Some persons can hardly conceal a secret, if they would. They will promise readily enough; but the moment they gain possession of the fact, its importance rises in their estimation, till it occupies so much of their waking thoughts, that it will be almost certain, in some form or other, to escape them.

Others are not very anxious to conceal things which are entrusted to them. They may not wish to make mischief, exactly; but there is a sort of recklessness about them, that renders them very unsafe confidants.

Others again, when they promise, mean to perform. But no sooner do they possess the *treasure* committed to their charge, than they begin to grow forgetful of the *manner* of coming by it. And before they are aware, they reveal it.

There are not many then, whom it is safe to trust. These you will value as they do diamonds, in proportion to their scarcity.

But there *are* individuals who merit your highest confidence, if you can but find them. Husbands, where a union is founded as it ought to be, can usually trust their wives. This is one of the prominent advantages of matrimony. It gives us an opportunity of unbosoming our feelings and views and wishes not only with safety, but often with *sympathy*.

But confidence may sometimes be reposed, in other circumstances. Too much reserve makes us miserable. Perhaps it were better that we should suffer a little, now and then, than that we should never trust.

As an instance of the extent to which mankind can sometimes be confided in, and to show that celibacy, too, is not without this virtue, you will allow me to relate, briefly, an anecdote.

A certain husband and wife had difficulties. They both sought advice of a single gentleman, their family physician. For some time there was hope of an amicable adjustment of all grievances; but at length every effort proved vain, and an open quarrel ensued. But what was the surprise of each party to learn by accident, some time afterward, that both of them had sought counsel of the same individual, and yet he had not betrayed the trust.

In a few instances, too, secrets have been confided to husbands, without their communicating them to their wives; and the contrary. This was done, however, by particular request. It is a requisition which, for my own part, I should be very unwilling to make.

SECTION XV. *Fear of Poverty.* - The ingenious but sometimes fanciful Dr. Darwin, reckons the fear of poverty as a disease, and goes on to prescribe for it.

The truth is, there is not much *real* poverty in this country. Our very paupers are rich, for they usually have plenty of wholesome food, and comfortable clothing, and what could a Crœsus, with all *his* riches, have more? Poverty exists much more in imagination than in reality. The *shame of being thought poor*, is a great and fatal weakness, to say the least. It depends, it is true, much upon the fashion.

So long as the phrase 'he is a good man,' means that the person spoken of is rich, we need not wonder that every one wishes to be thought richer than he is. When adulation is sure to follow wealth, and when contempt would be sure to follow many if they were not wealthy; when people are spoken of with deference, and even lauded to the skies because their riches are very great; when this is the case, I say, we need not wonder if men are ashamed to be thought poor. But this is one of the greatest dangers which young people have to encounter in setting out in life. It has brought thousands and hundreds of thousands to pecuniary ruin.

One of the most amiable features of *good* republican society is this; that men seldom boast of their riches, or disguise their poverty, but speak of both, as of any other matters that are proper for conversation. No man shuns another because he is poor; no man is preferred to another because he is rich. In hundreds and hundreds of instances have men in this country, not worth a shilling, been chosen by the people to take care of their rights and interests, in preference to men who ride in their carriages.

The shame of being thought poor leads to everlasting efforts to *disguise* one's poverty. The carriage—the domestics—the wine—the spirits—the decanters—the glass;—all the table apparatus, the horses, the dresses, the dinners, and the parties, must be kept up; not so much because he or she who keeps or gives them has any pleasure arising therefrom, as because not to keep and give them, would give rise to a suspicion of *a want of means.* And thus thousands upon thousands are yearly brought into a state of real poverty, merely by their great anxiety not to be thought poor. Look around you carefully, and see if this is not so.

In how many instances have you seen amiable and industrious families brought to ruin by nothing else but the fear they *should* be? Resolve, then, from the first, to set this false shame at defiance. When you have done that, effectually, you have laid the corner-stone of mental tranquillity.

There are thousands of families at this very moment, struggling to keep up appearances. They feel that it makes them miserable; but you can no more induce them to change their course, than you can put a stop to the miser's laying up gold.

Farmers accommodate themselves to their condition more easily than merchants, mechanics, and professional men. They live at a greater distance from their neighbors; they can change their style of living without being perceived; they can put away the decanter, change the china for something plain, and the world is none the wiser for it. But the mechanic, the doctor, the attorney, and the trader cannot make the change so quietly and unseen.

Stimulating drink, which is a sort of criterion of the scale of living,—(or scale to the plan,)—a sort of key to the tune;—this is the thing to banish first of all, because all the rest follow; and in a short time, come down to their proper level.

Am I asked, what is a glass of wine? I answer, *it is every thing*. It creates a demand for all the other unnecessary expenses; it is injurious to health, and must be so. Every bottle of wine that is drank contains a portion of *spirit*, to say nothing of other drugs still more poisonous; and of all friends to the doctors, alcoholic drinks are the greatest. It is nearly the same, however, with strong tea and coffee. But what adds to the folly and wickedness of using these drinks, the parties themselves do not always drink them by *choice*, and hardly ever because they believe they are useful;—but from mere ostentation, or the fear of being thought either *rigid* or *stingy*. At this very moment, thousands of families daily use some half a dozen drinks, *besides the best*, because if they drank water only, they might not be regarded as genteel; or might be suspected of poverty. And thus they waste their property and their health.

Poverty frequently arises from the very virtues of the impoverished parties. Not so frequently, I admit, as from vice, folly, and indiscretion; but still very frequently. And as it is according to scripture not to 'despise the poor, *because* he is poor,' so we ought not to honor the rich merely because he is rich. The true way is to take a fair survey of the character of a man as exhibited in his conduct; and to respect him, or otherwise, according to a due estimate of that character.

Few countries exhibit more of those fatal terminations of life, called suicides, than *this*. Many of these unnatural crimes arise from an unreasonable estimate of the evils of poverty. Their victims, it is true, may be called insane; but their insanity almost always arises from the dread of poverty. Not, indeed, from the dread of the want of means for sustaining life, or even *decent* living; but from the dread of being thought or known to be poor;—from the dread of what is called falling in the scale of society.[8]

Viewed in its true light, what is there in poverty that can tempt a man to take away his own life? He is the same man that he was before; he has the same body and the same mind. Suppose he can foresee an alteration in his *dress* or his *diet*, should he kill himself on that account? Are these all the things that a man wishes to live for?

I do not deny that we ought to take care of our means, use them prudently and sparingly, and keep our expenses always within the limits of our income, be that what it may. One of the effectual means of doing this, is to purchase with ready money. On this point, I have already remarked at length, and will only repeat here the injunction of St. Paul; 'Owe no man any thing;' although the fashion of the whole world should be against you.

Should you regard the advice of this section, the counsels of the next will be of less consequence; for you will have removed one of the strongest inducements to speculation, as well as to overtrading.

SECTION XVI. *On Speculation.* - Young men are apt to be fond of *speculation*. This propensity is very early developed—first in the family—and afterwards at the school. By *speculation*, I mean the purchasing of something which you do not want for use, solely with a view to sell it again at a large profit; but on the sale of which there is a hazard.

When purchases of this sort are made with the person's own cash, they are not so unreasonable, but when they are made by one who is deeply indebted to his fellow beings, or with money borrowed for the purpose, it is not a whit better than gambling, let the practice be defended by whom it may: and has been in every country, especially in this, a fruitful source of poverty, misery, and suicide. Grant that this species of gambling has arisen from the facility of obtaining the fictitious means of making the purchase, still it is not the less necessary that I beseech you not to practise it, and if engaged in it already, to disentangle yourself as soon as you can. Your life, while thus engaged, is that of a gamester—call it by what smoother name you may. It is a life of constant anxiety, desire to overreach, and general gloom; enlivened now and then, by a gleam of hope or of success. Even that success is sure to lead to farther adventures; till at last, a thousand to one, that your fate is that of 'the pitcher to the well.'

The great temptation to this, as well as to every other species of gambling, is, the *success of the few*. As young men, who crowd to the army in search of rank and renown, never look into the ditch that holds their slaughtered companions, but have their eye constantly fixed on the commander-in-chief; and as each of them belongs to the *same profession*, and is sure to be conscious that he has equal merit, every one dreams himself the suitable successor of him who is surrounded with *aides-de-camp*, and who moves battalions and columns by his nod;—so with the rising generation of 'speculators.' They see those whom they suppose nature and good laws made to black shoes, or sweep chimneys or streets, rolling in carriages, or sitting in palaces, surrounded by servants or slaves; and they can see no earthly reason why they should not all do the same. They forget the thousands, and tens of thousands, who in making the attempt, have reduced themselves to beggary.

SECTION XVII. *On Lawsuits.* - In every situation in life, avoid the law. Man's nature must be changed, perhaps, before lawsuits will entirely cease; and yet it is in the power of most men to avoid them, in a considerable degree.

One excellent rule is, to have as little as possible to do with those who are *fond* of litigation; and who, upon every slight occasion, talk of an appeal to the law. This may be called a *disease*; and, like many other diseases, it is contagious. Besides, these persons, from their frequent litigations, contract a habit of using the technical terms of the courts, in which they take a pride, and are therefore, as companions, peculiarly disgusting to men of sense. To such beings a lawsuit is a luxury, instead of being regarded as a source of anxiety, and a real scourge. Such men are always of a quarrelsome disposition, and avail themselves of every opportunity to indulge in that which is mischievous to their neighbors.

In thousands of instances, men go to law for the indulgence of mere anger. The Germans are *said* to bring *spite-actions* against one another, and to harass their poorer neighbors from motives of pure revenge. But I hope this is a mistake; for I am unwilling to think so ill of that intelligent nation.

Before you decide to go to law, consider well the *cost*, for if you win your suit and are poorer than you were before, what do you gain by it? You only imbibe a little additional anger against your opponent; you injure him, but at the same time, injure yourself more. Better to put up with the loss of one dollar than of two; to which is to be added, all the loss of time, all the trouble, and all the mortification and anxiety attending a lawsuit. To set an attorney at work to worry and torment another man, and alarm his family as well as himself, while you are sitting quietly at home, is baseness. If a man owe you money which he cannot pay, why add to his distress, without even the *chance* of benefiting yourself? Thousands have injured themselves by resorting to the law, while very few, indeed, ever bettered their condition by it.

Nearly a million of dollars was once expended in England, during the progress of a single lawsuit. Those who brought the suit expended $444,000 to carry it through; and the opposite party was acquitted, and only sentenced to pay the cost of prosecution, amounting to $318,754. Another was sustained in court fifty years, at an enormous expense. In Meadville, in Pennsylvania, a petty law case occurred in which the damages recovered were only ten dollars, while the costs of court were one hundred. In one of the New England States, a lawsuit occurred, which could not have cost the parties less than $1,000 each; and yet after all this expense, they mutually agreed to take the matter out of court, and suffer it to end where it was. Probably it was the wisest course they could possibly have taken. It is also stated that a quarrel occurred between two persons in Middlebury, Vermont, a few years since, about *six eggs*, which was carried from one court to another, till it cost the parties $4,000.

I am well acquainted with a gentleman who was once engaged in a lawsuit, (than which none perhaps, was ever more just) where his claim was one to two thousand dollars; but it fell into such a train that a final decision could not have been expected in many months;—perhaps not in years. The gentleman was unwilling to be detained and perplexed with waiting for a trial, and he accordingly paid the whole amount of costs to that time, amounting to $150, went about his business, and believes, to this hour, that it was the wisest course he could have pursued.

A spirit of litigation often disturbs the peace of a whole neighborhood, perpetually, for several generations; and the hostile feeling thus engendered seems to be transmitted, like the color of the eyes or the hair, from father to son. Indeed it not unfrequently happens, that a lawsuit in a neighborhood, a society, or even a church, awakens feelings of discord, which never terminate, but at the death of the parties concerned.

How ought young men, then, to avoid, as they would a pestilence, this fiend-like spirit! How ought they to labor to settle all disputes—should disputes unfortunately arise,—without this tremendous resort! On the strength of much observation,—*not experience*, for I have been saved the pain of learning in that painful school, on this subject,—I do not hesitate to recommend the settlement of such difficulties by arbitration. One thing however should be remembered. Would you dry up the river of discord, you must first exhaust the fountains and rills which form it. The moment you indulge one impassioned or angry feeling against your fellow being, you have taken a step in the high road which leads to litigation, war and murder. Thus it is, as I have already told you, that 'He that hateth his brother is a murderer.' I have heard a father—for he hath the name of parent, though he little deserved it—gravely contend that there was no such thing as avoiding quarrels and lawsuits. He thought there was one thing, however, which might prevent them, which was to take the litigious individual and 'tar and feather' him without ceremony. How often is it true that mankind little know 'what manner of spirit they are of;' and to how many of us will this striking reproof of the Saviour apply! Multitudes of men have been in active business during a long life, and yet avoided every thing in the shape of a lawsuit. 'What man has done, man may do;' in this respect, at the least.

SECTION XVIII. *On Hard Dealing.* - Few things are more common among business-doing men, than *hard dealing*, yet few things reflect more dishonor on a Christian community. It seems, in general, to be regarded as morally right,—in defiance of all rules, whether *golden* or not,—to get as 'good a bargain' in trade, as possible; and this is defended as unavoidable, on account of the *state of society!* But what *produced* this state of society? Was it not the spirit of avarice? What will change it for the better? Nothing but the renunciation of this spirit, and a willingness to sacrifice, in this respect, for the public welfare. We are *pagans* in this matter, in spite of our professions. It would be profitable for us to take lessons on this subject from the Mohammedans. They never have, it is said, but one price for an article; and to ask the meanest shopkeeper to lower his price, is to *insult* him. Would this were the only point, in which the Christian community are destined yet to learn even from Mohammedans. To ask one price and take another, or to offer one price and give another, besides being a loss of time, is highly dishonorable to the parties. It is, in fact, a species of lying; and it answers no one advantageous purpose, either to the buyer or seller. I hope that every young man will start in life with a resolution never to be *hard in his dealings*. 'It is an evil which will correct itself;' say those who wish to avail themselves of its present advantages a little longer. But when and where did a general evil correct itself? When or where was an erroneous practice permanently removed, except by a change of public sentiment? And what has ever produced a change in the public sentiment but the determination of individuals, or their combined action?

While on this topic, I will hazard the assertion—even at the risk of its being thought misplaced—that great effects are yet to be produced on public opinion, in this country, by associations of spirited and intelligent young men. I am not now speaking of associations for political purposes, though I am not sure that even these *might* not be usefully conducted; but of associations for mutual improvement, and for the correction and elevation of the public morals. The "Boston Young Men's Society," afford a specimen of what may be done in this way; and numerous associations of the kind have sprung up and are springing up in various parts of the country. Judiciously managed, they must inevitably do great good;—though it should not be forgotten that they *may* also be productive of immense evil.

# CHAPTER III.

On Amusements and Indulgences. - SECTION I. *On Gaming.*

Even Voltaire asserts that 'every gambler is, has been, or will be a robber.' Few practices are more ancient, few more general, and few, if any, more pernicious than gaming. An English writer has ingeniously suggested that the Devil himself might have been the first player, and that he contrived the plan of introducing games among men, to afford them temporary amusement, and divert their attention from themselves. 'What numberless disciples,' he adds, 'of his sable majesty, might we not count in our own metropolis!'

Whether his satanic majesty has any very direct agency in this matter or not, one thing is certain;— gaming is opposed to the happiness of mankind, and ought, in every civilized country, to be suppressed by public opinion. By gaming, however, I here refer to those cases only in which property is at stake, to be won or lost. The subject of *diversions* will be considered in another place.

Gaming is an evil, because, in the first place, it is a practice which *produces* nothing. He who makes two blades of grass grow where but one grew before, has usually been admitted to be a public benefactor; for he is a *producer.* So is he who combines or arranges these productions in a useful manner,—I mean the mechanic, manufacturer, &c. He is equally a public benefactor, too, who produces *mental* or *moral* wealth, as well as physical. In gaming, it is true, property is shifted from one individual to another, and here and there one probably gains more than he loses; but nothing is actually *made*, or *produced.* If the whole human family were all skilful gamesters, and should play constantly for a year, there would not be a dollar more in the world at the end of the year, than there was at its commencement. On the contrary, is it not obvious that there would be much *less*, besides even an immense loss of time?[9]

But, secondly, gaming favors corruption of manners. It is difficult to trace the progress of the gamester's mind, from the time he commences his downward course, but we know too well the goal at which he is destined to arrive. There may be exceptions, but not many; generally speaking, every gamester, sooner or later travels the road to perdition, and often adds to his own wo, by dragging others along with him.

Thirdly, it discourages industry. He who is accustomed to receive large sums at once, which bear no sort of proportion to the labor by which they are obtained, will gradually come to regard the moderate but constant and certain rewards of industrious exertion as insipid. He is also in danger of falling into the habit of paying an undue regard to hazard or chance, and of becoming devoted to the doctrine of fatality.

As to the few who are skilful enough to gain more, on the whole, than they lose, scarcely one of them pays any regard to prudence or economy in his expenditures. What is thus lightly acquired, is lightly disposed of. Or if, in one instance in a thousand, it happens otherwise, the result is still unfavorable. It is but to make the miser still more a miser, and the covetous only the more so. Man is so constituted as to be unable to bear, with safety, a rapid accumulation of property. To the truth of this, all history attests, whether ancient or modern, sacred or profane.

The famous philosopher Locke, in his 'Thoughts on Education,' thus observes: 'It is certain, gaming leaves no satisfaction behind it to those who reflect when it is over; and it no way profits either body or mind. As to their estates, if it strike so deep as to concern them, it is a *trade* then, and not a *recreation*, wherein few thrive; and at best a thriving gamester has but a poor trade of it, who fills his pockets at the price of his reputation.'

In regard to the *criminality* of the practice, a late writer has the following striking remarks.

'As to gaming, it is always *criminal*, either in itself or in its tendency. The basis of it is covetousness; a desire to take from others something for which you have neither given, nor intend to give an equivalent. No gambler was ever yet a happy man, and few gamblers have escaped being positively miserable. Remember, too, that to game for *nothing* is still *gaming*; and naturally leads to gaming for *something*. It is sacrificing time, and that, too, for the worst of purposes.

'I have kept house for nearly forty years; I have reared a family; I have entertained as many friends as most people; and I never had cards, dice, a chess board, nor any implement of gaming under my roof. The hours that young men spend in this way, are hours murdered; precious hours that ought to be spent either in reading or in writing; or in rest; preparatory to the duties of the dawn.

'Though I do not agree with those base flatterers who declare the army to be *the best school for statesmen*, it is certainly a school in which we learn, experimentally, many useful lessons; and in this school I learned that men fond of gaming, are rarely, if ever, trust-worthy. I have known many a decent man rejected in the way of promotion, only because he was addicted to gaming. Men, in that state of life, cannot *ruin* themselves by gaming, for they possess no fortune, nor money; but the taste for gaming is always regarded as an indication of a radically bad disposition; and I can truly say that I never in my whole life—and it has been a long and eventful one—knew a man fond of gaming, who was not, in some way or other, unworthy of confidence. This vice creeps on by very slow degrees, till, at last, it becomes an ungovernable passion, swallowing up every good and kind feeling of the heart.'

For my own part I know not the *names* of cards; and could never take interest enough in card-playing to remember them. I have always wondered how sober and intelligent people, who have consciences, and believe the doctrine of accountability to God—how professing Christians even, as is the case in some parts of this country, can sit whole evenings at cards. Why, what notions have they of the value of time? Can they conceive of Him, whose example we are bound to follow, as engaged in this way? The thought should shock us! What a Herculean task Christianity has yet to accomplish!

The excess of this vice has caused even the overthrow of empires. It leads to conspiracies, and creates conspirators. Men overwhelmed with debt, are always ready to obey the orders of any bold chieftain who may attempt a decisive stroke, even against government itself. Catiline had very soon under his command an army of scoundrels. 'Every man,' says Sallust, 'who by his follies or losses at the gaming table had consumed the inheritance of his fathers, and all who were sufferers by such misery, were the friends of this perverse man.'

Perhaps this vice has nowhere been carried to greater excess than in France. There it has its administration, its chief, its stockholders, its officers, and its priests. It has its domestics, its pimps, its spies, its informers, its assassins, its bullies, its aiders, its abettors,—in fact, its scoundrels of every description; particularly its hireling swindlers, who are paid for decoying the unwary into this 'hell upon earth,' so odious to morality, and so destructive to virtue and Christianity.

In England, this vice has at all times been looked upon as one of pernicious consequence to the commonwealth, and has, therefore, long been prohibited. The money lost in this way, is even recoverable again by law. Some of the laws on this subject were enacted as early as the time of Queen Anne, and not a few of the penalties are very severe. Every species of gambling is strictly forbidden in the British army, and occasionally punished with great severity, by order of the commander in chief. These facts show the state of public opinion in that country, in regard to the evil tendency of this practice.

Men of immense wealth have, in some instances, entered gambling houses, and in the short space of an hour have found themselves reduced to absolute beggary. 'Such men often lose not only what their purses or their bankers can supply, but houses, lands, equipage, jewels; in fine, every thing of which they call themselves masters, even to their very clothes; then perhaps a pistol terminates their mortal career.'

Fifteen hours a day are devoted by many infatuated persons in some countries to this unhappy practice. In the middle of the day, while the wife directs with prudence and economy the administration of her husband's house, he abandons himself to become the prey of rapacious midnight and *mid-day* robbers. The result is, that he contracts debts, is stripped of his property, and his wife and children are sent to the alms-house, whilst he, perhaps, *perishes in a prison*.

My life has been chiefly spent in a situation where comparatively little of this vice prevails. Yet, I have known one individual who divided his time between hunting and gaming. About four days in the week were regularly devoted to the latter practice. From breakfast to dinner, from dinner to tea, from tea to nine o'clock, this was his regular employment, and was pursued incessantly. The man was about seventy years of age. He did not play for very large sums, it is true; seldom more than five to twenty dollars; and it was his uniform practice to retire precisely at nine o'clock, and without supper.

Generally, however, the night is more especially devoted to this employment. I have occasionally been at public houses, or on board vessels where a company was playing, and have known many hundreds of dollars lost in a single night. In one instance, the most horrid midnight oaths and blasphemy were indulged. Besides, there is an almost direct connection between the gambling table and brothel; and the one is seldom long unaccompanied by the other.

Scarcely less obvious and direct is the connection between this vice and intemperance. If the drunkard is not always a gamester, the gamester is almost without exception intemperate. There is for the most part a union of the three—horrible as the alliance may be—I mean gambling, intemperance, and debauchery.

There is even a species of intoxication attendant on gambling. *Rede*, in speaking of one form of this vice which prevails in Europe, says; 'It is, in fact, a PROMPT MURDERER; irregular as all other games of hazard—rapid as lightning in its movements—its strokes succeed each other with an activity that redoubles the ardor of the player's blood, and often deprives him of the advantage of reflection. In fact, a man after half an hour's play, who for the whole night may not have taken any thing stronger than water, has all the appearance of drunkenness.' And who has not seen the flushed cheek and the red eye, produced simply by the excitement of an ordinary gaming table?

It is an additional proof of the evil of gaming that every person devoted to it, *feels* it to be an evil. Why then does he not refrain? Because he has sold himself a slave to the deadly habit, as effectually as the drunkard to his cups.

Burgh, in his Dignity of Human Nature, sums up the evils of this practice in a single paragraph:

'Gaming is an amusement wholly unworthy of rational beings, having neither the pretence of exercising the body, of exerting ingenuity, or of giving any natural pleasure, and owing its entertainment wholly to an unnatural and vitiated taste;—the cause of infinite loss of time, of enormous destruction of money, of irritating the passions, of stirring up avarice, of innumerable sneaking tricks and frauds, of encouraging idleness, of disgusting people against their proper employments, and of sinking and debasing all that is truly great and valuable in the mind.'

Let me warn you, then, my young readers,—nay, more, let me *urge* you never to enter this dreadful road. Shun it as you would the road to destruction. Take not the first step,—the moment you do, all may be lost. Say not that you can command yourselves, and can stop when you approach the confines of danger. So thousands have thought as sincerely as yourselves—and yet they fell. 'The probabilities that we shall fall where so many have fallen,' says Dr. Dwight, 'are millions to one; and the contrary opinion is only the dream of lunacy.'

When you are inclined to think yourselves safe, consider the multitudes who once felt themselves equally so, have been corrupted, distressed, and ruined by gaming, both for this world, and that which is to come. Think how many families have been plunged by it in beggary, and overwhelmed by it in vice. Think how many persons have become liars at the gaming table; how many perjured; how many drunkards; how many blasphemers; how many suicides. 'If Europe,' said Montesquieu, 'is to be ruined, it will be ruined by gaming.' If the United States are to be ruined, gaming in some of its forms will be a very efficient agent in accomplishing the work.

Some of the most common games practised in this country, are cards, dice, billiards, shooting matches, and last, though not *least*, lotteries. Horse-racing and cockfighting are still in use in some parts of the United States, though less so than formerly. In addition to the general remarks already made, I now proceed to notice a few of the particular forms of this vice.

1. CARDS, DICE, AND BILLIARDS. - The foregoing remarks will be applicable to each of these three modes of gambling. But in regard to cards, there seems to be something peculiarly enticing. It is on this account that youth are required to be doubly cautious on this point. So bewitching were cards and dice regarded in England, that penalties were laid on those who should be found playing with them, as early as the reign of George II. Card playing, however, still prevails in Europe, and to a considerable extent in the United States. There is a very common impression abroad, that the mere *playing* at cards is in itself innocent: that the danger consists in the tendency to excess; and against excess most people imagine themselves sufficiently secure. But as 'the best throw at dice, is to throw them away,' so the best move with cards would be, to commit them to the flames.

2. SHOOTING MATCHES. - This is a disgraceful practice, which was formerly in extensive use in these States at particular seasons, especially on the day preceding the annual Thanksgiving. I am sorry to say, that there are places where it prevails, even now. Numbers who have nothing better to do, collect together, near some tavern or grog-shop, for the sole purpose of trying their skill at shooting fowls. Tied to a stake at a short distance, a poor innocent and helpless fowl is set as a mark to furnish sport for idle men and boys.

Could the creature be put out of its misery by the first discharge of the musket, the evil would not appear so great. But this is seldom the case. Several discharges are usually made, and between each, a running, shouting and jumping of the company takes place, not unfrequently mingled with oaths and curses.

The object of this infernal torture being at length despatched, and suspended on the muzzle of the gun as a trophy of victory, a rush is made to the bar or counter, and brandy and rum, accompanied by lewd stories, and perhaps quarrelling and drunkenness, often close the scene.

It rarely fails that a number of children are assembled on such occasions, who listen with high glee to the conversation, whether in the field or at the inn. If it be the grossest profaneness, or the coarsest obscenity, they will sometimes pride themselves in imitating it, thinking it to be manly; and in a like spirit will partake of the glass, and thus commence the drunkard's career.—This practice is conducted somewhat differently in different places, but not essentially so.

It is much to the credit of the citizens of many parts of New England that their good sense will not, any longer, tolerate a practice so brutal, and scarcely exceeded in this respect by the cockfights in other parts of the country. As a substitute for this practice a circle is drawn on a board or post, of a certain size, and he who can hit within the circle, gains the fowl. This is still a species of *gaming*, but is divested of much of the ferocity and brutality of the former.

3. HORSERACING AND COCKFIGHTING. - It is only in particular sections of the United States that public opinion tolerates these practices extensively. A horserace, in New England, is a very rare occurrence. A cockfight, few among us have ever witnessed. Wherever the cruel disposition to indulge in seeing animals fight together is allowed, it is equally degrading to human nature with that fondness which is manifested in other countries for witnessing a bull fight. It is indeed the *same* disposition, only existing in a smaller degree in the former case than in the latter.

Montaigne thinks it a reflection upon human nature itself that few people take delight in seeing beasts caress and play together, while almost every one is pleased to see them lacerate and worry one another.

Should your lot be cast in a region where any of these inhuman practices prevail, let it be your constant and firm endeavor, not merely to keep aloof from them yourselves, but to prevail on all those over whom God may have given you influence, to avoid them likewise. To enable you to face the public opinion when a point of importance is at stake, it will be useful to consult carefully the first chapter of this work.

I am sorry to have it in my power to state that in the year 1833 there was a *bull fight* four miles southward of Philadelphia. It was attended by about 1500 persons; mostly of the very lowest classes from the city. It was marked by many of the same evils which attend these cruel sports in other countries, and by the same reckless disregard of mercy towards the poor brutes who suffered in the conflict. It is to be hoped, however, for the honor of human nature, that the good sense of the community will not permit this detestable custom to prevail.

SECTION II. *On Lotteries.* - Lotteries are a species of gambling; differing from other kinds only in being tolerated either by the law of the land, or by that of public opinion. The proofs of this assertion are innumerable. Not only young men, but even married women have, in some instances, become so addicted to ticket buying, as to ruin themselves and their families.

From the fact that efforts have lately been made in several of the most influential States in the Union to suppress them, it might seem unnecessary, at first view, to mention this subject. But although the letter of the law may oppose them, there is a portion of our citizens who will continue to buy tickets clandestinely; and consequently somebody will continue to sell them in the same manner. Penalties will not suppress them at once. It will be many years before the evil can be wholly eradicated. The flood does not cease at the moment when the windows of heaven are closed, but continues, for some time, its ravages. It is necessary, therefore, that the young should guard themselves against the temptations which they hold out.

It may be said that important works, such as monuments, and churches, have been completed by means of lotteries. I know it is so. But the profits which arise from the sale of tickets are a tax upon the community, and generally upon the poorer classes: or rather they are a species of swindling. That good is sometimes done with these ill-gotten gains, is admitted; but money procured in any other unlawful, immoral, or criminal way, could be applied to build bridges, roads, churches, &c. Would the advantages thus secured, however, justify an unlawful means of securing them? Does the end sanctify the means?

It is said, too, that individuals, as well as associations, have been, in a few instances, greatly aided by prizes in lotteries. Some bankrupts have paid their debts, *like* honest men, with them. This they might do with stolen money. But cases of even this kind, are rare. The far greater part of the money drawn in the form of prizes in lotteries, only makes its possessor more avaricious, covetous, or oppressive than before. Money obtained in this manner commonly ruins mind, body, or estate; sometimes all three.

Lottery schemes have been issued in the single State of New York, in twelve years, to the amount of $37,000,000. If other States have engaged in the business, in the same proportion to their population, the sum of all the schemes issued in the United States within that time has been $240,000,000. A sum sufficient to maintain in comfort, if not affluence, the entire population of some of the smaller States for more than thirty years.

Now what has been gained by all this? It is indeed true, that the discount on this sum, amounting to $36,000,000, has been expended in paying a set of men for *one* species of labor. If we suppose their average salary to have been $500, no less than 6,000 clerks, managers, &c., may have obtained by this means, a support during the last twelve years. But what have the 6,000 men *produced* all this while?

Has not their whole time been spent in receiving small sums (from five to fifty dollars) from individuals, putting them together, as it were, in a heap, and afterwards distributing a part of it in sums, with a few exceptions, equally small?—Have they added one dollar, or even one cent to the original stock? I have already admitted, that he who makes two blades of grass grow where only one grew before, is a benefactor to his country; but these men have not done so much as that.

A few draw prizes, it has been admitted. Some of that few make a good use of them. But the vast majority are injured. They either become less active and industrious, or more parsimonious and miserly; and not a few become prodigals or bankrupts at once. In any of these events, they are of course unfitted for the essential purposes of human existence. It is not given to humanity to *bear* a sudden acquisition of wealth. The best of men are endangered by it. As in knowledge, so in the present case, what is gained by hard digging is usually retained; and what is gained easily usually goes quickly. There is this difference, however, that the moral character is usually lost with the one, but not always with the other.

These are a part of the evils connected with lotteries. To compute their sum total would be impossible. The immense waste of money and time (and time is money) by those persons who are in the habit of buying tickets, to say nothing of the cigars smoked, the spirits, wine, and ale drank, the suppers eaten, and the money lost at cards, while lounging about lottery offices, although even this constitutes but a *part* of the waste, is absolutely incalculable. The suffering of wives, and children, and parents, and brothers, and sisters, together with that loss of health, and temper, and reputation, which is either directly or indirectly connected, would swell the sum to an amount sufficient to alarm every one, who intends to be an honest, industrious, and respectable citizen.

It is yours, my young friends, to put a stop to this tremendous evil. It is your duty, and it should be your pleasure, to give that *tone* to the public sentiment, without which, in governments like this, written laws are powerless.

Do not say that the influence of *one person* cannot effect much. Remember that the power of example is almost omnipotent. In debating whether you may not venture to buy one more ticket, remember that if you do so, you adopt a course which, if taken by every other individual in the United States (and who out of thirteen millions has not the same *right* as yourself?) would give abundant support to the whole lottery system, with all its horrors. And could you in that case remain guiltless? Can the fountains of such a sickly stream be pure? You would not surely condemn the waters of a mighty river while you were one of a company engaged in filling the springs and rills that unite to form it. Remember that just in proportion as you contribute, by your example, to discourage this species of gambling, just in the same proportion will you contribute to stay the progress of a tremendous scourge, and to enforce the execution of good and salutary laws.

With this pernicious practice, I have always been decidedly at war. I believe the system to be wholly wrong, and that those who countenance it, in any way whatever, are wholly inexcusable.

SECTION III. *On Theatres.* - Much is said by the friends of theatres about what they *might* be; and not a few persons indulge the hope that the theatre may yet be made a school of morality. But my business at present is with it *as it is*, and as it has hitherto been. The reader will be more benefited by existing *facts* than sanguine anticipations, or visionary predictions.

A German medical writer calculates that one in 150 of those who frequently attend theatres become diseased and die, from the impurity of the atmosphere. The reason is, that respiration contaminates the air; and where large assemblies are collected in close rooms, the air is corrupted much more rapidly than many are aware. Lavoisier, the French chemist, states, that in a theatre, from the commencement to the end of the play, the oxygen or vital air is diminished in the proportion of from 27 to 21, or nearly one fourth; and consequently is in the same proportion less fit for respiration, than it was before. This is probably the general truth; but the number of persons present, and the amount of space, must determine, in a great measure, the rapidity with which the air is corrupted. The pit is the most unhealthy part of a play-house, because the carbonic acid which is formed by respiration is heavier than atmospheric air, and accumulates near the floor.

It is painful to look round on a gay audience of 1500 persons, and consider that ten of this number will die in consequence of breathing the bad air of the room so frequently, and so long. But I believe this estimate is quite within bounds.

There are however other results to be dreaded. The practice of going out of a heated, as well as an impure atmosphere late in the evening, and often without sufficient clothing, exposes the individual to cold, rheumatism, pleurisy, and fever. Many a young lady,—and, I fear, not a few young gentlemen,—get the consumption by taking colds in this manner.

Not only the health of the body, but the mind and morals, too, are often injured. Dr. Griscom, of New York, in a report on the causes of vice and crime in that city, made a few years since, says; 'Among the causes of vicious excitement in our city, none appear to be so powerful in their nature as theatrical amusements. The number of boys and young men who have become determined thieves, in order to procure the means of introduction to the theatres and circuses, would appal the feelings of every virtuous mind, could the whole truth be laid open before them.

'In the case of the feebler sex, the result is still worse. A relish for the amusements of the theatre, without the means of indulgence, becomes too often a motive for listening to the first suggestion of the seducer, and thus prepares the unfortunate captive of sensuality for the haunts of infamy, and a total destitution of all that is valuable in the mind and character of woman.'

The following fact is worthy of being considered by the friends and patrons of theatres. During the progress of one of the most ferocious revolutions which ever shocked the face of heaven, theatres, in Paris alone, multiplied from six to twenty-five. Now one of two conclusions follow from this: Either the spirit of the times produced the institutions, or the institutions cherished the spirit of the times; and this will certainly prove that they are either the parents of vice or the offspring of it.

The philosopher Plato assures us, that 'plays raise the passions, and prevent the use of them; and of course are dangerous to morality.'

'The seeing of *Comedies*,' says Aristotle, 'ought to be forbidden to young people, till age and discipline have made them proof against debauchery.'

Tacitus says, 'The German women were guarded against danger, and preserved their purity by having no play-houses among them.'

Even Ovid represents theatrical amusements as a grand source of corruption, and he advised Augustus to suppress them.

The infidel philosopher Rousseau, declared himself to be of opinion, that the theatre is, in all cases, a school of vice. Though he had himself written for the stage, yet, when it was proposed to establish a theatre in the city of Geneva, he wrote against the project with zeal and great force, and expressed the opinion that every friend of pure morals ought to oppose it.

Sir John Hawkins, in his life of Johnson, observes:—'Although it is said of plays that they teach morality, and of the stage that it is the mirror of human life, these assertions are mere declamation, and have no foundation in truth or experience. On the contrary, a play-house, and the regions about it, are the very hot-beds of vice.'

Archbishop Tillotson, after some pointed and forcible reasoning against it, pronounces the play-house to be 'the devil's chapel,' 'a nursery of licentiousness and vice,' and 'a recreation which ought not to be allowed among a civilized, much less a Christian people.'

Bishop Collier solemnly declared, that he was persuaded that 'nothing had done more to debauch the age in which he lived, than the stage poets and the play-house.'

Sir Matthew Hale, having in early life experienced the pernicious effects of attending the theatre, resolved, when he came to London, never to see a play again, and to this resolution he adhered through life.

Burgh says; 'What does it avail that the piece itself be unexceptionable, if it is to be interlarded with lewd songs or dances, and tagged at the conclusion with a ludicrous and beastly farce? I cannot therefore, in conscience, give youth any other advice than to avoid such diversions as cannot be indulged without the utmost danger of perverting their taste, and corrupting their morals.'

Dr. Johnson's testimony on this subject is nearly as pointed as that of Archbishop Tillotson; and Lord Kaimes speaks with much emphasis of the 'poisonous influence,' of theatres.

Their evil tendency is seldom better illustrated than by the following anecdote, from an individual in New York, on whose statements we may place the fullest reliance.

'F. B. a young man of about twenty-two, called on the writer in the fall of 1831 for employment. He was a journeyman printer; was recently from Kentucky; and owing to his want of employment, as he said, was entirely destitute, not only of the comforts, but the necessaries of life. I immediately procured him a respectable boarding house, gave him employment, and rendered his situation as comfortable as my limited means would permit.

'He had not been with me long, before he expressed a desire to go to the theatre. Some great actor was to perform on a certain night, and he was very anxious to see him. I warned him of the consequences, and told him, my own experience and observation had convinced me that it was a very dangerous place for young men to visit. But my warning did no good. He neglected his business, and went. I reproved him gently, but retained him in my employment. He continued to go, notwithstanding all my remonstrances to the contrary. At length my business suffered so much from his neglecting to attend to it as he ought, that I was under the necessity of discharging him in self-defence. He got temporary employment in different offices of the city, where the same fault was found with him. Immediately after, he accepted a situation of bar-keeper in a porter house or tavern attached to the theatre. His situation he did not hold long—from what cause, I know not.

'He again applied to me for work; but as his habits were not reformed, I did not think it prudent to employ him, although I said or did nothing to injure him in the estimation of others. Disappointed in procuring employment in a business to which he had served a regular apprenticeship, being pennyless, and seeing no bright prospect for the future, he enlisted as a common soldier in the United States' service.

'He had not been in his new vocation long, before he was called upon, with other troops, to defend our citizens from the attacks of the Indians. But when the troops had nearly reached their place of destination, that 'invisible scourge,' the cholera, made its appearance among them. Desertion was the consequence, and among others who fled, was the subject of this article.

'He returned to New York—made application at several different offices for employment, without success. In a few days news came that he had been detected in pilfering goods from the house of his landlord. A warrant was immediately issued for him—he was seized, taken to the police office—convicted, and sentenced to six months' hard labor in the penitentiary. His name being published in the newspapers, in connection with those of other convicts—was immediately recognised by the officer under whom he had enlisted.—This officer proceeds to the city—claims the prisoner—and it is at length agreed that he shall return to the United States' service, where he shall, for the first six months, be compelled to roll sand as a punishment for desertion, serve out the five years for which he had enlisted, and then be given up to the city authorities, to suffer for the crime of pilfering.

'It is thus that we see a young man, of good natural abilities, scarcely twenty-three years of age, compelled to lose six of the most valuable years of his life, besides ruining a fair reputation, and bringing disgrace upon his parents and friends, from the apparently harmless desire of seeing dramatic performances. Ought not this to be a warning to others, who are travelling on, imperceptibly in the same road to ruin?'

Theatres are of ancient date. One built of wood, in the time of Cicero and Cæsar, would contain 80,000 persons. The first stone theatre in Rome, was built by Pompey, and would contain 40,000. There are one or two in Europe, at the present time, that will accommodate 4,000 or 5,000.

In England, until 1660, public opinion did not permit *females* to perform in theatres, but the parts were performed by boys.

If theatres have a reforming tendency, this result might have been expected in France, where they have so long been popular and flourishing. In 1807, there were in France 166 theatres, and 3968 performers. In 1832 there were in Paris alone 17, which could accommodate 21,000 persons. But we do not find that they reformed the Parisians; and it is reasonable to expect they never will.

Let young men remember, that in this, as well as in many other things, there is only one point of security, viz. total abstinence.

SECTION IV. *Use of Tobacco.* - 1. SMOKING.

Smoking has every where, in Europe and America, become a tremendous evil; and if we except Holland and Germany, nowhere more so than in this country. Indeed we are already fast treading in the steps of those countries, and the following vivid description of the miseries which this filthy practice entails on the Germans will soon be quite applicable to the people of the United States, unless we can induce the rising generation to turn the current of public opinion against it.

'This plague, like the Egyptian plague of frogs, is felt every where, and in every thing. It poisons the streets, the clubs, and the coffee-houses;—furniture, clothes, equipage, persons, are redolent of the abomination. It makes even the dulness of the newspapers doubly narcotic: every eatable and drinkable, all that can be seen, felt, heard or understood, is saturated with tobacco;—the very air we breathe is but a conveyance for this poison into the lungs; and every man, woman, and child, rapidly acquires the complexion of a boiled chicken. From the hour of their waking, if nine-tenths of their population can be said to awake at all, to the hour of their lying down, the pipe is never out of their mouths. One mighty fumigation reigns, and human nature is smoked dry by tens of thousands of square miles. The German physiologists compute, that of 20 deaths, between eighteen and thirty-five years, 10 originate in the waste of the constitution by smoking.'

This is indeed a horrid picture; but when it is considered that the best estimates which can be made concur in showing that tobacco, to the amount of $16,000,000, is consumed in the United States annually, and that by far the greater part of this is in smoking cigars, there is certainly room for gloomy apprehensions. What though we do not use the dirty pipe of the Dutch and Germans? If we only use the *tobacco*, the mischief is effectually accomplished. Perhaps it were even better that we should lay out a part of our money for pipes, than to spend the whole for tobacco.

Smoking is indecent, filthy, and rude, and to many individuals highly offensive. When first introduced into Europe, in the 16th century, its use was prohibited under very severe penalties, which in some countries amounted even to cutting off the nose. And how much better is the practice of voluntarily burning up our noses, by making a chimney of them? I am happy, however, in being able to state, that this unpardonable practice is now abandoned in many of the fashionable societies in Europe.

There is one remarkable fact to be observed in speaking on this subject. No parent ever teaches his child the use of tobacco, or even encourages it, except by his example. Thus the smoker virtually condemns himself in the very 'thing which he alloweth.' It is not precisely so in the case of spirits; for many parents directly encourage the use of that.

Tobacco is one of the most powerful poisons in nature. Even the physician, some of whose medicines are so active that a few grains, or a few drops, will destroy life at once, finds tobacco too powerful for his use; and in those cases where it is most clearly required, only makes it a last resort. Its daily use, in any form, deranges, and sometimes destroys the stomach and nerves, produces weakness, low spirits, dyspepsy, vertigo, and many other complaints. These are its more immediate effects.

Its remoter effects are scarcely less dreadful. It dries the mouth and nostrils, and probably the brain; benumbs the senses of smell and taste, impairs the hearing, and ultimately the eye-sight. Germany, a *smoking* nation, is at the same time, a *spectacled* nation. More than all this; it dries the blood; creates thirst and loss of appetite; and in this and other ways, often lays the foundation of intemperance. In fact, not a few persons are made drunkards by this very means. Dr. Rush has a long chapter on this subject in one of his volumes, which is well worth your attention. In addition to all this, it has often been observed that in fevers and other diseases, medicines never operate well in constitutions which have been accustomed to the use of tobacco.

Of the expense which the use of it involves, I have already spoken. Of the $16,000,000 thus expended, $9,000,000 are supposed to be for smoking Spanish cigars; $6,500,000 for smoking American tobacco, and for chewing it; and $500,000 for snuff.

Although many people of real intelligence become addicted to this practice, as is the case especially among the learned in Germany, yet it cannot be denied that in general, those individuals and *nations* whose mental powers are the weakest, are (in proportion to their means of acquiring it) most enslaved to it. To be convinced of the truth of this remark, we have only to open our eyes to facts as they exist around us.

All ignorant and savage *nations* indulge in extraordinary stimulants, (and tobacco among the rest,) whenever they have the means of obtaining them; and in proportion to their degradation. Thus it is with the native tribes of North America; thus with the natives of Africa, Asia, and New Holland; thus with the Cretins and Gypsies. Zimmerman says, that the latter 'suspended their predatory excursions, and on an appointed evening in every week, assemble to enjoy their guilty spoils in the fumes of *strong waters* and *tobacco.*' Here they are represented as indulging in idle tales about the character and conduct of those around them; a statement which can very easily be believed by those who have watched the effects produced by the fumes of stimulating beverages much more '*respectable*' than spirits or tobacco smoke.

The quantity which is used in civilized nations is almost incredibly great. England alone imported, in 1829, 22,400,000 lbs. of unmanufactured tobacco. There is no narcotic plant—not even the tea plant—in such extensive use, unless it is the *betel* of India and the adjoining countries. *This* is the leaf of a climbing plant resembling ivy, but of the pepper tribe. The people of the east chew it so incessantly, and in such quantities, that their lips become quite red, and their teeth black—showing that it has affected their whole systems. They carry it about them in boxes, and offer it to each other in compliment, as the Europeans do snuff; and it is considered uncivil and unkind to refuse to accept and chew it. This is done by the women as well as by the men. Were we disposed, we might draw from this fact many important lessons on our own favored stimulants.

In view of the great and growing evil of smoking, the practical question arises; 'What shall be done?' The answer is—Render it unfashionable and disreputable. Do you ask, '*How* is this to be accomplished?' Why, how has alcohol been rendered unpopular? Do you still say, 'One person alone cannot effect much?' But so might any person have said a few years ago, in regard to spirits. Individuals must commence the work of reformation in the one case, as well as in the other; and success will then be equally certain.

2. CHEWING. - Many of the remarks already made apply with as much force to the use of tobacco in every form, as to the mere habit of smoking. But I have a few additional thoughts on chewing this plant.

There are never wanting excuses for any thing which we feel strongly inclined to do. Thus a thousand little frivolous pleas are used for chewing tobacco. One man of reputed good sense told me that his tobacco probably cost him nothing, for if he did not use it, he 'should be apt to spend as much worth of time in *picking and eating summer fruits*, as would pay for it.' Now I do not like the practice of eating even summer fruits between meals; but they are made to be eaten moderately, no doubt; and if people will not eat them *with* their food, it is generally a less evil to eat them between meals, than not at all. But the truth is, tobacco chewers never relish these things at any time.

The only plea for chewing this noxious plant, which is entitled to a serious consideration is, that it tends to preserve the teeth. This is the strong hold of tobacco chewers—not, generally, when they commence the practice, but as soon as they find themselves slaves to it.

Now the truth appears to be this:

1. 'When a tooth is decayed in such a manner as to leave the nerve exposed, there is no doubt that the powerful stimulus of tobacco must greatly diminish its sensibility. But there are very many other substances, less poisonous, whose occasional application would accomplish the same result, and without deadening, at the same time, the sensibilities of the whole system, as tobacco does.

2. The person who chews tobacco, generally puts a piece in his mouth immediately after eating. This is immediately moved from place to place, and not only performs, in some measure, the offices of a brush and toothpick, but produces a sudden flow of saliva; and in consequence of both of these causes combined, the teeth are effectually cleansed; and cleanliness is undoubtedly one of the most effectual preventives of decay in teeth yet known. Yet there are far better means of cleansing the mouth and teeth after eating than by means of tobacco.

If there be any other known reasons why tobacco should preserve teeth, I am ignorant of them. There are then no arguments of any weight for using it; while there are a multitude of very strong reasons against it. I might add them, in this place, but it appears to me unnecessary.

3. TAKING SNUFF. - I have seen many individuals who would not, on any account whatever, use spirits, or chew tobacco; but who would not hesitate to dry up their nasal membranes, injure their speech, induce catarrhal affections, and besmear their face, clothes, books, &c. with *snuff*. This, however common, appears to me ridiculous. Almost all the serious evils which result from smoking and chewing, follow the practice of snuffing powdered tobacco into the nose. Even Chesterfield opposes it, when after characterizing all use of tobacco or snuff, in any form, as both vulgar and filthy, he adds: 'Besides, snuff-takers are generally very dull and shallow people, and have recourse to it merely as a fillip to the brain; by all means, therefore, avoid the filthy custom.' This censure, though rather severe, is equally applicable to smoking and chewing.

Naturalists say there is one species of maggot fly that mistakes the odor of some kinds of snuff for that of putrid substances, and deposits its eggs in it. In warm weather therefore, it must be dangerous to take snuff which has been exposed to these insects; for the eggs sometimes hatch in two hours, and the most tremendous consequences might follow. And it is not impossible that some of the most painful diseases to which the human race are liable, may have been occasionally produced by this or a similar cause. The 'tic douloureux' is an example.

A very common disease in sheep is known to be produced by worms in cavities which communicate with the nose. Only a little acquaintance with the human structure would show that there are a number of cavities in the bones of the face and head, some of which will hold half an ounce each, which communicate with the nose, and into which substances received into this organ occasionally fall, but cannot escape as easily as they enter.

SECTION V. *Useful Recreations.* - The young, I shall be told, must and will have their recreations; and if they are to be denied every species of gaming, what shall they do? 'You would not, surely, have them spend their leisure hours in gratifying the senses; in eating, drinking, and licentiousness.'

By no means. Recreations they must have; active recreation, too, in the open air. Some of the most appropriate are playing ball, quoits, ninepins, and other athletic exercises; but in no case for money, or any similar consideration. *Skating* is a good exercise in its proper season, if followed with great caution. *Dancing*, for those who sit much, such as pupils in school, tailors and shoemakers, would be an appropriate exercise, if it were not perpetually abused. By assembling in large crowds, continuing it late at evening, and then sallying out in a perspiration, into the cold or damp night air, a thousand times more mischief has been done, than all the benefit which it has afforded would balance. It were greatly to be wished that this exercise might be regulated by those rules which human experience has indicated, instead of being subject to the whim and caprice of fashion. It is a great pity an exercise so valuable to the sedentary, and especially those who *sit* much, of both sexes, should be so managed as to injure half the world, and excite against it the prejudices of the other half.

I have said that the young must have recreations, and generally in the open air. The reason why they should usually be conducted in the open air, is, that their ordinary occupations too frequently confine them within doors, and of course in an atmosphere more or less vitiated. Farmers, gardeners, rope makers, and persons whose occupations are of an active nature, do not need out-of-door sports at all. Their recreations should be by the fire side. Not with cards or dice, nor in the company of those whose company is not worth having. But the book, the newspaper, conversation, or the lyceum, will be the appropriate recreations for these classes, and will be found in the highest degree satisfactory. For the evening, the lyceum is particularly adapted, because laboring young men are often too much fatigued at night, to think, closely; and the lyceum, or conversation, will be more agreeable, and not less useful. But the family circle may of itself constitute a lyceum, and the book or the newspaper may be made the subject of discussion. I have known the heads of families in one neighborhood greatly improved, and the whole neighborhood derive an impulse, from the practice of meeting one evening in the week, to read the news together, and converse on the more interesting intelligence of the day.

Some strongly recommend 'the sports of the field,' and talk with enthusiasm of 'hunting, coursing, fishing;' and of 'dogs and horses.' But these are no recreations for me. True they are *healthy* to the body; but not to the morals. This I say confidently, although some of my readers may smile, and call it an affectation of sensibility. Yet with Cowper,

'I would not enter on my list of friends

The man who needlessly sets foot upon a worm.'

If the leading objects of field sports were to procure sustenance, I would not say a word. But the very term *sports*, implies something different. And shall we sport with *life*—even that of the inferior animals? That which we cannot give, shall we presumptuously dare to take away, and as our only apology say, 'Am I not in sport?'

Besides, other amusements equally healthy, and if we are accustomed to them, equally pleasant, and much more rational, can be substituted. What they are, I have mentioned, at least in part. How a sensible man, and especially a Christian, can hunt or fish, when he would not do it, were it not for the pleasure he enjoys in the cruelty it involves;—how, above all, a wise father can recommend it to his children, or to others, I am utterly unable to conceive!

# CHAPTER IV.

Improvement of the Mind. - SECTION I. *Habit of Observation.*

'Your eyes open, your thoughts close, will go safe through the world,' is a maxim which some have laid down; but it savors rather too much of selfishness. 'You may learn from others all you can, but you are to give them as little opportunity as possible for learning from you,' seems to be the language, properly interpreted. Suppose every one took the advice, and endeavored to keep his thoughts close, for fear he should either be misunderstood, or thought wanting in wisdom; what would become of the pleasures of conversation? Yet these make up a very considerable item of the happiness of human life.

I have sometimes thought with Dr. Rush, that taciturnity, though often regarded as a mark of wisdom, is rather the effect of a 'want of ideas.' The doctor mentions the taciturnity of the American Indians as a case in point. Even in civilized company, he believes that with one or two exceptions, an indisposition to join in conversation 'in nine cases out of ten, is a mark of stupidity,' and presently adds; 'Ideas, whether acquired from books or by reflection, produce a *plethora* in the mind, which can only be relieved by depletion from the pen or tongue.'

'Keep your eyes open,' however, is judicious advice. How many who have the eyes of their body open, keep the eyes of the soul perpetually shut up. 'Seeing, they see not.' Such persons, on arriving at the age of three or four score, *may* lay claim to superior wisdom on account of superior age, but their claims ought not to be admitted. A person who has the eyes both of his mind and body open, will derive more wisdom from one year's experience, than those who neglect to observe for themselves, from ten. Thus at thirty, with ten years acquaintance with men, manners and things, a person *may* be wiser than another at three times thirty, with seven times ten years of what he calls experience. Sound practical wisdom, cannot, it is true, be rapidly acquired any where but in the school of experience, but the world abounds with men who are old enough to be wise, and yet are very ignorant. Let it be your fixed resolution not to belong to this class.

But in order to have the mental eyes open, the external eyes should be active. We should, as a general rule, see what is going on around us. There are indeed seasons, occurring in the school or the closet, when abstraction is desirable; but speaking generally, we should 'keep our eyes open.'

It is hence easy to see why some men who are accounted learned, are yet in common life very great fools. Is it not because their eyes have been shut to every thing but books, and schools, and colleges, and universities?

The late Dr. Dwight was an eminent instance of keeping up an acquaintance both with books, and the world in which he lived and acted. In his walks, or wherever he happened to be, nothing could escape his eye. 'Not a bird could fly up,' says one of his students, 'but he observed it.' And he endeavored to establish the same habit of observation in others. Riding in a chaise, one day, with a student of his, who was apt to be abstracted from surrounding things, he suddenly exclaimed, almost indignant at his indifference, 'S—— keep your eyes open!' The lesson was not lost. It made a deep impression on the mind of the student. Though by no means distinguished in his class, he has outstripped many, if not the most of them, in actual and practical usefulness; and to this hour, he attributes much of his success to the foregoing circumstance.

There is a pedantry in these things, however, which is not only fulsome, but tends to defeat our very purpose. It is not quite sufficient that we merely bestow a passing glance on objects, they must strike deep. If they do not, they had better not have been seen at all; since the habit of 'seeing not,' while we appear to 'see,' has been all the while strengthening.

It cannot be denied that a person who shall take the advice I have given, may, with a portion of his fellow men, gain less credit than if he adopted a different course. There is a certain surgeon, in one of the New England States, who has acquired much popularity by reading as he travels along. Seldom or never, say his admirers, is he seen in his carriage without a book in his hand, or at his side. But such popularity is usually of a mushroom character. There may be pressing occasions which render it the *duty* of a surgeon to consult his books, while in his carriage; but these occasions can never be of frequent occurrence. It is far better that he should be reading lessons from the great and open volume of nature.

Nor does it add, in any degree, to the just respect due to the wisdom of either of the Plinys, that the elder 'never travelled without a book and a portable writing desk by his side,' and that the younger read upon all occasions, whether riding, walking, or sitting.' I cannot doubt that, wise as they were in books and philosophy, they would have secured a much greater fund of practical wisdom, had they left their books and writing desks at home, and 'kept their eyes open' to surrounding objects.

There is another thing mentioned of Pliny the elder, which is equally objectionable. It is said that a person read to him during his meals. I have given my views on this point in Chapter I.

SECTION II. *Rules for Conversation.* - The bee has the art of extracting honey from every flower which contains it, even from some which are not a little nauseous or poisonous. It has also been said that the conversation of every individual, whatever may be the condition of his mind or circumstances, may be made a means of improvement. How happy would it be, then, if man possessed the skill of the bee, and knew how to extract the good, and reject the bad or useless!

Something on this subject is, indeed, known. There are rules, by the observance of which we may derive much valuable information from the conversation of those among whom we live, even though it should relate to the most ordinary subjects and concerns. And not only so, we may often devise means to *change* the conversation, either directly, by gradually introducing other topics of discourse, or indirectly, by patient attempts to enlarge and improve and elevate the minds of our associates.

Every individual has excellences; and almost every person, however ignorant, has thought upon some one subject more than many,—perhaps *most*—others. Some excel in the knowledge of husbandry, some in gardening, some in mechanics, or manufactures, some in mathematics, and so on. In all your conversation, then, it will be well to ascertain as nearly as you can wherein the skill and excellence of an individual lies, and put him upon his favorite subject. Nor is this difficult. Every one *will*, of his own accord, fall to talking on his favorite topic, if you will follow, and not attempt to *lead* him.

Except in a few rare cases, every one wishes to be the hero of the circle where he is conversing. If, therefore, you seek to improve in the greatest possible degree, from the conversation of those among whom you may be thrown, you will suffer a companion to take his own course, and 'out of the abundance of his heart,' let his 'mouth speak.' By this means you may easily collect the worth and excellence of every one you meet with; and be able to put it together for your own use upon future occasions.

The common objections to the views here presented, are, that they encourage dissimulation. But this does not appear to me to be the fact. In suffering a person, for the space of a single conversation, to be the hero of the circle, we do not of necessity concede his superiority generally; we only help him to be useful to the company. It often happens that you are thrown among persons whom you cannot benefit by becoming the hero of the circle yourself, for they will not listen to you; and perhaps will not understand your terms, if they do. If, however, there appear to be others in the company whose object, like your own, is improvement, you might expose yourself to the just charge of being selfish, should you refuse to converse upon your own favorite topics in your turn; and thus to let the good deed go round.

Never interrupt another, but hear him out. You will understand him the better for it, and be able to give him the better answer. If you only give him an opportunity, he may say something which you have not yet heard, or explain what you did not fully understand, or even mention something which you did not expect.

There are individuals with whom you may occasionally come in contact, from whose conversation you will hardly derive much benefit at all. Such are those who use wanton, or obscene, or profane language. For, besides the almost utter hopelessness of deriving any benefit from such persons, and the pain you must inevitably suffer in hearing them, you put your own reputation at hazard. 'A man is known by the company he keeps;' take care therefore how you frequent the company of the swearer or the sensualist. Avoid, too, the known liar, for similar reasons.

If you speak in company, it is not only modest but wise to speak late; for by this means, you will be able to render your conversation more acceptable, and to weigh beforehand the importance of what you utter; and you will be less likely to violate the good old rule, 'think twice before you speak once.' Let your words be as few as will express the sense which you wish to convey, especially when strangers or men of much greater experience than yourself are present; and above all, be careful that what you say be strictly *true*.

Do not suffer your feelings to betray you into too great earnestness, or vehemence; and never be overbearing. Avoid triumphing over an antagonist, even though you might reasonably do so. You gain nothing. On the contrary, you often confirm him in his erroneous opinions. At least, you prejudice him against yourself. Zimmerman insists that we should suffer an antagonist to get the victory over us occasionally, in order to raise his respect for himself. All *finesse* of this kind, however, as Christians, I think it better to avoid.

SECTION III. *On Books, and Study.* - It may excite some surprise that books, and study, do not occupy a more conspicuous place in this work. There are several reasons for this circumstance. The first is, a wish to counteract the prevailing tendency to make too much of books as a means of forming character. The second is, because the choice of these depends more upon parents and teachers than upon the individual himself; and if *they* have neglected to lay the foundation of a desire for mental improvement, there is less probability that any advice I may give on this subject will be serviceable, than on most others.

And yet, no young man, at any age, ought to despair of establishing such habits of body and mind as he believes would contribute to his usefulness. He hates the sight of a book perhaps; but what then? This prejudice may, in a measure, be removed. Not at once, it is true, but gradually. Not by compelling himself to read or study against his inclination; for little will be accomplished when it goes 'against the grain.' But there are means better and more effective than these; some of which I will now proceed to point out.

Let him attach himself to some respectable lyceum or debating society. Most young men are willing to attend a lyceum, occasionally; and thanks to the spirit of the times and those who have zealously labored to produce the present state of things, these institutions every where abound. Let him now and then take part in a discussion, if it be, at first, only to say a few words. The moment he can awaken an interest in almost any subject whatever, that moment he will, of necessity, seek for information in regard to it. He will seek it, not only in conversation, but in newspapers. These, if well selected, will in their turn refer him to books of travels. Gradually he will find histories, if not written in too dry a manner, sources of delight. Thus he will proceed, step by step, till he finds himself quite attached to reading of various descriptions.

There is one caution to be observed here, which is, not to read too long or too much at once. Whenever a book, or even a newspaper, begins to be irksome, let it be laid aside for the time. In this way you will return to it, at the next leisure moment, with increased pleasure.

A course not unlike that which I have been describing, faithfully and perseveringly followed, would in nine cases in ten, be successful. Indeed, I never yet knew of a single failure. One great point is, to be thoroughly convinced of its importance. No young man can reasonably expect success, unless he enters upon his work with his whole heart, and pursues it with untiring assiduity.

Of the *necessity* of improvement, very few young men seem to have doubts. But there is a difficulty which many feel, which it will require no little effort to remove, because it is one of long standing, and wrought into all the arrangements of civilized society. I allude to the prevailing impression that very little can be done to improve the mind beyond a certain age, and the limit is often fixed at eighteen or twenty years. We hear it, indeed, asserted, that nothing can be done after thirty; but the general belief is that most men cannot do much after twenty: or at least that it will cost much harder effort and study.

Now, I would be the last to encourage any young person in wasting, or even undervaluing his early years; for youth is a golden period, and every moment well spent will be to the future what good seed, well planted in its season, is to the husbandman.

The truth is, that what we commonly call a course of education, is only a course which prepares a young man to educate himself. It is giving him the keys of knowledge. But who will sit down contentedly and cease to make effort, the moment he obtains the keys to the most valuable of treasures? It is strange, indeed, that we should so long have talked of finishing an education, when we have only just prepared ourselves to begin it.

If any young man at twenty, twenty-five, or thirty, finds himself ignorant, whether the fault is his own or that of others, let him not for one single moment regard his age as presenting a serious obstacle to improvement. Should these remarks meet the eye of any such individual, let me prevail with him, when I urge him to make an effort. Not a momentary effort, either; let him *take time* for his experiment. Even Rome was not built in a day; and he who thinks to build up a well regulated and highly enlightened mind in a few weeks, or even months, has yet to learn the depths of his own ignorance.

It would be easy to cite a long list of men who commenced study late in life, and yet finally became eminent; and this, too, with no instructors but themselves and their books. Some have met with signal success, who commenced after forty years of age. Indeed, no reason can be shown, why the mind may not improve as long, at least, as the body. But all experience goes to prove that with those whose habits are judicious, the physical frame does not attain perfection, in every respect, till thirty-five or forty.

It is indeed said that knowledge, if it could be acquired thus late in life, would be easily forgotten. This is true, if it be that kind of knowledge for which we have no immediate use. But if it be of a practical character, it will not fail to be remembered. Franklin was always learning, till death. And what he learned he seldom forgot, because he had an immediate use for it. I have said, it is a great point to be convinced of the importance of knowledge. I might add that it is a point of still greater consequence to feel our own ignorance. 'To know ourselves diseased, (morally) is half our cure.' To know our own ignorance is the first step to knowledge; and other things being alike, our progress in knowledge will generally be in proportion to our sense of the want of it.

The strongest plea which indolence is apt to put in, is, that we have no *time* for study. Many a young man has had some sense of his own ignorance, and a corresponding thirst for knowledge, but alas! the idea was entertained that he had no time to read—no time to study—no time to think. And resting on this plea as satisfactory, he has gone down to the grave the victim not only of indolence and ignorance, but perhaps of vice;—vice, too, which he might have escaped with a little more general intelligence.

No greater mistake exists than that which so often haunts the human mind, that we cannot find *time* for things; things, too, which we have previously decided for ourselves that we ought to do. Alfred, king of England, though he performed more business than almost any of his subjects, found time for study. Franklin, in the midst of all his labors, found time to dive into the depths of philosophy, and explore an untrodden path of science. Frederick the Great, with an empire at his direction, in the midst of war, and on the eve of battles, found time to revel in all the charms of philosophy, and to feast himself on the rich viands of intellect. Bonaparte, with Europe at his disposal, with kings at his ante-chamber begging for vacant thrones, and at the head of thousands of men whose destinies were suspended on his arbitrary pleasure, had time to converse with books. Cæsar, when he had curbed the spirits of the Roman people, and was thronged with visitors from the remotest kingdoms, found time for intellectual cultivation. The late Dr. Rush, and the still later Dr.

Dwight, are eminent instances of what may be done for the cultivation of the mind, in the midst of the greatest pressure of other occupation.

On this point, it may be useful to mention the results of my own observation. At no period of my life am I conscious of having made greater progress than I have sometimes done while laboring in the summer; and almost incessantly too. It is true, I read but little; yet that little was well understood and thoroughly digested. Almost all the knowledge I possess of ancient history was obtained in this way, in one year. Of course, a particular knowledge could not be expected, under such circumstances; but the general impressions and leading facts which were imbibed, will be of very great value to me, as I trust, through life. And I am acquainted with one or two similar instances.

It is true that mechanics and manufacturers, as well as men of most other occupations, find fewer leisure hours than most farmers. The latter class of people are certainly more favorably situated than any other. But it is also true that even the former, almost without exception, can command a small portion of their time every day, for the purposes of mental improvement, if they are determined on it. Few individuals can be found in the community, who have not as much leisure as I had during the summer I have mentioned. The great point is to have the necessary disposition to improve it; and a second point, of no small importance, is to have at hand, proper means of instruction. Of the latter I shall speak presently.

The reason why laboring men make such rapid progress in knowledge, in proportion to the number of hours they devote to study, appears to me obvious. The mental appetite is keen, and they devour with a relish. What little they read and understand, is thought over, and perhaps conversed upon, during the long interval; and becomes truly the property of the reader. Whereas those who make study a business, never possess a healthy appetite for knowledge; they are always cloyed, nothing is well digested; and the result of their continued effort is either a superficial or a distorted view of a great many things, without a thorough or practical understanding of any.

I do not propose, in a work of this kind, to recommend to young men what particular books on any subject they ought to study. First, because it is a matter of less importance than many others, and I cannot find room to treat of every thing.

He who has the determination to make progress, will do so, either with or without books, though these are certainly useful. But an old piece of newspaper, or a straggling leaf from some book, or an inscription on a monument, or the monument itself—and works of nature as well as of art, will be books to him. Secondly, because there is such an extensive range for selection. But, thirdly, because it may often be left to the reader's own taste and discretion. He will probably soon discover whether he is deriving solid or permanent benefit from his studies, and govern himself accordingly. Or if he have a friend at hand, who will be likely to make a judicious selection, with a proper reference to his actual progress and wants, he would do wrong not to avail himself of that friend's opinion.

I will now mention a *few* of the particular studies to which he who would educate himself for usefulness should direct his attention.

I. GEOGRAPHY. - As it is presumed that every one whom I address reads newspapers more or less, I must be permitted to recommend that you read them with good maps of every quarter of the world before you, and a geography and correct gazetteer at hand. When a place is mentioned, observe its situation on the map, read an account of it in the gazetteer, and a more particular description in the geography. Or if you choose to go through with the article, and get some general notions of the subject, and afterwards go back and read it a second time, in the manner proposed, to this I have no objection.

Let me insist, strongly, on the importance of this method of reading. It may seem slow at first; but believe me, you will be richly repaid in the end. Even in the lyceum, where the subject seems to demand it, and the nature of the case will admit, it ought to be required of lecturers and disputants, to explain every thing in passing, either by reference to books themselves on the spot, or by maps, apparatus, diagrams, &c; with which, it is plain, that every lyceum ought to be furnished. The more intelligent would lose nothing, while the less so, would gain much, by this practice. The expense of these things, at the present time, is so trifling, that no person, or association of persons, whose object is scientific improvement, should, by any means, dispense with them.

No science expands the mind of a young man more, at the same time that it secures his cheerful attention, than geography—I mean if pursued in the foregoing manner. Its use is so obvious that the most stupid cannot fail to see it. Much is said, I know, of differences of taste on this, as well as every other subject; but I can hardly believe that any young person can be entirely without taste for geographical knowledge. It is next to actual travels; and who does not delight in seeing new places and new objects?

2. HISTORY. - Next in order as regards both interest and importance, will be a knowledge of history, with some attention at the same time to chronology. Here, too, the starting point will be the same as in the former case. Some circumstance or event mentioned at the lyceum, or in the newspaper, will excite curiosity, and lead the way to inquiry. I think it well, however, to have but one leading science in view at a time; that is, if geography be the object, let history and almost every thing else be laid aside for that time, in order to secure, and hold fast the geographical information which is needed. After a few weeks or months, should he wish to pursue history, let the student, for some time confine himself chiefly, perhaps exclusively, to that branch.

The *natural* order of commencing and pursuing this branch without an instructor, and I think in schools also, is the following. For example, you take up a book, or it may be a newspaper, since these are swarming every where at the present time, and read that a person has just deceased, who was at *Yorktown*, in Virginia, during the whole *siege*, in the American *revolution*. I am supposing here that you have already learned where Yorktown is; for geography, to some extent at least, should precede history; but if not, I would let it pass for the moment, since we cannot do every thing at once, and proceed to inquire about the siege, and revolution. If you have any books whatever, on history, within your reach, do not give up the pursuit till you have attained a measure of success. Find out, *when* the *siege* in question *happened*, by *whom*, and by *how many thousand troops* it was carried on; and *who* and *how many* the besieged were.

He who follows out this plan, will soon find his mind reaching beyond the mere events alluded to in the newspaper, both forward and backward. As in the example already mentioned, for I cannot think of a better;—What were the consequences of this siege?—Did it help to bring about peace, and how soon?—And did the two nations ever engage in war afterward?—If so, how soon, and with what results? What became of the French troops and of the good La Fayette? This would lead to the study of French history for the last forty years. On the other hand, Where had Washington and La Fayette and Cornwallis been employed, previous to the siege of Yorktown? What battles had they fought, and with what success? What led to the quarrel between Great Britain and the United States? &c. Thus we should naturally go backward, step by step, until we should get much of modern history clustered round this single event of the siege of Yorktown. The same course should be pursued in the case of any other event, either ancient or modern. If newspapers are not thus read, they dissipate the mind, and probably do about as much harm as good.

It is deemed disgraceful—and ought to be—for any young man at this day to be ignorant of the geography and history of the country in which he lives. And yet it is no uncommon occurrence. However it argues much against the excellence of our systems of education, that almost every child should be carried apparently through a wide range of science, and over the whole material universe, and yet know nothing, or next to nothing, practically, of his own country.

3. ARITHMETIC. - No young man is excusable who is destitute of a knowledge of Arithmetic. It is probable, however, that no individual will read this book, who has not some knowledge of the fundamental branches; numeration, addition, subtraction, multiplication, and division. But with these, every person has the key to a thorough acquaintance with the whole subject, so far as his situation in life requires. To avail himself of these keys to mathematical knowledge, he must pursue a course not unlike that which I have recommended in relation to geography and history. He must seize on every circumstance which occurs in his reading, where reckoning is required, and if possible, stop at once and compute it. Or if not, let the place be marked, and at the first leisure moment, let him turn to it, and make the estimates.

Suppose he reads of a shipwreck. The crew is said to consist of thirty men besides the captain and mate, with three hundred and thirteen passengers, and a company of sixty grenadiers. The captain and mate, and ten of the crew escaped in the long boat. The rest were drowned, except twelve of the grenadiers, who clung to a floating fragment of the wreck till they were taken off by another vessel. Now is there a single person in existence, who would read such an account, without being anxious to know how many persons in the whole were lost? Yet nine readers in ten would *not* know; and why? Simply because they will not stop to use what little addition and subtraction they possess.

I do not say that, in reading to a company, who did not expect it, a young man would be required to stop and make the computation; but I do say that in all ordinary cases, no person is excusable who omits it, for it is a flagrant wrong to his own mind. Long practice, it is true, will render it unnecessary for an individual to *pause*, in order to estimate a sum like that abovementioned. Many, indeed most persons who are familiar with figures, might compute these numbers while reading, and without the slightest pause; but it certainly requires some practice. And the most important use of arithmetical studies (except as a discipline to the mind) is to enable us to reckon without slates and pencils. He has but a miserable knowledge of arithmetic, who is no arithmetician without a pen or pencil in his hand. These are but the ladders upon which he should ascend to the science, and not the science itself.

4. CHEMISTRY AND OTHER NATURAL SCIENCES. - If I were to name one branch, as more important to a young man than any other,—next to the merest elements of reading and writing—it would be chemistry. Not a mere smattering of it, however; for this usually does about as much harm as good. But a thorough knowledge of a few of the simple elements of bodies, and some of their most interesting combinations, such as are witnessed every day of our lives, but which, for want of a little knowledge of chemistry, are never understood, would do more to interest a young man in the business in which he may be employed, than almost any thing I could name. For there is hardly a single trade or occupation whatever, that does not embrace a greater or less number of chemical processes. Chemistry is of very high importance even to the gardener and the farmer.

There are several other branches which come under the general head of NATURAL SCIENCE, which I recommend to your attention. Such are BOTANY, or a knowledge of plants; NATURAL HISTORY, or a knowledge of animals; and GEOLOGY, or a general knowledge of the rocks and stones of which the earth on which we live is composed. I do not think these are equally important with the knowledge of chemistry, but they are highly interesting, and by no means without their value.

5. GRAMMAR AND COMPOSITION. - The foundation of a knowledge of Grammar is, in my view, Composition; and composition, whether learned early or late, is best acquired by *letter writing*. This habit, early commenced, and judiciously but perseveringly followed, will in time, ensure the art not only of composing well, but also grammatically. I know this position is sometimes doubted, but the testimony is so strong, that the point seems to me fully established.

It is related in Ramsay's Life of Washington, that many individuals, who, before the war of the American Revolution, could scarcely write their names, became, in the progress of that war, able to compose letters which were not only intelligible and correct, but which would have done credit to a profound grammarian. The reason of this undoubtedly was, that they were thrown into situations where they were obliged to write much and often, and in such a manner as to be clearly understood. Perhaps the misinterpretation of a single doubtful word or sentence might have been the ruin of an army, or even of the *cause*. Thus they had a motive to write accurately; and long practice, with a powerful motive before them, rendered them successful.

Nor is it necessary that motives so powerful should always exist, in order to produce this result;—it is sufficient that there be a motive to *write well*, and to *persevere* in writing well. I have known several pedlars and traders, whose business led to the same consequences.

6. LETTER WRITING. - But what I have seen most successful, is, the practice of common *letter writing*, from friend to friend, on any topic which happened to occur, either ordinary, or extraordinary; with the mutual understanding and desire that each should criticise freely on the other's composition. I have known more than one individual, who became a good writer from this practice, with little aid from grammatical rules; and without any direct instruction at all.

These remarks are not made to lessen the value which any young man may have put upon the studies of grammar and composition, as pursued in our schools; but rather to show that a course at school is not absolutely indispensable; and to encourage those who are never likely to enjoy the latter means, to make use of means not yet out of their reach, and which have often been successful. But lest there should be an apparent contradiction in some of my remarks, it will be necessary to say that I think the practice of familiar letter writing from our earliest years, even at school, should, in every instance, have a much more prominent place than is usually assigned it; and the study of books on Grammar and Composition one much *less* prominent.

7.   VOYAGES, TRAVELS, AND BIOGRAPHY.   -   For mere READING, well selected *Voyages* and *Travels* are among the best works for young men; particularly for those who find little taste for reading, and wish to enkindle it; and whose geographical knowledge is deficient.

Well written BIOGRAPHY is next in importance, and usually so in interest; and so improving to the character is this species of composition, that it really ought to be regarded as a separate branch of education, as much as history or geography; and treated accordingly. In the selection of both these species of writing the aid of an intelligent, experienced and judicious friend would be of very great service; and happy is he who has such a treasure at hand.

8. NOVELS. - As to NOVELS it is difficult to say what advice ought to be given. At first view they seem unnecessary, wholly so; and from this single consideration. They interest and improve just in proportion as the fiction they contain is made to resemble reality; and hence it might be inferred, and naturally enough, too, that reality would in all cases be preferable to that which imitates it. But to this it may be replied, that we have few books of narrative and biography, which are written with so much spirit as some works of fiction; and that until those departments are better filled, fiction, properly selected, should be admissible. But if fiction be allowable at all, it is only under the guidance of age and experience;—and here there is even a more pressing need of a friend than in the cases already mentioned.

On the whole, it is believed to be better for young men who have little leisure for reading, and who wish to make the most they can of that little, to abandon novels wholly. If they begin to read them, it is difficult to tell to what an excess they may go; but if they never read one in their whole lives, they will sustain no great loss. Would not the careful study of a single chapter of Watts's Improvement of the Mind, be of more real practical value than the perusal of all that the best novel writers,—Walter Scott not excepted,—have ever written?

9. OF NEWSPAPERS. - Among other means both of mental and moral improvement at the present day, are periodical publications. The multiplicity and cheapness of these sources of knowledge renders them accessible to all classes of the community. And though their influence were to be as evil as the frogs of Egypt we could not escape it.

Doubtless they produce much evil, though their tendency on the whole is believed to be salutary. But wisdom is necessary, in order to derive the greatest amount of benefit from them; and here, perhaps, more than any where else, do the young need the counsels of experience. I am not about to direct what particular newspapers and magazines they ought to read; this is a point which their friends and relatives must assist them in determining. My purpose is simply to point to a few principles which should guide both the young and those who advise them, in making the selection.

I. In the first place, do not seek for your guide a paper which is just commencing its existence, unless you have reason to think the character of its conductors is such as you approve.

2. Avoid, unless your particular occupation requires it, a *business* paper. Otherwise your head will become so full of 'arrivals' and 'departures,' and 'prices current,' and 'news,' that you will hardly find room for any thing else.

3. Do not take a paper which dwells on nothing but the details of human depravity. It will indeed, for a time, call forth a sensibility to the woes of mankind; but the final result will probably be a stupidity and insensibility to human suffering which you would give much to remove.

4. Avoid those papers which, awed by the cry for *short* and *light* articles, have rendered their pages mere columns of insulated facts or useless scraps, or what is still worse, of unnatural and sickening love stories.

Lastly, do not take a paper which sneers at religion. It is quite enough that many periodicals do, in effect, take a course which tends to irreligion, by leaving this great subject wholly out of sight. But when they openly sneer at and ridicule the most sacred things, leave them at once. 'Evil communications corrupt' the best 'manners;' and though the sentiment may not at once be received, I can assure my youthful readers that there are no publications which have more direct effect upon their lives, than these unpretending companions; and perhaps the very reason is because we least suspect them. Against receiving deep or permanent impressions from the Bible, the sermon, or the *book* of any kind, we are on our watch, but who thinks of having his principles contaminated, or affected much in any way, merely by the newspaper? Yet I am greatly mistaken, if these very monitors do not have more influence, after all, in forming the minds, the manners, and the morals (shall I add, the *religious character*, even?) of the rising generation, than all the other means which I have mentioned, put together.

How important, in this view, it becomes, that your newspaper reading should be well selected. Let me again repeat the request, that in selecting those papers which sustain an appropriate character, you will seek the advice of those whom you deem most able and judicious; and so far as you think them disinterested, and worthy of your confidence, endeavor to follow it.

*Politics.* As to the study of politics, in the usual sense of the term, it certainly cannot be advisable. Nothing appears to me more disgusting than to see young men rushing into the field of political warfare, and taking sides as fiercely as if they laid claim to infallibility, where their fathers and grandfathers modestly confess ignorance.

At the same time, in a government like ours, where the highest offices are in the gift of the people, and within the reach of every young man of tolerable capacity, it would be disgraceful not to study the history and constitution of our own country, and closely to watch all legislative movements, at least in the councils of the nation. The time is not far distant, it is hoped, when these will be made every day subjects in our elementary schools; and when no youth will arrive at manhood, as thousands, and, I was going to say, millions now do, without understanding clearly a single article in the Constitution of the United States, or even in that of the State in which he resides: nor even how his native state is represented in Congress.

Again, most young men will probably, sooner or later, vote for rulers in the town, state, and nation to which they belong. Should they vote at random? Or what is little better, take their opinions upon trust? Or shall they examine for themselves; and go to the polls with their eyes open? At a day like the present, nothing appears to me more obvious than that young men ought to understand what they are doing when they concern themselves with public men or public measures.

10. KEEPING A JOURNAL. - I have already spoken of the importance of letter writing. The keeping of a journal is scarcely less so, provided it be done in a proper manner. I have seen journals, however, which, aside from the fact that they improve the *handwriting*, and encourage *method*, could have been of very little use. A young agriculturist kept a journal for many years, of which the following is a specimen.

1813.

July 2. Began our haying. Mowed in the forenoon, and raked in the afternoon. Weather good.

3. Continued haying. Mowed. Got in one load. Cloudy.

4. Independence. Went, in the afternoon, to ——.

5. Stormy. Did nothing out of doors.

This method of keeping a journal was continued for many years; and only discontinued, because it was found useless. A better and more useful sort of journal for these four days, would have read something like the following.

1813.

July 2. Our haying season commenced. How fond I am of this employment! How useful an article hay is, too, especially in this climate, during our long and cold winters! We have fine weather to begin with, and I hope it will continue.

I think a very great improvement might be made in our rakes. Why need they be so heavy for light raking? We could take up the heavier ones when it became necessary.

July 3. To-day I have worked rather too hard in order to get in some of our hay, for there is a prospect of rain. I am not quite sure, however, but I hurt myself more by drinking too much cold water than by over-working. Will try to do better to-morrow.

4. Have heard a few cannon fired, and a spouting oration delivered, and seen a few toasts drank; and what does it all amount to? Is this way of keeping the day of independence really useful? I doubt it. Who knows but the value of the wine which has been drank, expended among the poor, would have done more towards *real* independence, than all this parade?

5. Rainy. Would it not have been better had I staid at home yesterday, while the weather was fair, and gone on with haying? Several acres of father's grass want cutting very much. I am more and more sick of going to independence. If I live till another year, I hope I shall learn to 'make hay while the sun shines.'

I selected a common agricultural employment to illustrate my subject, first, because I suppose a considerable proportion of my readers are farmers, and secondly, because it is an employment which is generally supposed to furnish little or nothing worth recording. The latter, however, is a great mistake. Besides writing down the real incidents that occur, many of which would be interesting, and some of them highly important facts, the *thoughts*, which the circumstances and incidents of an agricultural life are calculated to elicit, are innumerable. And these should always be put down. They are to the mere detail of facts and occurrences, what leaves and fruit are to the dry trunk and naked limbs of a tree. The above specimen is very dry indeed, being intended only as a hint. Pages, instead of a few lines, might sometimes be written, when our leisure permitted, and thoughts flowed freely.

One useful method of improving the mind, and preparing ourselves for usefulness, would be, to carry a small blank book and pencil in our pockets, and when any interesting fact occurred, embrace the first spare moment to put it down, say on the right hand page; and either then, or at some future time, place on the left hand page, our own reflections about it. Some of the most useful men in the world owe much of their usefulness to a plan like this, promptly and perseveringly followed. Quotations from books or papers might also be preserved in the same manner.[10]

Perhaps it may be thought, at first, that this advice is not in keeping with the caution formerly given, not to read as we travel about; but if you reflect, you will find it otherwise. Reading as we travel, and at meals, and the recording of facts and thoughts which occur, are things as different as can well be conceived. The latter creates and encourages a demand for close observation, the former discourages and even suppresses it.

II. PRESERVATION OF BOOKS AND PAPERS. - Let books be covered as soon as bought. Never use them without clean hands. They show the dirt with extreme readiness, and it is not easily removed. I have seen books in which might be traced the careless thumbs and fingers of the last reader, for half a dozen or a dozen pages in succession.

I have known a gentleman—quite a literary man, too—who, having been careful of his books in his earlier years, and having recently found them occasionally soiled, charged the fault on those who occasionally visited his library. At last he discovered that the coal dust (for he kept a coal fire) settled on his hands, and was rubbed off upon his book leaves by the slight friction of his fingers upon the leaves in reading.

Never wet your finger or thumb in order to turn over leaves. Many respectable people are addicted to this habit, but it is a vulgar one. Besides, it is entirely useless. The same remarks might be applied to the habit of suffering the corners of the leaves to turn up, in 'dog's ears.' Keep every leaf smooth, if you can. Never hold a book very near the fire, nor leave it in the hot sun. It injures its cover materially, and not a few books are in one or both of these ways entirely ruined.

It is a bad practice to spread out a book with the back upwards. It loosens the leaves, and also exposes it in other respects. You will rarely find a place to lay it down which is *entirely* clean, and the least dust on the leaves, is readily observed.

The plan of turning down a leaf to enable us to remember the place, I never liked. It indulges the memory in laziness. For myself, if I take much interest in a book, I can remember where I left off and turn at once to the place without a mark. If a mark must be used at all, however, a slip of paper, or a piece of tape or ribbon is the best.

When you have done using a book for the time, have a place for it, and put it in its place. How much time and patience might be saved if this rule were universally followed! Many find it the easiest thing in the world to have a place for every book in their library, and to keep it in its place. They can put their hands upon it in the dark, almost as well as in the light.

Never allow yourselves to use books for any other purpose but reading. I have seen people recline after dinner and at other times, with books under their heads for a pillow. Others will use them to cover a tumbler, bowl, or pitcher. Others again will raise the window, and set them under the sash to support it; and next, perhaps, the book is wet by a sudden shower of rain, or knocked out of the window, soiled or otherwise injured, or lost. I have seen people use large books, such as the family-bible, or encyclopedia, to raise a seat, especially for a child at table.

# CHAPTER V.

Social and Moral Improvement. - SECTION I. *Of Female Society, in general.*

No young man is fully aware how much he is indebted to female influence in forming his character. Happy for him if his mother and sisters were his principal companions in infancy. I do not mean to exclude the society of the father, of course; but the father's avocations usually call him away from home, or at least from the immediate presence of his children, for a very considerable proportion of his time.

It would be easy to show, without the possibility of mistake, that it is those young men who are shut out either by accident or design, from female society, that most despise it. And on this account, I cannot but regret the supposed necessity which prevails of having separate schools for the two sexes; unless it were *professional* ones—I mean for the study of law, medicine, &c. There is yet too much practical Mohammedanism and Paganism in our manner of educating the young.

If we examine the character and conduct of woman as it now is, and as history shows it to have been in other periods of the world, we shall see that much of the good and evil which has fallen upon mankind has been through her influence. We may see that man has often been influenced *directly* by the soft warning words, or the still more powerful weapons—tears—of woman, to do that to which whole legions of soldiers never could have driven him.

Now the same influence which is exerted by mothers and wives is also exerted, in a smaller degree, by sisters; and indeed by the female sex generally. When, therefore, I find a young man professing a disregard for their society, or frequenting only the worst part of it, I always expect to find in him a soul which would not hesitate long, in the day of temptation, to stoop to vicious if not base actions. Who would despise the fountain at which he is refreshed daily? Above all, who would willingly contaminate it? But how much better than this is it to show by our language, as well as deeds, that we hold this portion of the world in disdain; and only meet with them, if we meet them at all, to comply with custom, or for purposes still more unworthy; instead of seeking their society as a means of elevating and ennobling the character?

When, therefore, a young man begins to affect the *wit*, and to utter sarcasms against the female character, it may be set down as a mark, either of a weak head, or a base heart; for it cannot be good sense or gratitude, or justice, or honorable feeling of any kind. There are indeed nations, it is said, where a boy, as soon as he puts off the dress of a child, beats his mother, to show his manhood. These people live in the interior of Africa, and there let them remain. Let us be careful that we do not degrade the sex, in the same manner, by disrespectful language, or actions, or *thoughts*. We should '*think* no evil,' on this subject; for let it never be forgotten, that our own happiness and elevation of character must ever be in exact proportion to that of females. Degrade *them*, and we degrade ourselves; neglect to raise their moral and intellectual condition as much as possible, and you neglect the readiest and most certain means of promoting, in the end, your own comfort and happiness.

If any of your elder associates defame the sex, you can hardly be mistaken when you suspect them of having vitiated their taste for what is excellent in human character by improper intimacies, or still more abominable vices. The man who says he has never found a virtuous female character, you may rely upon it, cannot himself be virtuous.

In civilized society much of our time must *necessarily* be spent among females. These associations will have influence upon us. Either they are perpetually improving our character, or, on the other hand, by increasing our disregard or disgust, debasing it. Is it not wisdom, then, to make what we can of the advantages and opportunities which their society affords us?

The very presence of a respectable female will often restrain those from evil whose hearts are full of it. It is not easy to talk or to look obscenely, or even to behave with rudeness and ill manners under such restraint. Who has not seen the jarring and discordant tones of a company of rude men and boys hushed at once by the sudden arrival of a lady of dignified manners and appearance?

The frequent, the habitual society of one whom a youth respects, must have a happy tendency to make him love honorable conduct; and restrain his less honorable feelings. Frequent restraint tends to give the actual mastery; therefore every approach towards this must be of great value. There is a delicacy, too, in female society, which serves well to check the boisterous, to tame the brutal, and to embolden the timid. Whatever be the innate character of a youth, it may be polished, and exalted, by their approbation. He must be unusually hardened that can come from some shameful excess, or in a state of inebriety, into the company of the ladies.

Sometimes a diffident youth has been taken under the *protection*, if it may be so called, of a considerate and respectable woman. A woman of proper dignity of manners and character, especially with a few years' advantage, can do this without the least injury to herself, and without stepping a hair's breadth beyond the bounds which should surround her sex. Happy is the young man who enjoys a fostering care so important; he may learn the value of the sex; learn to discriminate among them, to esteem many of them, and prize their approbation; and in time, deserve it. It is obvious that the favor of silly, flirting girls, (and there are some such) is not what I am here recommending.

Where the character of such society is pure, where good sense, cultivation, intellect, modesty, and superior age, distinguish the parties, it is no small honor to a young man to enjoy it. Should he be conscious that epithets of a different and of a contrary quality belong to them, it is no honor to him to be their favorite. He must be *like* them, in some degree, or they would not approve him.

SECTION II. *Advice and Friendship of Mothers.* - When you seek female society for the sake of improvement, it is proper you should begin where nature begun with you. You have already been encouraged to respect your mother; I go a step farther; and say, Make her your friend. Unless your own misconduct has already been very great, she will not be so far estranged from you, as not to rejoice at the opportunity of bestowing that attention to you which the warmest wishes for your welfare would dictate. If your errors *have*, on the contrary, created a wide distance between you, endeavor to restore the connection as soon as possible. I do not undervalue a father's counsel and guidance; yet however excellent his judgment may be, your mother's opinion is not only a help to your own; but as a *woman's*, it has its peculiar character, and may have its appropriate value. *Women* sometimes see at a glance, what a *man* must go round through a train of argument to discover. Their *tact* is delicate, and therefore quicker in operation. Sometimes, it is true, their judgment will not only be prompt, but premature. Your *own* judgment must assist you here. Do not, however, proudly despise your mother's;—but examine it. It will generally well repay the trouble; and the habit of consulting her will increase habits of consideration, and self command; and promote propriety of conduct.

If a mother be a woman of sense, why should you not profit by her long exercised intelligence? Nay, should she even be deficient in cultivation, or in native talent, yet her experience is something, and her love for you will, in part, make up for such deficiency. It cannot be worthiness to despise, or wisdom to neglect your mother's opinion.

SECTION III. *Society of Sisters.* - Have you a sister?—Have you several of them? Then you are favorably situated; especially if one of them is older than yourself. She has done playing with dolls, and you with bats and balls. She is more womanly; her carriage becomes dignified. Do not oblige her, by your boyish behavior, to keep you at a distance. Try to deserve the character of her friend. She will sometimes look to you for little services, which require strength and agility; let her look up to you for judgment, steadiness, and counsel too. You may be mutually beneficial. Your affection, and your intertwining interest in each other's welfare, will hereby be much increased.

A sister usually present, is that sort of second conscience, which, like the fairy ring, in an old story, pinches the wearer whenever he is doing any thing amiss. Without occasioning so much awe as a mother, or so much reserve as a stranger, her sex, her affection, and the familiarity between you will form a compound of no small value in itself, and of no small influence, if you duly regard it, upon your growing character. Never for one moment suppose *that* a good joke at which a sister blushes, or turns pale, or even looks anxious. If you should not at first perceive what there is in it which is amiss, it will be well worth your while to examine all over again. Perhaps a single glance of her eye will explain your inconsiderateness; and as you value consistency and propriety of conduct, let it put you on your guard.

There is a sort of attention due to the sex which is best attained by practising at home. Your mother may sometimes require this attention, your sisters still oftener. Do not require calling, or teasing, or even persuading to go abroad with them when their safety, their comfort, or their respectability require it. It is their due; and stupid or unkind is he who does not esteem it so. In performing this service, you are only paying a respect to yourself. Your sister could, indeed, come home alone, but it would be a sad reflection on you were she obliged to do so. Accustom yourself, then, to wait upon her; it will teach you to wait upon others by and by; and in the meantime, it will give a graceful polish to your character.

It will be well for you, if your sisters have young friends whose acquaintance with them may bring you sometimes into their society. The familiarity allowable with your sisters, though it may well prepare you to show suitable attention to other ladies, yet has its disadvantages. You need sometimes to have those present who may keep you still more upon your guard; and render your manners and attention to them still more respectful.

SECTION IV. *General Remarks and Advice.* - Never seek, then, to avoid respectable female society. Total privation has its dangers, as well as too great intimacy. One of the bad results of such a privation, is, that you run the risk of becoming attached to unworthy objects because they first fall in your way. Human nature is ever in danger of perversion. Those passions which God has given you for the wisest and noblest purposes may goad you onward, and, if they do not prove the occasion of your destruction in one way, they may in another. If you should be preserved in solitude, you will not be quite safe abroad. Having but a very imperfect conception of the different shades of character among the sex, you will be ready to suppose all are excellent who appear fair and all good who appear gentle.

I have alluded to the dangers of too great intimacy. Nothing here advanced is intended to make you a mere trifler, or to sink the dignity of your own sex. Although you are to respect females because of their sex, yet there are some who bestow upon them a species of attention extremely injurious to themselves, and unpleasant and degrading to all sensible ladies.

There is still another evil sometimes resulting from too great intimacy. It is that you lead the other party to mistake your object. This mistake is easily made. It is not necessary, to this end, that you should make any professions of attachment, in word or deed. Looks, nay even something less than this, though it may be difficult to define it, may indicate that sort of preference for the society of a lady, that has sometimes awakened an attachment in her which you never suspected or intended. Or what is a far less evil, since it falls chiefly on yourself, it may lead her and others to ridicule you for what they suppose to be the result, on your part, of intention.

Let me caution you, then, if you would obey the golden rule of doing to others as you would wish others should do to you, in the same circumstances, and if you value, besides this, your own peace, to beware of injuring those whom you highly esteem, by leading them by words, looks, or actions, to that misapprehension of your meaning which may be the means of planting thorns in their bosoms, if not in your own.

There is another error to which I wish to call your attention, in this place, although it might more properly be placed under the head, *Seduction*. I allude to the error of too great familiarity with others, after your heart is already pledged to a particular favorite. Here, more, if possible, than in the former case, do you need to set a guard over all your ways, words, and actions; and to resolve, in the strength, and with the aid of Divine grace, that you will never deviate from that rule of conduct toward others,—which Divine Goodness has given, as the grand text to the book of human duty.

The general idea presented in the foregoing sections, of what a woman ought to be, is sufficient to guide you, with a little care in the application. Such as are forward, soon become tedious. Their character is what no man of taste will bear. Some are even anglers, aiming to catch gudgeons by every look; placing themselves in attitudes to allure the vagrant eye. Against such it is quite unnecessary that I should warn you; they usually give you sufficient notice themselves. The trifler can scarcely amuse you for an evening. The company of a lady who has nothing to say but what is commonplace, whose inactive mind never for once stumbles upon an idea of its own, must be dull, as a matter of course. You can learn nothing from her, unless it be the folly of a vacant mind. Come away, lest you catch the same disorder.

The artful and manœuvring, on the contrary, will, at a glance, penetrate your inmost mind, and become any thing which they perceive will be agreeable to you.

Should your lot be cast where you can enjoy the society of a few intelligent, agreeable, and respectable females, remember to prize the acquisition. If you do not derive immense advantage from it, the fault must be your own. If, in addition to the foregoing qualifications, these female friends happen to have had a judicious and useful, rather than a merely polite education, your advantages are doubly valuable.

The genial influence of such companions must unavoidably be on the side of goodness and propriety. Loveliness of mind will impart that agreeableness of person which recommends to the heart every sentiment, gives weight to every argument, justifies every opinion, and soothes to recollection and recovery those who, were they reproved by any other voice, might have risen to resistance, or sunk into despair. The only necessary caution in the case is, 'Beware of *idolatry*.' Keep yourself clear from fascination, and call in the aid of your severest judgment to keep your mind true to yourself, and to principle.

SECTION V. *Lyceums and other Social Meetings.* - The course of my remarks has given occasion, in several instances, to speak of the importance of lyceums as a means of mental and social improvement. It will not be necessary therefore, in this place, to dwell, at *length*, on their importance. My principal object will be to call your attention to the subject in general, and urge it upon your consideration. I hope no young person who reads these pages, will neglect to avail himself of the advantages which a good lyceum affords; or if there are none of that character within his reach, let him make unremitting efforts till one exists.

Although these institutions are yet in their infancy, and could hardly have been expected to accomplish more within the same period than they have, it is hoped they will not hereafter confine their inquiries so exclusively to matters of mere intellect, as has often been done. There are other subjects nearer home, if I may so say, than these. How strangely do mankind, generally, stretch their thoughts and inquiries abroad to the concerns of other individuals, states and nations, and forget themselves, and the objects and beings near by them, and their mutual relations, connections, and dependencies!

Lyceums, when they shall have obtained a firmer footing among us, may become a most valuable means of enlightening the mass of the community, in regard to the structure and laws of the human body, and its relation to surrounding objects; of discussing the philosophy of dress, and its different materials for different seasons; of food, and drink, and sleep and exercise; of dwellings and other buildings; of amusements and employments;—in short, of the ten thousand *little things*, as many call them, which go to make up human life, with its enjoyments or miseries. These things have been surprisingly overlooked by most men, for the sake of attending to others, whose bearing on human happiness, if not often questionable, is at least more remote.

In some of our larger cities there are respectable courses of useful lectures established during the months of winter, and sometimes throughout the year. Added to this are reading-rooms, and various sorts of libraries, which are accessible for a small sum, and sometimes for almost nothing. There have been three valuable courses of Franklin Lectures delivered in Boston, during the three last winters, of twenty lectures each, for only fifty cents a course. In most large towns, benevolent and spirited individuals might establish something of the same kind, at least every winter.

SECTION VI. *Moral Instruction.* - It was not my intention, at first, to say a single word, directly, on the subject of religion, but I should leave this chapter very incomplete indeed, as well as do violence to my own feelings, should I say nothing at all of Bible classes, and other means of religious instruction, with which the age, and especially this part of the country abounds, not only on Sundays, but during the long evenings of leisure which, for a part of the year, many young men enjoy.

Viewed merely as a means of improving the *mind*, and acquiring much authentic historical information to be found nowhere else, the study of the Bible is a most valuable exercise, and ought to be encouraged. To adults who labor, a walk to church, and prompt attention to the Bible lesson, is happily adapted to the health of the body, no less than to intellectual improvement; and whatever objections might be urged against subjecting infants and young children who attend other schools during the week, to the present routine of Sabbath instruction, I am quite sure that the class of young persons for whom I am writing, would derive the most lasting benefit from studying the Bible.

I have made these remarks on the presumption that they were to derive no *moral* improvement from Bible instruction. However, I see not how these schools can be long attended by ingenuous minds without inspiring a *respect*, at the least, for that book which is superior to all other books, and for that religion which it inculcates; which is above all sect, and beyond all price.

SECTION VII. *Of Female Society in reference to Marriage.* - It is now time to consider the subject of female society in reference to matrimony. I shall find it necessary, however, to make a division of my subject, reserving a more *complete* view of female qualifications for a succeeding chapter.

Whatever advice may be given to the contrary by friends or foes, it is my opinion that you ought to keep matrimony steadily in view. For this end, were it for no other, you ought to mingle much in society. Never consider yourself complete without this other half of yourself. It is too much the fashion among young men at the present day to make up their minds to dispense with marriage;—an unnatural, and therefore an unwise plan. Much of our character, and most of our comfort and happiness depend upon it. Many have found this out too late; that is, after age and fixed habits had partly disqualified them for this important duty.

All that has been hitherto said of female influence bears upon this point. According to the character of the person you select, in a considerable degree, will be your own. Should a mere face fascinate you to a *doll*, you will not need much mental energy to please her; and the necessity of exertion on this account being small, your own self will sink, or at least not rise, as it otherwise might do.

But were I personally acquainted with you, and should I perceive an *honorable* attachment taking possession of your heart, I should regard it as a happy circumstance. Life then has an object. The only thing to be observed is that it be managed with prudence, honor, and good sense.

The case of John Newton is precisely in point. In very early life this man formed a strong attachment to a lady, under circumstances which did not permit him to make it known; which was probably well for both parties. It did not diminish *her* happiness, so long as she remained in ignorance on the subject; and in scenes of sorrow, suffering, and temptation, the hope of one day obtaining her soothed him, and kept him from performing many dishonorable actions. 'The bare possibility,' he says, 'of seeing her again, was the only obvious means of restraining me from the most horrid designs, against myself and others.'

The wish to marry, if *prudently* indulged, will lead to honest and persevering exertions to obtain a reasonable income—one which will be satisfactory to the object of your hopes, as well as to her friends. He who is determined on living a single life, very naturally contracts his endeavors to his own narrow personal wants, or else squanders freely, in the belief that he can always procure enough to support himself. Indeed it cannot have escaped even the careless observer that in proportion as an individual relinquishes the idea of matrimony, just in the same proportion do his mind and feelings contract. On the contrary, that hope which aims at a beloved partner—a family—a fireside,—will lead its possessor to activity in all his conduct. It will elicit his talents, and urge them to their full energy, and probably call in the aid of economy; a quality so indispensable to every condition of life. The single consideration, 'What would she think were she now to see me?' called up by the obtrusion of a favorite image,—how often has it stimulated a noble mind and heart to deeds which otherwise had never been performed!

I repeat it, I am aware that this advice is liable to abuse. But what shall be done? Images of some sort will haunt the mind more or less—female influence in some shape or other will operate. Is it not better to give the imagination a virtuous direction than to leave it to range without control, and without *end?*

I repeat it, nothing is better calculated to preserve a young man from the contamination of low pleasures and pursuits, than frequent intercourse with the more refined and virtuous of the other sex. Besides, without such society his manners can never acquire the true polish of a gentleman,—general character, dignity, and refinement;—nor his mind and heart the truest and noblest sentiments of a man. Make it an object then, I again say, to spend some portion of every week of your life in the company of intelligent and virtuous ladies. At all events, flee solitude, and especially the exclusive society of your own sex. The doctrines even of Zimmerman, the great apostle of solitude, would put to shame many young men, who seldom or never mix in female society.

If you should be so unfortunate as not to have among your acquaintance any ladies whose society would, in these points of view, be profitable to you, do not be in haste to mix with the ignorant and vulgar; but wait patiently till your own industry and good conduct shall give you admission to better circles; and in the meantime cultivate your mind by reading and thinking, so that when you actually gain admission to good society, you may know how to prize and enjoy it. Remember, too, that you are not to be so selfish as to think nothing of contributing to the happiness of others. It is blessed to *give* as well as to *receive*.

When you are in the company of ladies, beware of silliness. It is true that they will sooner forgive foolishness than ill manners, but you will, of course, avoid both. I know one young gentleman of great promise, who adopted the opinion that in order to qualify himself for female society, he had only to become as foolish as possible, while in their presence. That young man soon lost the favor of all whose friendship might have operated as a restraint; but unwilling to associate with the despicable, and unable to live in absolute solitude, he chose the bottle for his companion; and made himself, and the few friends he had, miserable.

Nothing, unless it be the coarsest flattery, will give more offence, in the end, than to treat ladies as mere playthings or children. On the other hand, do not become pedantic, and lecture them on difficult subjects. They readily see through all this. Neither is it good manners or policy to talk much of yourself. They can penetrate this also; and they despise the vanity which produces it. In detecting deception, they are often much quicker than we apprehend.

A young gentleman, in one of the New England States, who had assumed the chair of the pedagogue, paid his addresses to the beautiful and sensible daughter of a respectable farmer. One day, as she was present in his school, he read to her a hymn, which he said was from his own pen. Now it was obvious to this lady, and even to some of the pupils, that the hymn was none other than that usually known by the name of the 'Harvest Hymn,' modified by the change of a few words only. How much effect this circumstance might have had I cannot say with certainty; but I know it disgusted *one*, at least, of the pupils; and I know, too, that his addresses to the lady were soon afterwards discontinued.

A young man who would profit from the society of young ladies, or indeed from any society, must preserve a modest and respectful spirit; must seek to conciliate their good will by quiet and unostentatious attentions, and discover more willingness to avail himself of their stock of information, than to display his own knowledge or abilities.

He should observe, and learn to admire, that purity and ignorance of evil, which is the characteristic of well-educated young ladies, and which, while we are near them, raises us above those sordid and sensual considerations which hold such sway over *men*, in their intercourse with each other. He should treat them as spirits of a purer sphere, and try to be as innocent, if not as ignorant of evil as they are; remembering that there is no better way of raising himself in the scale of intellectual and moral being. But to whatever degree of intimacy he may arrive, he should never forget those little acts of courtesy and kindness, as well as that respect, and self-denial, which lend a charm to every kind of polite intercourse, and especially to that of which I am now speaking.

Whenever an opportunity occurs, however, it is the duty of a young man to introduce topics of conversation which are decidedly favorable to mental and moral improvement. Should he happen to be attending to the same study, or reading the same book with a female acquaintance, an excellent opportunity will be afforded for putting this rule in practice.

## CHAPTER VI.

Marriage. - SECTION I. *Why Matrimony is a Duty.*

Matrimony is a subject of high importance and interest. It is *important*, because it was among the earliest institutions of the great Creator; because it has always existed in some form or other, and must continue to exist, or society cannot be sustained; and because in proportion as the ends of the Creator are answered by its establishment, just in the same proportion does the happiness of society rise or fall. It points out the condition of society in this respect as accurately as a thermometer shows the temperature of the surrounding atmosphere. I might even go farther, and say, that in proportion as the original and real ends of marriage are answered, do the interests of religion also rise or sink.[11]

This institution is peculiarly interesting from the fact that it involves so many items of human happiness. We often speak of the value of *friendship*. What friendship like that which results from a happy union of the sexes? We talk of *education*. What school so favorable to improvement as the domestic circle may be rendered? Whether we consider education in a physical, mental or moral point of view, all its plans are imperfect without this. No man or woman is, as a general rule, fully prepared for the humblest sphere of action on earth, without the advantages which are peculiar to this institution. Nor has any man done his whole duty to God, who has left this subject out of consideration.

It has sometimes been said, and with much truth, that 'no unmarried person was ever thoroughly and completely educated.' It appears to me that were we to consider the intellectual and physical departments of education, merely, this would be true; but how much more so when we take in morals? Parents,—teachers,—what are they? Their labors are indeed of infinite value, in themselves considered; but it is only in a state of matrimony, it is only when we are called to the discharge of those multiplied duties which are involved in the endearing relations of husband, wife, parent and guardian, that our characters are fully tested and established. Late in life as these relations commence, the circumstances which they involve are so peculiar that they modify the character of the parties much more than has usually been considered.

I am fond, therefore, of contemplating the married state as a school;—not merely for a short term, but for *life*,—not one whose teachers are liable to be changed once or twice a year to the great disadvantage of all who are concerned, but whose instructors are as permanent as the school itself. It is true, that like other schools, it may result in the formation of bad character; but in proportion to its power to accomplish either good or bad results, will be its value, if wisely improved.

It is not to be denied that this view of the subject is in favor of *early* marriage. And I can truly say, indeed, that every thing considered, early marriage does appear to me highly desirable. And it would require stronger arguments than any which I have yet seen adduced, even by some of our political economists, to make me surrender this opinion.

The only serious objection, of a popular kind, to early marriage, arises from the difficulty of supporting a family. But the parties themselves must be supported at all events, whether married or single. 'But the consequences'—And what are the consequences? An *earlier* family, indeed; but not of necessity a larger. I believe that facts will bear me out in stating that the sum total of the progeny of every thousand families who commence at from twenty-five to thirty, is as great as that of one thousand who begin at from twenty to twenty-five. I have even seen pretty large families where the eldest was thirty-five years younger than both the parents; and one or two instances of numerous families where marriage did not take place till the age of forty. Physiologists have long observed this singular fact, and it has sometimes been explained by saying, if indeed it be an explanation, that Nature, in these cases, unwilling to be cheated out of her rights, endeavors to make up in energy and activity what has been lost in time.

The question, however, will recur, whether families, though equally large, cannot be better maintained when marriage is deferred to a later period. And it certainly is a question of immense importance; For nothing is more painful than to see large families, whose parents, whether young or more advanced, have not the means of educating them properly. It is also not a little painful to find instances of poverty so extreme that there is absolute suffering, for want of food and clothing.

But the question must be determined by facts. And it would be greatly aiding the cause of humanity if extensive comparisons were made between the pecuniary condition of those who marry early and those who defer the subject to a later period. But from my own limited observation I am fully of opinion that the result of the comparison would be greatly in favor of early marriages. Should this prove to be true, the position which I have assumed is, I think, established; for it appears to me that no other argument for delay has any claim to our notice.

On the other hand, the following, among other evils, are the results of deferring marriage.

1. The temper and habits of the parties become stiff and unyielding when advanced in life, and they learn to adapt themselves to each other with difficulty. In the view which I have taken above they become miserable as teachers, and still more miserable as scholars.

2. Youth are thus exposed to the danger of forming habits of criminal indulgence, as fatal to the health and the character, as they are ruinous to the soul.

3. Or if they proceed not so far, they at least acquire the habit of spending time in vain or pernicious amusements. All mankind must and will seek for gratifications of some sort or other. And aside from religious principle, there is no certain security against those amusements and indulgences which are pernicious and destructive, but early and virtuous attachments, and the pleasures afforded by domestic life. He can never want for amusement or rational gratification who is surrounded by a rising family for whom he has a genuine affection.

4. Long continued celibacy *contracts* the mind, if it does not enfeeble it. For one openhearted liberal old bachelor, you will find ten who are parsimonious, avaricious, cold-hearted, and too often destitute of those sympathies for their fellow beings which the married life has a tendency to elicit and perpetuate.[12]

5. Franklin says that late marriages are attended with another inconvenience, viz.; that the chance of living to see our children educated, is greatly diminished.

6. But I go much farther than I have hitherto done, and insist that other things being equal, the young married man has the advantage in a *pecuniary* point of view. This is a natural result from the fact that he is compelled to acquire habits of industry, frugality, and economy; and is under less temptation to waste his time in trifling or pernicious amusements. But I may appeal to facts, even here. Look around you in the world, and see if out of a given number of single persons, say one thousand, of the age of thirty-five, there be not a greater number in poverty, than of the same number who settled in life at twenty.

Perhaps I ought barely to notice another objection to these views. It is said that neither the mind nor the body come to full maturity so early as we are apt to suppose. But is complete maturity of body or mind indispensable? I am not advocating the practice of marrying in childhood. It takes sometime for the affections toward an individual to ripen and become settled. This is a matter involving too high responsibilities to justify haste. The consequences, speaking generally, are not confined to this life; they extend to eternity.

SECTION II. *General Considerations.* - We are now to enter on a most important part of our subject. Hitherto it had been my object to point out the proper course for you to pursue in reference to yourself, your own improvement, and consequent usefulness. In the remarks of the preceding chapter, and in those which follow, you are regarded as seeking a *companion*, as anxious to assume new relations, such as involve new duties and new responsibilities.

If you are successful, instead of educating yourself alone, you are to be concerned in improving the mental, moral, and social condition of two persons; and in the end, perhaps *others*. You are to be a *teacher*; you cannot avoid this station if you would. But you are also to be a *learner*. Dr. Rush says we naturally imitate the manners, and gradually acquire the tempers of persons with whom we live, provided they are objects of our affection and respect. 'This,' he adds, 'has been observed in husbands and wives who have lived long and happily together; and even in servants.' And nothing can be more true.

Not only your temper and that of your companion, but your whole character, considered as physical, mental, and moral beings, will be mutually improved or injured through life. You will be placed, as I have already intimated, at a school of mutual instruction, which is to continue without vacation or change of monitors,—perhaps half a century;—during every one of the earliest years of which, your character will be more really and more permanently modified than in the same amount of time at any prior period of your education, unless it were in the veriest infancy.

Surely then it is no light affair to make preparation for a school like this. There is no period in the life of a young man so important; for there is none on which his happiness and the happiness of others so essentially depend.

Before I advert to the particular qualifications which it is necessary for you to seek in so intimate a friend, I shall mention a few considerations of a general nature.

Settle it, in the first place, that absolute perfection is not to be found. There are not a few young men of a romantic turn of mind, fostered and increased by reading the fictitious writings of the day, who have pictured to themselves for companions in life unreal forms and angelic characters, instead of beings who dwell in 'houses of clay,' and are 'crushed before the moth.' Such 'exalted imaginations' must sooner or later be brought down: happy will it be with those who are chastened in due season.

In the second place, resolve never to be misled by any adventitious circumstances. Wealth, beauty, rank, friends, &c, are all proper considerations, but they are not of the *first* importance. They are merely secondary qualifications. Marriage must never be a matter of bargain and sale; for

In the third place, no marriage engagement should ever be thought of unless there is first a genuine and rational attachment. No cold calculations of profit or loss, no hereditary estates or other adventitious circumstances, though they were equivalent to a peerage, or a realm, should ever, for one moment, even in thought, be substituted for love. It is treason to Him who ordained this most blessed institution.

But fourthly, though wealth, however valuable in itself, is by no means a recommendation in the present case, yet the means of a comfortable support are certainly to be regarded. It is painful to see a very young couple, with a large family, and destitute of the means of support.

In the fifth place, a *suitable age* is desirable.

When we consider the varying tastes, habits and feelings of the same person at different periods of his life, is it not at once obvious that, other things being equal, those persons are most likely to find that happiness which is sought in matrimony, by associating with those whose age does not differ greatly from their own? It is true, some of the happiest human connexions that ever were formed were between persons of widely differing ages; but is this the general rule? Would not those who have found happiness under other circumstances, have been *still happier*, had their ages been more nearly equal?

There is little doubt that a person advanced in life may lengthen his days by a connection with a person much younger than himself. Whether the life of the other party is not shortened, in an equal degree, at the same time, and by the same means, remains to be determined; but probably it is so.

Some men and women are as old, in reality, whatever their *years* may indicate, at twenty, as others at twenty-five. The matrimonial connection then may be safely formed between parties whose ages differ a few years; but I think that as a general rule, the ages of the parties ought to be nearly equal.

Lastly, it was believed by a great observer of human nature, the late Dr. Spurzheim, that no person was fit for the domestic relations who had not undergone trials and sufferings. The gay reader may smile at this opinion, but I can assure him that many wise men besides Spurzheim have entertained it. Chateaubriand, among others, in his 'Genius of Christianity,' advances the same opinion. Some, as we have seen, hold that no person can be well educated without suffering. Such persons, however, use the term education as meaning something more than a little scientific instruction;—as a means of forming *character*. In this point of view no sentiment can be more true. Even the Bible confirms it, when it assures us, that the 'Captain of our Salvation was made perfect through sufferings.'

SECTION III. *Female Qualifications for Marriage.* - I. MORAL EXCELLENCE.

94

The highest as well as noblest trait in female character, is love to God. When we consider what are the tendencies of Christianity to elevate woman from the state of degradation to which she had, for ages, been subjected—when we consider not only what it has done, but what it is destined yet to do for her advancement,—it is impossible not to shrink from the presence of an impious, and above all an unprincipled atheistical female, as from an ungrateful and unnatural being.

Man is under eternal obligations to Christianity and its Divine Author, undoubtedly; but woman seems to be more so.

That charge against females which in the minds of some half atheistical men is magnified into a stigma on Christianity itself, namely that they are more apt to become religious than men; and that we find by far the greater part of professing Christians to be females, is in my own view one of the highest praises of the sex. I rejoice that their hearts are more susceptible than ours, and that they do not war so strongly against that religion which their nature demands. I have met with but one female, whom I knew to be an avowed atheist.

Indeed there are very few men to be found, who are skeptical themselves, who do not prefer pious companions of the other sex. I will not stop to adduce this as an evidence of the truth of our religion itself, and of its adaptation to the wants of the human race, for happily it does not need it. Christianity is based on the most abundant evidence, of a character wholly unquestionable. But this I do and will say, that to be consistent, young men of loose principles ought not to rail at females for their piety, and then whenever they seek for a constant friend, one whom they can love,—for they never really love the abandoned—always prefer, other things being equal, the society of the pious and the virtuous.

2. COMMON SENSE. - Next on the list of particular qualifications in a female, for matrimonial life, I place COMMON SENSE. In the view of some, it ought to precede moral excellence. A person, it is said, who is deficient in common sense, is, in proportion to the imbecility, unfit for *social* life, and yet the same person might possess a kind of negative excellency, or perhaps even a species of piety. This view appears to me, however, much more specious than sound.

By *common sense*, as used in this place, I mean the faculty by means of which we see things *as they* really are. It implies judgment and discrimination, and a proper sense of propriety in regard to the common concerns of life. It leads us to form judicious plans of action, and to be governed by our circumstances in such a way as will be generally approved. It is the exercise of reason, uninfluenced by passion or prejudice. To man, it is nearly what instinct is to brutes. It is very different from genius or talent, as they are commonly defined; but much better than either. It never blazes forth with the splendor of noon, but shines with a constant and useful light. To the housewife—but, above all, to the mother,—it is indispensable.

3. DESIRE FOR IMPROVEMENT. - Whatever other recommendations a lady may possess, she should have an inextinguishable thirst for improvement. No sensible person can be truly happy in the world, without this; much less qualified to make others happy. But the genuine spirit of improvement, wherever it exists, atones for the absence of many qualities which would otherwise be indispensable: in this respect resembling that 'charity' which covers 'a multitude of sins.' Without it,

almost everything would be of little consequence,—with it, every thing else is rendered doubly valuable.

One would think that every sensible person, of either sex, would aspire at improvement, were it merely to avoid the shame of being stationary like the brutes. Above all, it is most surprising that any lady should be satisfied to pass a day or even an hour without mental and moral progress. It is no discredit to the lower animals that—'their little all flows in at once,' that 'in ages they no more can know, or covet or enjoy,' for this is the legitimate result of the physical constitution which God has given them. But it is far otherwise with the masters and mistresses of creation; for

'Were man to live coeval with the sun,

The patriarch pupil *should* be learning still,

And dying, leave his lessons half unlearnt.'

There are,—I am sorry to say it—not a few of both sexes who never appear to breathe out one hearty desire to rise, intellectually or morally, with a view to the government of themselves or others. They love themselves supremely—their friends subordinately—their neighbors, perhaps not at all. But neither the love they bear to themselves or others ever leads them to a single series of any sort of action which has for its ultimate object the improvement of any thing higher than the condition of the mere animal. Dress, personal appearance, equipage, style of a dwelling or its furniture, with no other view, however, than the promotion of mere physical enjoyment, is the height of their desires for improvement!

Talk to them of elevating the intellect or improving the heart, and they admit it is true; but they go their way and pursue their accustomed round of folly again. The probability is, that though they assent to your views, they do not understand you. It requires a stretch of charity to which I am wholly unequal, to believe that beings who ever conceived, for one short moment, of the height to which their natures may be elevated, should sink back without a single struggle, to a mere selfish, unsocial, animal life;—to lying in bed ten or twelve hours daily, rising three or four hours later than the sun, spending the morning in preparation at the glass, the remainder of the time till dinner in unmeaning calls, the afternoon in yawning over a novel, and the evening in the excitement of the tea table and the party, and the ball room, to retire, perhaps at midnight, with the mind and body and soul in a feverish state, to toss away the night in vapid or distressing dreams.

How beings endowed with immortal souls can be contented to while away precious hours in a manner so useless, and withal so displeasing to the God who gave them their time for the improvement of themselves and others, is to me absolutely inconceivable! Yet it is certainly done; and that not merely by a few solitary individuals scattered up and down the land; but in some of our most populous cities, by considerable numbers.

A philanthropic individual not long since undertook with the aid of others, to establish a weekly or semi-weekly gazette in one of our cities, for almost the sole purpose, as I have since learned, of rousing the drones among her sex to benevolent action in some form or other, in behalf of members of their families, their friends or their neighbors. She hoped, at first, to save them from many hours of ennui by the perusal of her columns; and that their *minds* being opened to instruction, and their *hearts* made to vibrate in sympathy with the cries of ignorance, poverty, or absolute distress, their *hands* might be roused to action. But alas, the articles in the paper were *too long*, or *too dry*. They could not task their minds to go through with an argument.

Should the young man who is seeking an 'help meet,' chance to fall in with such *beings* as these—and some we fear there are in almost every part of our land,—let him shun them as he would the 'choke damp' of the cavern.

Their society would extinguish, rather than fan the flame of every generous or benevolent feeling that might be kindling in his bosom. *With* the fond, the ardent, the never failing desire to improve, physically, intellectually, and morally, there are few females who may not make tolerable companions for a man of sense;—*without* it, though a young lady were beautiful and otherwise lovely beyond comparison, wealthy as the Indies, surrounded by thousands of the most worthy friends, and even talented, let him beware! Better remain in celibacy a thousand years (could life last so long) great as the evil may be, than form a union with such an object. He should pity, and seek her reformation, if not beyond the bounds of possibility; but love her he should not! The penalty will be absolutely insupportable.

One point ought to be settled,—I think unalterably settled—before matrimony. It ought indeed so be settled in early life, but it is better late, perhaps, than never. Each of the parties should consider themselves as sacredly pledged, in all cases, to yield to conviction. I have no good opinion of the man who expects his wife to yield her opinion to his, on every occasion, unless she is convinced. I say on *every occasion*; for that she sometimes ought to do so, seems to be both scriptural and rational. It would be very inconvenient to call in a third person as an umpire upon every slight difference of opinion between a young couple, besides being very humiliating. But if each maintain, with pertinacity, their opinion, what can be done? It does seem to me that every sensible woman, who feels any good degree of confidence in her husband, will perceive the propriety of yielding her opinion to his in such cases, where the matter is of such a nature that it cannot be delayed.

But there are a thousand things occurring, in which there is no necessity of forming an immediate opinion, or decision, except from conviction. I should never like the idea of a woman's conforming to her husband's views to please him, merely, without considering whether they are correct or not. It seems to me a sort of treason against the God who gave her a mind of her own, with an intention that she should use it. But it would be higher treason still, in male, or female, not to yield, when actually convinced.

4. FONDNESS FOR CHILDREN. - Few traits of female character are more important than this. Yet there is much reason to believe that, even in contemplating an engagement that is expected to last for life, it is almost universally overlooked. Without it, though a woman should possess every accomplishment of person, mind, and manners, she would be poor indeed; and would probably render those around her miserable. I speak now generally. There may be exceptions to this, as to other general rules. A dislike of children, even in men, is an unfavorable omen; in woman it is insupportable; for it is grossly unnatural. To a susceptible, intelligent, virtuous mind, I can scarcely conceive of a worse situation in this world or any other, than to be chained for life to a person who

hates children. You can purchase, if you have the pecuniary means, almost every thing but *maternal love*. This no gold can buy. Wo to the female who is doomed to drag out a miserable existence with a husband who 'can't bear children;' but thrice miserable is the doom of him who has a wife and a family of children, but whose children have no *mother*! If there be orphans any where in the wide world, they are these.[13]

The more I reflect on the four last mentioned traits of female character, the more they rise in my estimation, eclipsing all others; unless perhaps, a good temper.

It is said that after every precaution, the choice of a wife is like buying a ticket in a lottery. If we were absolutely deaf and blind in the selection, and were so from necessity, the maxim might be just. But this is not so. We shut our eyes and stop our ears voluntarily, and then complain of the imperfection of our means of forming a judgment. In truth we impeach the goodness of Him who was the author of the *institution*.

No young man is worthy of a wife who has not sense enough to determine, even after a few interviews, what the bent of a lady's mind is;—whether she listens with most pleasure to conversation which is wholly unimproving, or whether she gladly turns from it, when an opportunity offers, to subjects which are above the petty chit-chat or common but fashionable scandal of the day; and above all, avoids *retailing* it. He knows, or *may* know, without a 'seven years' acquaintance, whether she spends a part of her leisure time in reading, or whether the whole is spent in dressing, visiting, or conversing about plays, actors, theatres, &c. And if she reads a part of the time, the fault must be his own, if he does not know whether she relishes any thing but the latest novel, or the most light—not to say empty—periodical. Let it be remembered, then, by every young man that the fault is his own, if he do not give himself time, before he forms an engagement that is to last for life, to ascertain whether his friendship is to be formed with a person who is desirous of improvement, or with one who, living only for pleasure, is 'dead while she liveth.'

You will say it is difficult to ascertain whether she is fond of children or not. But I doubt it. Has she then no young brothers, or sisters, or cousins? Are there no children in the neighborhood? For if there are,—if there is but one, and she sees that individual but once a week,—the fact may easily be ascertained. If she loves that child, the child will love her; and its eye will brighten when it sees her, or hears her name mentioned. Children seldom fail to keep debt and credit in these matters, and they know how to balance the account, with great ingenuity.

These remarks are made, not in the belief that they will benefit those who are already blinded by fancy or passion, but with the hope that some more fortunate reader may reflect on the probable chances of happiness or misery, and pause before he leaps into the vortex of matrimonial discord. No home can ever be a happy one to any of its inmates, where there is no maternal love, nor any desire for mental or moral improvement. But where these exist, in any considerable degree, and the original attachment was founded on correct principles, there is always hope of brighter days, even though clouds at present obscure the horizon. No woman who loves her husband, and desires to make continual improvement, will long consent to render those around her unhappy.

5. LOVE OF DOMESTIC CONCERNS. - Without the knowledge and the love of domestic concerns, even the wife of a peer, is but a poor affair. It was the fashion, in former times, for ladies to

understand a great deal about these things, and it would be very hard to make me believe that it did not tend to promote the interests and honor of their husbands.

The concerns of a great family never can be *well* managed, if left *wholly* to hirelings; and there are many parts of these affairs in which it would be unseemly for husbands to meddle. Surely, no lady can be too high in rank to make it proper for her to be well acquainted with the character and general demeanor of all the female servants. To receive and give character is too much to be left to a servant, however good, whose service has been ever so long, or acceptable.

Much of the ease and happiness of the great and rich must depend on the character of those by whom they are assisted. They live under the same roof with them; they are frequently the children of their tenants, or poorer neighbors; the conduct of their whole lives must be influenced by the examples and precepts which they here imbibe; and when ladies consider how much more weight there must be in one word from them, than in ten thousand words from a person who, call her what you like, is still a *fellow servant*, it does appear strange that they should forego the performance of this at once important and pleasing part of their duty.

I am, however, addressing myself, in this work, to persons in the middle ranks of life; and here a knowledge of domestic affairs is so necessary in every wife, that the lover ought to have it continually in his eye. Not only a knowledge of these affairs—not only to know how things *ought to be done*, but how to *do them*; not only to know what ingredients ought to be put into a pie or a pudding, but to be able *to make* the pie or the pudding.

Young people, when they come together, ought not, unless they have fortunes, or are to do unusual business, to think about *servants*! Servants for what! To help them eat, and drink, and sleep? When they have children, there must be some *help* in a farmer's or tradesman's house, but until then, what call is there for a servant in a house, the master of which has to *earn* every mouthful that is consumed?

Eating and drinking come *three times every day*; they must come; and, however little we may, in the days of our health and vigor, care about choice food and about cookery, we very soon get *tired* of heavy or burnt bread, and of spoiled joints of meat. We bear them for once or twice perhaps; but about the third time, we begin to lament; about the fifth time, it must be an extraordinary affair that will keep us from complaining; if the like continue for a month or two, we begin to *repent*; and then adieu to all our anticipated delights. We discover, when it is too late, that we have not got a helpmate, but a burden; and, the fire of love being damped, the unfortunately educated creature, whose parents are more to blame than she is, unless she resolve to learn her duty, is doomed to lead a life very nearly approaching to that of misery; for, however considerate the husband, he never can esteem her as he would have done, had she been skilled in domestic affairs.

The mere *manual* performance of domestic labors is not, indeed, absolutely necessary in the female head of the family of professional men; but, even here, and also in the case of great merchants and of gentlemen living on their fortunes, surely the head of the household ought to be able to give directions as to the purchasing of meal, salting meat, making bread, making preserves of all sorts; and ought to see the things done.

The lady ought to take care that food be well cooked; that there be always a sufficient supply; that there be good living without waste; and that in her department, nothing shall be seen inconsistent with the rank, station, and character of her husband. If he have a skilful and industrious wife, he will, unless he be of a singularly foolish turn, gladly leave all these things to her absolute dominion, controlled only by the extent of the whole expenditure, of which he must be the best judge.

But, in a farmer's or a tradesman's family, the manual performance is absolutely necessary, whether there be domestics or not. No one knows how to teach another so well as one who has done, and can do, the thing himself. It was said of a famous French commander, that, in attacking an enemy, he did not say to his men '*go* on,' but '*come* on;' and, whoever has well observed the movements of domestics, must know what a prodigious difference there is in the effect of the words, *go* and *come*.

A very good rule would be, to have nothing to eat, in a farmer's or mechanic's house, that the mistress did not know how to prepare and to cook; no pudding, tart, pie or cake, that she did not know how to make. Never fear the toil to her: exercise is good for health; and without health there is no beauty. Besides, what is the labor in such a case? And how many thousands of ladies, who idle away the day, would give half their fortunes for that sound sleep which the stirring housewife seldom fails to enjoy.

Yet, if a young farmer or mechanic *marry* a girl, who has been brought up only to '*play music*,' to *draw*, to *sing*, to waste paper, pen and ink in writing long and half romantic letters, and to see shows, and plays, and read novels;—if a young man do marry such an unfortunate young creature, let him bear the consequences with temper. Let him be *just*. Justice will teach him to treat her with great indulgence; to endeavor to persuade her to learn her business as a wife; to be patient with her; to reflect that he has taken her, being apprized of her inability; to bear in mind, that he was, or seemed to be, pleased with her showy and useless acquirements; and that, when the gratification of his passion has been accomplished, he is unjust, and cruel, and unmanly, if he turn round upon her, and accuse her of a want of that knowledge, which he well knew, beforehand, she did not possess.

For my part, I do not know, nor can I form an idea of, a more unfortunate being than a girl with a mere boarding school education, and without a fortune to enable her to keep domestics, when married. Of what *use* are *her* accomplishments? Of what use her music, her drawing, and her romantic epistles? If she should chance to possess a sweet disposition, and good nature, the first faint cry of her first babe drives all the tunes and all the landscapes, and all the imaginary beings out of her head for ever.

The farmer or the tradesman's wife has to *help earn* a provision for her children; or, at the least, to help to earn a store for sickness or old age. She ought, therefore, to be qualified to begin, at once, to assist her husband in his earnings. The way in which she can most efficiently assist, is by taking care of his property; by expending his money to the greatest advantage; by wasting nothing, but by making the table sufficiently abundant with the least expense.

But how is she to do these things, unless she has been *brought up* to understand domestic affairs? How is she to do these things, if she has been taught to think these matters beneath her study? How is the man to expect her to do these things, if she has been so bred, as to make her habitually look upon them as worthy the attention of none but low and ignorant women?

*Ignorant*, indeed! Ignorance consists in a want of knowledge of those things which your calling or state of life naturally supposes you to understand. A ploughman is not an ignorant man because he does not know how to read. If he knows how to plough, he is not to be called an ignorant man; but a wife may be justly called an ignorant woman, if she does not know how to provide a dinner for her husband. It is cold comfort for a hungry man, to tell him how delightfully his wife plays and sings. *Lovers* may live on very aerial diet, but husbands stand in need of something more solid; and young women may take my word for it, that a constantly clean table, well cooked victuals, a house in order, and a cheerful fire, will do more towards preserving a husband's heart, than all the 'accomplishments' taught in all the 'establishments' in the world without them.

6. SOBRIETY. - Surely no reasonable young man will expect sobriety in a companion, when he does not possess this qualification himself. But by *sobriety*, I do not mean a habit which is opposed to *intoxication*, for if that be hateful in a man, what must it be in a woman? Besides, it does seem to me that no young man, with his eyes open, and his other senses perfect, needs any caution on that point. Drunkenness, downright drunkenness, is usually as incompatible with *purity*, as it is with *decency*.

Much is sometimes said in favor of a little wine or other fermented liquors, especially at dinner. No young lady, in health, needs any of these stimulants. Wine, or ale, or cider, at dinner! I would as soon take a companion from the *streets*, as one who must habitually have her glass or two of wine at dinner. And this is not an opinion formed prematurely or hastily.

But by the word SOBRIETY in a young woman, I mean a great deal more than even a rigid abstinence from a love of drink, which I do not believe to exist to any considerable degree, in this country, even in the least refined parts of it. I mean a great deal *more* than this; I mean sobriety of conduct. The word *sober* and its derivatives mean *steadiness, seriousness, carefulness, scrupulous propriety of conduct.*

Now this kind of sobriety is of great importance in the person with whom we are to live constantly. Skipping, romping, rattling girls are very amusing where all consequences are out of the question, and they may, perhaps, ultimately become *sober*. But while you have no certainty of this, there is a presumptive argument on the other side. To be sure, when girls are mere children, they are expected to play and romp *like* children. But when they are arrived at an age which turns their thoughts towards a situation for life; when they begin to think of having the command of a house, however small or poor, it is time for them to cast away, not the cheerfulness or the simplicity, but the *levity* of the child.

'If I could not have found a young woman,' says a certain writer, 'who I was not sure possessed *all* the qualities expressed by that word *sobriety*, I should have remained a bachelor to the end of life. Scores of gentlemen have, at different times, expressed to me their surprise that I was "*always in spirits*; that nothing *pulled me down*;" and the truth is, that throughout nearly forty years of troubles, losses, and crosses, assailed all the while by numerous and powerful enemies, and performing, at the same time, greater mental labors than man ever before performed; all those labors requiring mental exertion, and some of them mental exertion of the highest order, I have never known a single hour of *real anxiety*; the troubles have been no troubles to me; I have not known what *lowness of spirits* meant; and have been more gay, and felt less care than any bachelor that ever lived. "You are always in spirits!" To be sure, for why should I not be so? Poverty, I have always set at defiance, and I could, therefore, defy the temptations to riches; and as to *home* and *children*, I had taken care to provide myself with an inexhaustible store of that "sobriety" which I so strongly recommend to others.

'This sobriety is a title to trustworthiness; and this, young man, is the treasure that you ought to prize above all others. Miserable is the husband who, when he crosses the threshold of his house, carries with him doubts, and fears, and suspicions. I do not mean suspicions of the *fidelity* of his wife; but of her care, frugality, attention to his interests, and to the health and morals of his children. Miserable is the man who cannot leave all unlocked; and who is not *sure*, quite *certain*, that all is as safe as if grasped in his own hand.

'He is the happy husband who can go away at a moment's warning, leaving his house and family with as little anxiety as he quits an inn, no more fearing to find, on his return, any thing wrong, than he would fear a discontinuance of the rising and setting of the sun; and if, as in my case, leaving books and papers all lying about at sixes and sevens, finding them arranged in proper order, and the room, during the lucky interval, freed from the effects of his and his ploughman's or gardener's dirty shoes. Such a man has no *real cares—no troubles*; and this is the sort of life I have led. I have had all the numerous and indescribable delights of home and children, and at the same time, all the bachelor's freedom from domestic cares.

'But in order to possess this precious *trustworthiness*, you must, if you can, exercise your *reason* in the choice of your partner. If she be vain of her person, very fond of dress, fond of *flattery* at all, given to gadding about, fond of what are called *parties of pleasure*, or *coquetish*, though in the least degree,—she will never be trustworthy; she cannot change her nature; and if you marry her, you will be unjust, if you expect trustworthiness at her hands. But on the other hand, if you find in her that innate *sobriety* of which I have been speaking, there is required on your part, and that at once, too, confidence and trust without any limit. Confidence in this case is nothing, unless it be reciprocal. To have a trustworthy wife, you must begin by showing her, even before marriage, that you have no suspicions, fears, or doubts in regard to her. Many a man has been discarded by a virtuous girl, merely on account of his querulous conduct. All women despise jealous men, and if they marry them, their motive is other than that of affection.'

There is a tendency, in our very natures, to become what we are taken to be. Beware then of suspicion or jealousy, lest you produce the very thing which you most dread. The evil results of suspicion and jealousy whether in single or married, public or private life, may be seen by the following fact.

A certain professional gentleman had the misfortune to possess a suspicious temper. He had not a better friend on the earth than Mr. C., yet by some unaccountable whim or other, he began of a sudden to suspect he was his enemy;—and what was at first at the farthest possible remove from the truth, ultimately grew to be a reality. Had it not have been for his jealousy, Mr. C. might have been to this hour one of the doctor's warmest and most confidential friends, instead of being removed—and in a great measure through *his* influence—from a useful field of labor.

'Let any man observe as I frequently have,' says the writer last quoted, 'with delight, the excessive fondness of the laboring people for their children. Let him observe with what care they dress them out on Sundays with means deducted from their own scanty meals. Let him observe the husband, who has toiled, like his horse, all the week, nursing the babe, while the wife is preparing dinner. Let him observe them both abstaining from a sufficiency, lest the children should feel the pinchings of hunger. Let him observe, in short, the whole of their demeanor, the real mutual affection evinced, not in words, but in unequivocal deeds.

'Let him observe these things, and having then cast a look at the lives of the great and wealthy, he will say, with me, that when a man is choosing his partner for life, the dread of poverty ought to be cast to the winds. A laborer's cottage in a cleanly condition; the husband or wife having a babe in arms, looking at two or three older ones, playing between the flower borders, going from the wicket to the door, is, according to my taste, the most interesting object that eyes ever beheld; and it is an object to be seen in no country on earth but England.'

It happens, however, that the writer had not seen all the countries upon earth, nor even all in the interior of United America. There are as moving instances of native simplicity and substantial happiness here as in any other country; and occasionally in even the higher classes. The wife of a distinguished lawyer and senator in Congress, never left the society of her own children, to go for once to see her friends abroad, in *eleven years*! I am not defending the conduct of the husband who would doom his wife to imprisonment in his own house, even amid a happy group of children, for eleven years; but the example shows, at least, that there are women fitted for domestic life in other countries besides England.

Ardent young men may fear that great sobriety in a young woman argues a want of that warmth which they naturally so much desire and approve. But observation and experience attest to the contrary. They tell us that levity is ninety-nine times out of a hundred, the companion of a *want* of ardent feeling. But the *licentious* never *love*. Their passion is chiefly animal. Even better women, if they possess light and frivolous minds, have seldom any ardent passion.

I would not, however, recommend that you should be too severe in judging, when the conduct does not go beyond mere *levity*, and is not bordering on *loose* conduct; for something certainly depends here on constitution and animal spirits, and something on the manners of the country.

If any person imagine that the sobriety I have been recommending would render young women moping or gloomy, he is much mistaken, for the contrary is the fact. I have uniformly found—and I began to observe it in my very childhood—that your jovial souls, men or women, except when over the bottle, are of all human beings the most dull and insipid. They can no more exist—they may *vegetate*—but they can no more *live* without some excitement, than a fish could live on the top of the Alleghany. If it be not the excitement of the bottle, it must be that of the tea or the coffee cup, or food converted into some unwholesome form or other by condiments; or if it be none of these, they must have some excitement of the intellect, for intemperance is not confined to the use of condiments and poisons for the body; there are condiments and poisons to mind and heart. In fact, they usually accompany each other.

Show me a person who cannot live on plain and simple food and the only drink the Creator ever made, and as a general rule you will show me a person to whom the plain and the solid and the useful in domestic, social, intellectual, and moral life are insipid if not disgusting. 'They are welcome to all that sort of labor,' said one of these creatures—not rationals—this very day, to me, in relation to plain domestic employments.—Show me a female, as many, alas! very many in fashionable life are now trained, and you show me a person who has none of the qualities that fit her to be a help meet for man in a life of simplicity. She could recite well at the high school, no doubt; but the moment she leaves school, she has nothing to do, and is taught to do nothing. I have seen girls, of this description, and they may be seen by others.

But what is such a female—one who can hardly help herself—good for, at home or abroad; married, or single? The moment she has not some feast, or party, or play, or novel, or—I know not what—something to keep up a fever, the moment I say that she has not something of this sort to anticipate or enjoy, that moment she is miserable. Wo to the young man who becomes wedded for life to a creature of this description. She may stay at home, for want of a better place, and she may add one to the national census every ten years, but a companion, or a mother, she cannot be.

I should dislike a moping melancholy creature as much as any man, though were I tied to such a thing, I could live with her; but I never could enjoy her society, nor but half of my own. He is but half a man who is thus wedded, and will exclaim, in a literal sense, 'When shall I be delivered from the body of this death?'

One hour, an *animal* of this sort is moping, especially if nobody but her husband is present; the next hour, if others happen to be present, she has plenty of smiles; the next she is giggling or capering about; and the next singing to the motion of a lazy needle, or perhaps weeping over a novel. And this is called sentiment! *She* is a woman of feeling and good taste!

7. INDUSTRY. - Let not the individual whose eye catches the word *industry*, at the beginning of this division of my subject, condemn me as degrading females to the condition of mere wheels in a machine for money-making; for I mean no such thing. There is nothing more abhorrent to the soul of a sensible man than female *avarice*. The 'spirit of a man' may sustain him, while he sees avaricious and miserly individuals among his own sex, though the sight is painful enough, even here; but a female miser, 'who can bear?'

Still if woman is intended to be a 'help meet,' for the other sex, I know of no reason why she should not be so in physical concerns, as well as mental and moral. I know not by what rule it is that many resolve to remain for ever in celibacy, unless they believe their companion can 'support' them, without labor. I have sometimes even doubted whether any person who makes these declarations can be sincere. Yet when I hear people, of both sexes, speak of poverty as a greater calamity than death, I am led to think that this dread of poverty does really exist among both sexes. And there are reasons for believing that some females, bred in fashionable life, look forward to matrimony as a state, of such entire exemption from care and labor, and of such uninterrupted ease, that they would prefer celibacy and even death to those duties which scripture, and reason, and common sense, appear to me to enjoin.

Such persons, whatever may be their other qualifications, I call upon every young man to avoid, as he would a pestilence. If they are really determined to live and act as mere drones in society, let them live alone. Do not give them an opportunity to spread the infection of so wretched a disease, if you can honestly help it.

The woman who does not actually prefer action to inaction—industry to idleness—labor to ease—and who does not steadfastly resolve to labor moderately as long as she lives, whatever may be her circumstances, is unfit for life, social or domestic. It is not for me to say, in what *form* her labor shall be applied, except in rearing the young. But labor she ought—all she is able—while life and health lasts, at something or other; or she ought not to complain if she suffers the *natural penalty*; and she ought to do it with cheerfulness.

I like much the quaint remark of a good old lady of ninety. She was bred to labor, had labored through the whole of her long and eventful life, and was still at her 'wheel.' 'Why,' said she, 'people ought to strain *every nerve* to get property, as a matter of Christian duty.'

I should choose to modify this old lady's remark, and say that, people ought to do all they can *without straining* their *muscles* or *nerves*; not to get property, but because it is at once, their duty and their happiness.

The great object of life is to do good. The great object of society is to increase the power to good. Both sexes should aim, in matrimony, at a more extended sphere of usefulness. To increase an estate, merely, is a low and unworthy aim, from which may God preserve the rising generation. Still I must say, that I greatly prefer the avaricious being—a monster though she might be—to the stupid soul who would not lift a finger if she could help it, and who determines to fold her arms whenever she has a convenient opportunity.

If a female be lazy, there will be lazy domestics, and, what is a great deal worse, children will acquire this habit. Every thing, however necessary to be done, will be put off to the last moment, and then it will be done badly, and, in many cases, not at all. The dinner will be too late; the journey or the visit will be tardy; inconveniences of all sorts will be continually arising. There will always be a heavy arrear of things unperformed; and this, even among the most wealthy, is a great evil; for if they have no business imposed upon them by necessity, they *make* business for themselves. Life would be intolerable without it; and therefore an indolent woman must always be an evil, be her rank or station what it may.

But, *who is to tell* whether a girl will make an industrious woman? How is the pur-blind lover especially, to be able to ascertain whether she, whose smiles and dimples and bewitching lips have half bereft him of his senses; how is he to be able to judge, from any thing that he can see, whether the beloved object will be industrious or lazy? Why, it is very difficult; it is a matter that reason has very little to do with. Still there are indications which enable a man, not wholly deprived of the use of his reason, to form a pretty accurate judgment in this matter.

It was a famous story some years ago, that a young man, who was courting one of three sisters, happened to be on a visit to her, when all the three were present, and when one said to the others, 'I *wonder* where *our* needle is.' Upon which he withdrew, as soon as was consistent with the rules of politeness, resolving to think no more of a girl who possessed a needle only in partnership, and who, it appeared, was not too well informed as to the place where even that share was deposited.

This was, to be sure, a very flagrant instance of a want of industry; for, if the third part of the use of a needle satisfied her, when single, it was reasonable to anticipate that marriage would banish that useful implement altogether. But such instances are seldom suffered to come in contact with the eyes and ears of the lover. There are, however, as I have already said, certain *rules*, which, if attended to with care, will serve as pretty sure guides.

And, first, if you find the tongue lazy, you may be nearly certain that the hands and feet are not very industrious. By laziness of the tongue I do not mean silence; but, I mean, a *slow* and *soft* utterance; a sort of *sighing* out of the words, instead of *speaking* them; a sort of letting the sounds fall out, as if the party were sick at stomach. The pronunciation of an industrious person is generally *quick*, and *distinct*; the voice, if not strong, *firm* at the least. Not masculine, but as feminine as possible; not a *croak* nor a *bawl*, but a quick, distinct, and sound voice.

One writer insists that the motion of those little members of the body, the teeth, are very much in harmony with the operations of the mind; and a very observing gentleman assures me that he can judge pretty accurately of the temper, and indeed of the general character of a *child*, by his manner of eating. And I have no doubt of the fact. Nothing is more obvious than that the temper of the child who is so greedy as to swallow down his food habitually, without masticating it, must be very different from that of him who habitually eats slowly. Hunger, I know, will quicken the jaws in either case, but I am supposing them on an equal footing in this respect.

Another mark of industry is, a *quick step*, and a somewhat *heavy tread*, showing that the foot comes down with a *hearty good will*. If the body lean a little forward, and the eyes keep steadily in the same direction, while the feet are going, so much the better, for these discover *earnestness* to arrive at the intended point. I do not like, and I *never* liked, your *sauntering*, soft-stepping girls, who move as if they were perfectly indifferent as to the result. And, as to the *love* part of the story, who ever expects ardent and lasting affection from one of these sauntering girls, will, when too late, find his mistake. The character is much the same throughout; and probably no man ever yet saw a sauntering girl, who did not, when married, make an indifferent wife, and a cold-hearted mother; cared very little for, either by husband or children; and, of course, having no store of those blessings which are the natural resources to apply to in sickness and in old age.

8. EARLY RISING. - *Early rising* is another mark of industry; and though, in the higher stations of life, it may be of no importance in a mere pecuniary point of view, it is, even there, of importance in other respects; for it is rather difficult to keep love alive towards a woman who never sees the *dew*, never beholds the rising *sun*, and who constantly comes directly from a reeking bed to the breakfast table, and there chews, without appetite, the choicest morsels of human food. A man might, perhaps, endure this for a month or two, without being disgusted; but not much longer.

As to people in the middle rank of life, where a living and a provision for children is to be sought by labor of some sort or other, late rising in the wife is certain ruin; and rarely will you find an early-rising wife, who had been a late-rising girl. If brought up to late rising, she will like it; it will be her *habit*; she will, when married, never want excuses for indulging in the habit. At first she will be indulged without bounds; and to make a *change* afterwards will be difficult, for it will be deemed a *wrong* done to her; she will ascribe it to diminished affection. A quarrel must ensue, or, the husband must submit to be ruined, or, at the very least, to see half the fruit of his labor snored and lounged away.

And, is this being unreasonably harsh or severe upon woman? By no means. It arises from an ardent desire to promote the happiness, and to add to the natural, legitimate, and salutary influence of the female sex. The tendency of this advice is to promote the preservation of their health; to prolong the duration of their beauty; to cause them to be loved to the last day of their lives; and to give them, during the whole of those lives, that weight and consequence, and respect, of which laziness would render them wholly unworthy.

9. FRUGALITY. - This means the contrary of extravagance. It does not mean *stinginess*; it does not mean *pinching*; but it means an abstaining from all unnecessary expenditure, and all unnecessary use of goods of any and of every sort. It is a quality of great importance, whether the rank in life be high or low.

Some people are, indeed, so rich, they have such an over-abundance of money and goods, that how to get rid of them would, to a spectator, seem to be their only difficulty. How many individuals of fine estates, have been ruined and degraded by the extravagance of their wives! More frequently by their *own* extravagance, perhaps; but, in numerous instances, by that of those whose duty it is to assist in upholding their stations by husbanding their fortunes.

If this be the case amongst the opulent, who have estates to draw upon, what must be the consequences of a want of frugality in the middle and lower ranks of life? Here it must be fatal, and especially among that description of persons whose wives have, in many cases, the receiving as well as the expending of money. In such a case, there wants nothing but extravagance in the wife to make ruin as inevitable as the arrival of old age.

To obtain security against this is very difficult; yet, if the lover be not quite *blind*, he may easily discover a propensity towards extravagance. The object of his addresses will, nine times out of ten, never be the manager of a house; but she must have her *dress*, and other little matters under her control. If she be costly in these; if, in these, she step above her rank, or even to the top of it; if she purchase all she is able to purchase, and prefer the showy to the useful, the gay and the fragile to the less sightly and more durable, he may be sure that the disposition will cling to her through life. If he perceive in her a taste for costly food, costly furniture, costly amusements: if he find her love of gratification to be bounded only by her want of means; if he find her full of admiration of the trappings of the rich, and of desire to be able to imitate them, he may be pretty sure that she will not spare his purse, when once she gets her hand into it; and, therefore, if he can bid adieu to her charms, the sooner he does it, the better.

Some of the indications of extravagance in a lady are ear-rings, broaches, bracelets, buckles, necklaces, diamonds, (real or mock,) and nearly all the ornaments which women put upon their persons.

These things may be more proper in *palaces*, or in scenes resembling palaces; but, when they make their appearance amongst people in the middle rank of life, where, after all, they only serve to show that poverty in the parties which they wish to disguise; when the mean, tawdry things make their appearance in this rank of life, they are the sure indications of a disposition that will always be straining at what it can never attain.

To marry a girl of this disposition is really self-destruction. You never can have either property or peace. Earn her a horse to ride, she will want a gig: earn the gig, she will want a chariot: get her that, she will long for a coach and four: and, from stage to stage, she will torment you to the end of her or your days; for, still there will be somebody with a finer equipage than you can give her; and, as long as this is the case, you will never have rest. Reason would tell her, that she could never be at the *top*, that she must stop at some point short of that; and that, therefore, all expenses in the rivalship are so much thrown away. But, reason and broaches and bracelets seldom go in company. The girl who has not the sense to perceive that her person is disfigured and not beautified by parcels of brass and tin, or even gold and silver, as well to *regret*, if she dare not *oppose* the tyranny of absurd fashions, is not entitled to a full measure of the confidence of any individual.

10. PERSONAL NEATNESS. - There never yet was, and there never will be sincere and ardent love, of long duration, where personal neatness is wholly neglected. I do not say that there are not those who would live peaceably and even contentedly in these circumstances. But what I contend for is this: that there never can exist, for any length of time, ardent *affection*, in any man towards a woman who neglects neatness, either in her person, or in her house affairs.

Men may be careless as to their own person; they may, from the nature of their business, or from their want of time to adhere to neatness in dress, be slovenly in their own dress and habits; but, they do not relish this in their wives, who must still have *charms*; and charms and neglect of the person seldom go together. I do not, of course, approve of it even in men.

We may, indeed, lay it down as a rule of almost universal application, that supposing all other things to be equal, he who is most guilty of personal neglect; will be the most ignorant and the most vicious. *Why* there should be, universally, a connection between slovenliness, ignorance, and vice, is a question I have no room in this work to discuss.

I am well acquainted with one whole family who neglect their persons from principle. The gentleman, who is a sort of new light in religious concerns, will tell you that the true Christian *should* 'slight the hovel, as beneath his care.' But there is a want of intelligence, and even common refinement in the family, that certainly does not and *cannot* add much to their own happiness, or recommend religion—aside from the fact that it greatly annoys their neighbors. And though the head of the family observes many external duties with Jewish strictness, neither he nor any of its members are apt to bridle their tongues, or remember that on *ordinary* as well as *special* occasions they are bound to 'do all to the glory of God.' As to the connection of mind with matter—I mean the dependence of mind and soul on body, they are wholly ignorant.

It is not dress that the husband wants to be perpetual: it is not finery; but *cleanliness* in every thing. Women generally dress enough, especially when they *go abroad*. This *occasional* cleanliness is not the thing that a husband wants: he wants it always; in-doors as well as out; by night as well as by day; on the floor as well as on the table; and, however he may complain about the trouble and the 'expense' of it, he would complain more if it were neglected.

The indications of female neatness are, first, a clean *skin*. The hands and face will usually be clean, to be sure, if there be soap and water within reach; but if on observing other parts of the head besides the face, you make discoveries indicating a different character, the sooner you cease your visits the better. I hope, now, that no young woman who may chance to see this book, will be offended at this, and think me too severe on her sex. I am only telling that which all men think; and, it is a decided advantage to them to be fully informed of our thoughts on the subject. If any one, who reads this, shall find, upon self-examination, that she is defective in this respect, let her take the hint, and correct the defect.

In the *dress*, you can, amongst rich people, find little whereon to form a judgment as to cleanliness, because they have not only the dress prepared for them, but put upon them into the bargain. But, in the middle ranks of life, the dress is a good criterion in two respects: first, as to its *color*; for if the *white* be a sort of *yellow*, cleanly hands would have been at work to prevent that. A *white-yellow* cravat, or shirt, on a man, speaks at once the character of his wife; and, you may be assured, that she will not take with your dress pains which she has never taken with her own.

Then, the manner of *putting on* the dress, is no bad foundation for judging. If this be careless, and slovenly, if it do not fit properly,—no matter for its *mean quality*; mean as it may be, it may be neatly and trimly put on—if it be slovenly put on, I say, take care of yourself; for, you will soon find to your cost, that a sloven in one thing, is a sloven in all things. The plainer people, judge greatly from the state of the covering of the ankles; and, if that be not clean and tight, they conclude that the rest is not as it ought to be. Look at the shoes! If they be trodden on one side, loose on the foot, or run down at the heel, it is a very bad *sign*; and as to going *slipshod*, though at coming down in the morning, and even before daylight, make up your mind to a rope, rather than live with a slipshod woman.

How much do women lose by inattention to these matters! Men, in general, say nothing about it to their wives, but they *think* about it; they envy their more lucky neighbors, and in numerous cases, consequences the most serious arise from this apparently trifling cause. Beauty is valuable; it is one of the *ties*, and a *strong* one too; but it cannot last to old age; whereas the charm of cleanliness never ends but with life itself. It has been said that the sweetest flowers, when they really become putrid, are the most offensive. So the most beautiful woman, if found with an uncleansed skin, is, in my estimation, the most disagreeable.

II. A GOOD TEMPER. - This is a very difficult thing to ascertain beforehand. Smiles are cheap; they are easily put on for the occasion; and, besides, the frowns are, according to the lover's whim, interpreted into the contrary. By 'good temper,' I do not mean an easy temper, a serenity which nothing disturbs; for that is a mark of laziness. Sullenness, if you be not too blind to perceive it, is a temper to be avoided by all means. A sullen man is bad enough; what, then, must be a sullen woman, and that woman a *wife*, a constant inmate, a companion day and night! Only think of the delight of setting at the same table, and occupying the same chamber, for a week, without exchanging a word all the while! Very bad to be scolding for such a length of time; but this is far better than 'the *sulks*.'

But if you have your eyes, and look sharp, you will discover symptoms of this, if it unhappily exist. She will, at some time or other, show it towards some one or other of the family; or, perhaps, towards yourself; and you may be quite sure that, in this respect, marriage will not mend her. Sullenness arises from capricious displeasure not founded in reason. The party takes offence unjustifiably; is unable to frame a complaint, and therefore expresses displeasure by silence. The remedy for it is, to suffer it to take its *full swing*, but it is better not to have the disease in your house; and to be *married to it*, is little short of madness.

*Querulousness* is a great fault. No man, and, especially, no *woman*, likes to hear a continual plaintiveness. That she complain, and roundly complain, of your want of punctuality, of your coolness, of your neglect, of your liking the company of others: these are all very well, more especially as they are frequently but too just. But an everlasting complaining, without rhyme or reason, is a bad sign. It shows want of patience, and, indeed, want of sense.

But the contrary of this, a cold *indifference*, is still worse. 'When will you come again? You can never find time to come here. You like any company better than mine.' These, when groundless, are very teasing, and demonstrate a disposition too full of anxiousness; but, from a girl who always receives you with the same civil smile, lets you, at your own good pleasure, depart with the same; and who, when you take her by the hand, holds her cold fingers as straight as sticks, I should say, in mercy, preserve *me*!

*Pertinacity* is a very bad thing in anybody, and especially in a young woman; and it is sure to increase in force with the age of the party. To have the last word, is a poor triumph; but with some people it is a species of disease of the mind. In a wife it must be extremely troublesome; and, if you find an ounce of it in the maid, it will become a pound in the wife. A fierce *disputer* is a most disagreeable companion; and where young women thrust their *say* into conversations carried on by older persons, give their opinions in a positive manner, and court a contest of the tongue, those must be very bold men who will encounter them as wives.

Still, of all the faults as to *temper*, your melancholy ladies have the worst, unless you have the same mental disease yourself. Many wives are, at times, *misery-makers*; but these carry it on as a regular trade. They are always unhappy about something, either past, present, or to come. Both arms full of children is a pretty efficient remedy in most cases; but, if these ingredients be wanting, a little want, a little *real* trouble, a little *genuine affliction*, often will effect a cure.

12. ACCOMPLISHMENTS.  -  By accomplishments, I mean those things, which are usually comprehended in what is termed a useful and polite education. Now it is not unlikely that the fact of my adverting to this subject so late, may lead to the opinion that I do not set a proper estimate on this female qualification.

But it is not so. Probably few set too high an estimate upon it. Its *absolute* importance has, I am confident, been seldom overrated. It is true I do not like a *bookish* woman better than a bookish man; especially a great devourer of that most contemptible species of books with whose burden the press daily groans: I mean *novels*. But mental cultivation, and even what is called *polite* learning, along with the foregoing qualifications, are a most valuable acquisition, and make every female, as well as all her associates, doubly happy. It is only when books, and music, and a taste for the fine arts are substituted for other and more important things, that they should be allowed to change love or respect to disgust.

It sometimes happens, I know, that two persons are, in this respect, pretty equally yoked. But what of that? It only makes each party twofold more the child of misfortune than before. I have known a couple of intelligent persons who would sit with their 'feet in the ashes,' as it were, all day, to read some new and bewitching book, forgetting every want of the body; perhaps even forgetting that they *had* bodies. Were they therefore happy, or likely to be so?

Drawing, music, embroidery, (and I might mention half a dozen other things of the same class) where they do not exclude the more useful and solid matters, may justly be regarded as appropriate branches of female education; and in some circumstances and conditions of life, indispensable. Music,—vocal and instrumental—and drawing, to a certain extent, seem to me desirable in all. As for dancing, I do not feel quite competent to decide. As the world is, however, I am almost disposed to reject it altogether. At any rate, if a young lady is accomplished in every other respect, you need not seriously regret that she has not attended to dancing, especially as it is conducted in most of our schools.

# CHAPTER VII.

Criminal Behavior. - SECTION I. *Inconstancy and Seduction.*

In nineteen cases out of twenty, of illicit conduct, there is perhaps, no seduction at all; the passion, the absence of virtue, and the crime, being all mutual. But there are cases of a very different description. Where a young man goes coolly and deliberately to work, first to gain and rivet the affections of a young lady, then to take advantage of those affections to accomplish that which he knows must be her ruin, and plunge her into misery for life;—when a young man does this, I say he must be either a selfish and unfeeling brute, unworthy of the name of man, or he must have a heart little inferior, in point of obduracy, to that of the murderer. Let young women, however, be aware; let them be *well* aware, that few, indeed, are the cases in which this apology can possibly avail them. Their character is not solely theirs, but belongs, in part, to their family and kindred. They may, in the case contemplated, be objects of compassion with the world; but what contrition, what repentance, what remorse, what that even the tenderest benevolence can suggest, is to heal the wounded hearts of humbled, disgraced, but still affectionate parents, brethren, and sisters?

In the progress of an intimate acquaintance, should it be discovered that there are certain traits of character in one of the parties, which both are fully convinced will be a source of unhappiness, through life, there *may* be no special impropriety in separating. And yet even then I would say, avoid haste. Better consider for an hour than repent for a year, or for life. But let it be remembered, that before measures of this kind are even hinted at, there must be a full conviction of their necessity, and the mutual and hearty concurrence of both parties. Any steps of this kind, the reasons for which are not fully understood on both sides, and mutually satisfactory, as well as easily explicable to those friends who have a right to inquire on the subject, are criminal;—nay more; they are brutal.

I have alluded to *indirect* promises of marriage, because I conceive that the frequent opinion among young men that nothing is binding but a direct promise, in so many words, is not only erroneous, but highly dishonorable to those who hold it. The strongest pledges are frequently given without the interchange of words. Actions speak louder than words; and there is an attachment sometimes formed, and a confidence reposed, which would be, in effect, weakened by formalities. The man who would break a silent engagement, merely because it is a silent one, especially when he has taken a course of conduct which he knew would be likely to result in such engagement, and which perhaps he even designed, is deserving of the public contempt. He is even a monster unfit to live in decent society.

But there are such monsters on the earth's surface. There are individuals to be found, who boast of their inhuman depredations on those whom it ought to be their highest happiness to protect and aid, rather than injure. They can witness, almost without emotion, the heavings of a bosom rent with pangs which themselves have inflicted. They can behold their unoffending victim, as unmoved as one who views a philosophical experiment;—not expiring, it is true, but despoiled of what is vastly dearer to her than life—her reputation. They can witness all this, I say, without emotion, and without a single compunction of conscience. And yet they go on, sometimes with apparent prosperity and inward peace. At any rate, they *live.* No lightning blasts them; no volcano pours over them its floods of lava; no earthquake engulfs them. They are permitted to fill up the measure of their wickedness.

Perhaps they riot in ease, and become bloated with luxury. But let this description of beings—men I am almost afraid to call them—remember that punishment, though long deferred, cannot be always evaded. A day of retribution must and will arrive. For though they may not be visited by what a portion of the community call special 'judgments,' yet their punishment is not the less certain. The wretch who can commit the crime to which I have referred, against a fellow being, and sport with those promises, which, whether direct or indirect, are of all things earthly among the most sacred, will not, unless he repents, rest here. He will go on from step to step in wickedness. He will harden himself against every sensibility to the woes of others, till he becomes a fiend accursed, and whether on this side of the grave, or the other, cannot but be completely miserable. A single sin may not always break in upon habits of virtue so as to ruin an individual at once; but the vices go in gangs, or companies. One admitted and indulged, and the whole gang soon follow. And misery must follow sin, at a distance more or less near, as inevitably as a stone falls to the ground, or the needle points to the pole.

Some young men reason thus with themselves. If doubts about the future have already risen—if my affections already begin to waver at times—what is not to be expected after marriage? And is it not better to separate, even without a mutual concurrence, than to make others, perhaps many others, unhappy for life?

In reply, I would observe, in the first place, that though this is the usual reason which is assigned in such cases, it is not generally the true one. The fact is, the imagination is suffered to wander where it ought not; and the affections are not guarded and restrained, and confined to their proper object. And if there be a diminution of attachment, it is not owing to any change in others, but in ourselves. If our affection has become less ardent, let us look within, for the cause. Shall others suffer for our own fault?

But, secondly, we may do much to control the affections, even after they have begun to wander. We still seek the happiness of the object of our choice, more, perhaps, than that of any other individual. Then let us make it our constant study to promote it. It is a law of our natures, as irrevocable as that of the attraction of gravitation, that doing good to others produces love to them. And for myself I do not believe the affections of a young man *can* diminish towards one whose happiness he is constantly studying to promote by every means in his power, admitting there is no obvious change in her character. So that no young person of principle ought ever to anticipate any such result.

Nor has a man any right to *sport* with the affections of a young woman, in any way whatever. Vanity is generally the tempter in this case; a desire to be regarded as being admired by the women; a very despicable species of vanity, but frequently greatly mischievous, notwithstanding. You do not, indeed, actually, in so many words, promise to marry; but the general tenor of your language and deportment has that meaning; you know that your meaning is so understood; and if you have not such meaning; if you be fixed by some previous engagement with, or greater liking for another; if you know you are here sowing the seeds of disappointment; and if you persevere, in spite of the admonitions of conscience, you are guilty of deliberate deception, injustice and cruelty. You make to God an ungrateful return for those endowments which have enabled you to achieve this inglorious and unmanly triumph; and if, as is frequently the case, you *glory* in such triumph, you may have person, riches, talents to excite envy; but every just and humane man will abhor your heart.

The most direct injury against the spiritual nature of a fellow being is, by leading him into vice. I have heard one young man, who was entrusted six days in the week to form the immortal minds and hearts of a score or two of his fellow beings, deliberately boast of the number of the other sex he had misled. What can be more base? And must not a terrible retribution await such Heaven daring miscreants? Whether they accomplish their purposes by solicitation, by imposing on the judgment, or by powerful compulsion, the wrong is the same, or at least of the same nature; and nothing but timely and hearty repentance can save a wretch of this description from punishment, either here or hereafter.

'Some tempers,' says Burgh, (for nothing can be more in point than his own words) 'are so impotently ductile, that they can refuse nothing to repeated solicitation. Whoever takes the advantage of such persons is guilty of the lowest baseness. Yet nothing is more common than for the debauched part of our sex to show their heroism by a poor triumph, over weak, easy, thoughtless woman!—Nothing is more frequent than to hear them boast of the ruin of that virtue, of which they ought to have been the defenders. "Poor fool! she loved me, and therefore could refuse me nothing."—Base coward! Dost thou boast of thy conquest over one, who, by thy own confession, was disabled for resistance,— disabled by her affection for thy worthless self! Does affection deserve such a return Is superior understanding, or rather deeper craft, to be used against thoughtless simplicity, and its shameful success to be boasted of? Dost thou pride thyself that thou hast had art enough to decoy the harmless lamb to thy hand, that thou mightest shed its blood?'

And yet there are such monsters as Burgh alludes to. There are just such beings scattered up and down even the fairest portions of the world we live in, to mar its beauty. We may hope, for the honor of human nature, they are few. He who can bring himself to believe their number to be as great as one in a thousand, may well be disposed to blush

'And hang his head, to own himself a man.'

I have sometimes wished these beings—*men* they are not—would *reflect*, if it were but for one short moment. They will not deny the excellency of the golden rule, of doing to others as they wish others to do by themselves. I say they will not deny it, in theory; why then should they despise it in practice?

Let them *think* a moment. Let them imagine themselves in the place of the injured party. Could this point be gained; could they be induced to reflect long enough to see the enormity of their guilt as it really is, or as the Father in heaven may be supposed to see it, there might be hope in their case. Or if they find it difficult to view themselves as the injured, let them suppose, rather, a sister or a daughter. What seducer is so lost to all natural affection as not to have his whole soul revolt at the bare thought of having a beloved daughter experience the treatment which he has inflicted? Yet the being whom he has ruined had brothers or parents; and those brothers had a sister; and those parents a daughter!

SECTION II. *Licentiousness.* - I wish it were in my power to finish my remarks in this place, without feeling that I had made an important omission. But such is the tendency of human nature, especially in the case of the young and ardent, to turn the most valuable blessings conferred on man into curses,—and poison, at their very sources, the purest streams of human felicity,—that it will be necessary to advert briefly but plainly to some of the most frequent forms of youthful irregularity.

Large cities and thinly settled places are the *extremes* of social life. Here, of course, vice will be found in its worst forms. It is more difficult to say which extreme is worst, among *an equal number of individuals*; but probably the city; for in the country, vice is oftener solitary, and less frequently social; while in the city it is not only *social* but also *solitary*.

A well informed gentleman from New Orleans, of whose own virtue by the way, I have not the *highest* confidence, expressed, lately the strongest apprehension that the whole race of young men in our cities, of the present generation, will be ruined. Others have assured me that in the more northern cities, the prospect is little, if any, more favorable.

It is to be regretted that legislators have not found out the means of abolishing those haunts in cities which might be appropriately termed schools of licentiousness, and thus diminishing an aggregate of temptation already sufficiently large. But the vices, like their votaries, go in companies. Until, therefore, the various haunts of intemperance in eating and drinking, and of gambling and stage-playing, can be broken up, it may be considered vain to hope for the disappearance of those sties of pollution which are their almost inevitable results. We might as well think of drying up the channel of a mighty river, while the fountains which feed it continue to flow as usual.

There is now in Pennsylvania,—it seems unnecessary to name the place—a man thirty-five years old, with all the infirmities of 'three score and ten.' Yet his premature old age, his bending and tottering form, wrinkled face, and hoary head, might be traced to solitary and social *licentiousness*.

This man is not alone. There are thousands in every city who are going the same road; some with slow and cautious steps, others with a fearful rapidity. Thousands of youth on whom high expectations have been placed, are already on the highway that will probably lead down to disease and premature death.

Could the multitude of once active, sprightly, and promising young men, whose souls detested open vice, and who, without dreaming of danger, only found their way occasionally to a lottery office, and still more rarely to the theatre or the gambling house, until led on step by step they ventured down those avenues which lead to the chambers of death, from which few ever return, and none uninjured;—could the multitudes of such beings, which in the United States alone, (though admitted to be the paradise of the world,) have gone down to infamy through licentiousness, be presented to our view, at once, how would it strike us with horror! Their very numbers would astonish us, but how much more their appearance! I am supposing them to appear as they went to the graves, in their bloated and disfigured faces, their emaciated and tottering frames, bending at thirty years of age under the appearance of three or four score; diseased externally and internally; and positively disgusting,—not only to the eye, but to some of the other senses.

One such monster is enough to fill the soul of those who are but moderately virtuous with horror; what then would be the effect of beholding thousands? In view of such a scene, is there a young man in the world, who would not form the strongest resolution not to enter upon a road which ends in wo so remediless?

But it should be remembered that these thousands were once the friends—the children, the brothers,—yes, sometimes the *nearer* relatives of *other* thousands. They had parents, sisters, brothers;

sometimes (would it were not true) wives and infants. Suppose the young man whom temptation solicits, were not only to behold the wretched thousands already mentioned, but the many more thousands of dear relatives mourning their loss;—not by death, for that were tolerable—but by an everlasting destruction from the presence of all purity or excellence. Would he not shrink back from the door which he was about to enter, ashamed and aghast, and resolve in the strength of his Creator, never more to indulge a thought of a crime so disastrous in its consequences?

And let every one remember that the army of ruined immortals which have been here presented to the imagination, is by no means a mere fancy sketch. There is a day to come which will disclose a scene of which I have given but a faint picture. For though the thousands who have thus destroyed their own bodies and souls, with their agonized friends and relatives, are scattered among several millions of their fellow citizens, and, for a time, not a few of them elude the public gaze, yet their existence is much a reality, as if they were assembled in one place.

'All this,' it may be said, 'I have often heard, and it may be true. But it does not apply to me. I am in no danger. You speak of a path, I have never entered; or if I have ever done so, I have no idea of returning to it, habitually. I know my own strength; how far to go, and when and where to stop.'

But is there one of all the miserable, in the future world, who did not once think the same? Is there one among the thousands who have thus ruined themselves and those who had been as dear to them as themselves, that did not once feel a proud consciousness that he 'knew his own strength?' Yet now where is he?

Beware, then. Take not the first step. Nay, indulge not for an instant, the *thought* of a first step. Here you are safe. Every where else is danger. Take one step, and the next is more easy; the temptation harder to resist.

Do you call this preaching? Be it so then. I feel, and deeply too, that your immortal minds, those gems which were created to sparkle and shine in the firmament of heaven, are in danger of having their lustre for ever tarnished, and their brightness everlastingly hid beneath a thicker darkness than that which once covered the land of Egypt.

C. S. was educated by New England parents, in one of the most flourishing of New England villages. He was all that anxious friends could hope or desire; all that a happy community could love and esteem. As he rose to manhood he evinced a full share of 'Yankee' activity and enterprise. Some of the youth in the neighborhood were traders to the southern States, and C. concluded to try his fortune among the rest.

He was furnished with two excellent horses and a wagon, and every thing necessary to ensure success. His theatre of action was the low country of Virginia and North Carolina, and his head-quarters, N——, whither he used to return after an excursion of a month or six week, to spend a few days in that dissipated village.

Young C. gradually yielded to the temptations which the place afforded. First, he engaged in occasional 'drinking bouts,' next in gaming; lastly, he frequented a house of ill fame. This was about the year 1819.

At the end of the year 1820, I saw him, but—now changed! The eye that once beamed with health, and vigor, and cheerfulness, was now dimmed and flattened. The countenance which once shone with love and good-will to man, was pale and suspicious, or occasionally suffused with stagnant, and sickly, and crimson streams. The teeth, which were once as white as ivory, were now blackened by the use of poisonous medicine, given to counteract a still more poisonous and loathsome disease. The frame, which had once been as erect as the stately cedar of Lebanon, was, at the early age of thirty, beginning to bend as with years. The voice, which once spoke forth the sentiments of a soul of comparative purity, now not unfrequently gave vent to the licentious song, the impure jest, and the most shocking oaths, and heaven-daring impiety and blasphemy. The hands which were once like the spirit within, were now not unfrequently joined in the dance, with the vilest of the vile!

I looked, too, at his external circumstances Once he had friends whom he loved to see, and from whom he was glad to hear. Now it was a matter of indifference both to him and them whether they ever saw each other. The hopes of parents, and especially of 'her that bare him' were laid in the dust; and to the neighborhood of which he had once been the pride and the ornament, he was fast becoming as if he had never been.

He had travelled first with two horses, next with one; afterward on foot with a choice assortment of jewelry and other pedlar's wares; now his assortment was reduced to a mere handful. He could purchase to the value of a few dollars, take a short excursion, earn a small sum, and return—not to a respectable house, as once,—but to the lowest of resorts, to expend it.

Here, in 1821, I last saw him; a fair candidate for the worst contagious diseases which occasionally infest that region, and a pretty sure victim to the first severe attack. Or if he should even escape these, with the certainty before him of a very short existence, at best.

This is substantially the history of many a young man whose soul was once as spotless as that of C. S. Would that young men knew their strength, and their dignity; and would put forth but half the energy that God has given them. Then they would never approach the confines of those regions of dissipation, for when they have once entered them, the soul and the body are often ruined forever.

There are in every city hundreds of young men—I regret to say it,—who should heed this warning voice. *Now* they are happily situated, beloved, respected. They are engaged in useful and respectable avocations, and looking forward to brighter and better scenes. Let them beware lest there should be causes in operation, calculated to sap the foundations of the castle which fancy's eye has builded, (and which might even be realized); and lest their morning sun, which is now going forth in splendor, be not shrouded in darkness ere it has yet attained its meridian height.

Every city affords places and means of amusement, at once rational, satisfying, and improving. Such are collections of curiosities, natural and artificial, lectures on science, debating clubs, lyceums, &c. Then the libraries which abound, afford a source of never ending amusement and instruction. Let these suffice. At least, 'touch not, handle not' that which an accumulated and often sorrowful experience has shown to be accursed.

Neither resort to *solitary* vice. If this practice should not injure your system immediately, it will in the end. I am sorry to be obliged to advert to this subject; but I know there is occasion. Youth, especially those who lead a confined life, seek occasional excitement. Such sometimes resort to this lowest,—I may say most destructive of practices. Such is the constitution of things, as the Author of Nature has established it, that if every other vicious act were to escape its merited punishment in this world, the one in question could not. Whatever its votaries may think, it never fails, in a single instance, to injure them, personally; and consequently their posterity, should any succeed them.

It is not indeed true that the foregoing vices do of themselves, produce all this mischief *directly*; but as Dr. Paley has well said, *criminal intercourse* 'corrupts and *depraves the mind* more than any single vice whatsoever.' It gradually benumbs the conscience, and leads on, step by step, to those blacker vices at which the youth would once have shuddered.

But debasing as this vice is, it is scarcely more so than solitary gratification. The former is not always at hand; is attended, it may be, with expense; and with more or less danger of exposure. But the latter is practicable whenever temptation or rather imagination solicits, and appears to the morbid eye of sense, to be attended with no hazard. Alas! what a sad mistake is made here! It is a fact well established by medical men, that every error on this point is injurious; and that the constitution is often more surely or more effectually impaired by causes which do not appear to injure it in the least, than by occasional and heavier shocks, which rouse it to a reaction. The one case may be compared to daily *tippling*, the other to those *periodical* drunken frolics, which, having an interval of weeks or months between them, give the system time to recover, in part, (but *in part only*) from the violence it had sustained.

I wish to put the younger portion of my readers upon their guard against a set of wretches who take pains to initiate youth, while yet almost children, into the practice of the vice to which I have here adverted. Domestics—where the young are too familiar with them—*have* been known to be thus ungrateful to their employers. There are, however, people of several classes, who do not hesitate to mislead, in this manner.

But the misfortune is, that this book will not be apt to fall into the hands of those to whom *these* remarks apply, till the ruinous habit is already formed. And then it is that counsel sometimes comes too late. Should these pages meet the eye of any who have been misled, let them remember that they have begun a career which multitudes repent bitterly; and from which few are apt to return. But there have been instances of reform; therefore none ought to despair. 'What man has done, man may do.'

They should first set before their minds the nature of the practice, and the evils to which it exposes. But here comes the difficulty. What *are* its legitimate evils? They know indeed that the written laws of God condemn it; but the punishment which those laws threaten, appears to be remote and uncertain. Or if not, they are apt to regard it as the punishment of *excess*, merely. *They*, prudent souls, would not, for the world, plunge into excess. Besides, '*they* injure none but *themselves*,' they tell us.

Would it were true that they injured none but *themselves*! Would there were no generations yet unborn to suffer by inheriting feeble constitutions, or actual disease, from their progenitors!

Suppose, however, they really injured nobody but themselves. Have they a right to do even this? They will not maintain, for one moment, that they have a right to take away their own life. By what right, then, do they allow themselves to shorten it, or diminish its happiness while it lasts?

Here the question recurs again: *Does* solitary gratification actually shorten life, or diminish its happiness?

The very fact that the laws of God forbid it, is an affirmative answer to this question. For nothing is more obvious than that all other vices which that law condemns, stand in the way of our present happiness, as well as the happiness of futurity. Is this alone an exception to the general rule?

But I need not make my appeal to this kind of authority. You rely on human testimony. You believe a thousand things which yourselves never saw or heard. *Why* do you believe them, *except* upon testimony—I mean given either verbally, or, what is the same thing, in books?

Now if the accumulated testimony of medical writers from the days of Galen, and Celsus, and Hippocrates, to the present hour, could have any weight with you, it would settle the point at once. I have collected, briefly, the results of medical testimony on this subject, in the next chapter; but if you will take my statements for the present, I will assure you that I *have before me* documents enough to fill half a volume like this, from those who have studied deeply these subjects, whose united language is, that the practice in question, indulged in *any degree*, is destructive to body and mind; and that although, in vigorous young men, no striking evil may for some time appear, yet the punishment can no more be *evaded*, except by early death, than the motion of the earth can be hindered. And all this, too, without taking into consideration the terrors of a judgment to come.

But why, then, some may ask, are animal propensities given us, if they are not to be indulged? The appropriate reply is, they *are* to be indulged; but it is only in accordance with the laws of God; never otherwise. And the wisdom of these laws, did they not rest on other and better proof, is amply confirmed by that great body of medical experience already mentioned. God has delegated to man, a sort of *subcreative* power to perpetuate his own race. Such a wonderful work required a wonderful apparatus. And such is furnished. The texture of the organs for this purpose is of the most tender and delicate kind, scarcely equalled by that of the eye, and quite as readily injured; and this fact ought to be known, and considered. But instead of leaving to human choice or caprice the execution of the power thus delegated, the great Creator has made it a matter of *duty*; and has connected with the lawful discharge of that duty, as with all others, *enjoyment*. But when this enjoyment is sought in any way, not in accordance with the laws prescribed by reason and revelation, we diminish (whatever giddy youth may suppose,) the sum total of our own happiness. Now this is not the cold speculation of age, or monkish austerity. It is sober matter of fact.

It is said that young men are sometimes in circumstances which forbid their conforming to these laws, were they disposed to do so.

Not so often however, as is commonly supposed. Marriage is not such a mountain of difficulty as many imagine. This I have already attempted to show. One circumstance to be considered, in connection with this subject, is, that in any society, the more there is of criminal indulgence, whether secret or social, the more strongly are excuses for neglecting matrimony urged. Every step which a young man takes in forbidden paths, affords him a plea in behalf of the next. The farther he goes, the less the probability of his returning to the ways of purity, or entering those of domestic felicity.

People in such places as London and Paris, marry much later in life, upon the average, than in country places. And is not the cause obvious? And is not the same cause beginning to produce similar effects in our own American cities?

But suppose celibacy in some cases, to *be* unavoidable, can a life of continence, in the fullest sense of the term, be favorable to *health*? This question is answered by those to whose writings I have already referred, in the affirmative. But it is also answered by facts, though from the nature of the case these facts are not always easy of access. We have good reason to believe that Sir Isaac Newton and Dr. Fothergill, never for once in their lives deviated from the strict laws of rectitude on this point. And we have no evidence that they were sufferers for their rigid course of virtue. The former certainly enjoyed a measure of health and reached an age, to which few, in any circumstances, attain; and the latter led an active and useful life to nearly three-score and ten. There are living examples of the same purity of character, but they cannot, of course, be mentioned in this work.

Several erroneous views in regard to the animal economy which have led to the very general opinion that a life of celibacy—strictly so, I mean—cannot be a life of health, might here be exposed, did either the limits or the nature of the work permit. It is not that a state of celibacy—entirely so, I always mean—is positively *injurious*; but that a state of matrimony is more *useful*; and, as a general rule, attended with *more happiness*.

It is most ardently to be hoped, that the day is not far distant when every young man will study the laws and functions of the human frame for himself. This would do more towards promoting individual purity and public happiness, than all the reasoning in the world can accomplish without it. Men, old or young, must see for themselves how 'fearfully' as well as 'wonderfully' they are made, before they can have a thorough and abiding conviction of the nature of *disobedience*, or of the penalties that attend, as well as follow it. And in proportion, as the subject is studied and understood, may we not hope celibacy will become less frequent, and marriage—honorable, and, if you please, *early* marriage—be more highly estimated?

This work is not addressed to parents; but should it be read by any who have sons, at an age, and in circumstances, which expose them to temptation, and in a way which will be very apt to secure their fall, let them beware.[14]

Still, the matter must be finally decided by the young themselves. They, in short, must determine the question whether they will rise in the scale of being, through every period of their existence, or sink lower and lower in the depths of degradation and wo. They must be, after all, the arbiters of their own fate. No influences, human or divine, will ever *force* them to happiness.

The remainder of this section will be devoted to remarks on the causes which operate to form licentious feelings and habits in the young. My limits, however, will permit me to do little more than mention them. And if some of them might be addressed with more force to parents than to young men, let it be remembered that the young *may be* parents, and if they cannot recall the past, and correct the errors in their own education, they can, at least, hope to prevent the same errors in the education of others.

1. FALSE DELICACY. - Too much of real delicacy can never be inculcated; but in our early management, we seem to implant the *false*, instead of the true. The language we use, in answering the curious questions of children, often leads to erroneous associations of ideas; and it is much better to be silent. By the falsehoods which we think it necessary to tell, we often excite still greater curiosity, instead of satisfying that which already exists. I will not undertake to decide what ought to be done; but *silence*, I am certain, would be far better than falsehood.

There is another error, which is laid deeper still, because it begins earlier. I refer to the half Mohammedan practice of separating the two sexes at school. This practice, I am aware has strong advocates; but it seems to me they cannot have watched closely the early operations of their own minds, and observed how curiosity was awakened, and wanton imaginations fostered by distance, and apparent and needless reserve.

2. LICENTIOUS BOOKS, PICTURES, &C. - This unnatural reserve, and the still more unnatural falsehoods already mentioned, prepare the youthful mind for the reception of any thing which has the semblance of information on the points to which curiosity is directed. And now comes the danger. The world abounds in impure publications, which almost all children, (boys especially,) at sometime or other, contrive to get hold of, in spite of parental vigilance. If these books contained truth, and nothing but truth, their clandestine circulation would do less mischief. But they generally impart very little information which is really valuable; on the contrary they contain much falsehood; especially when they profess to instruct on certain important subjects. Let me repeat it then, they cannot be relied on; and in the language of another book, on another subject; 'He that trusteth' to them, 'is a fool.'

The same remarks might be extended, and with even more justice, to licentious paintings and engravings, which circulate in various ways. And I am sorry to include in this charge not a few which are publicly exhibited for sale, in the windows of our shops. You may sometimes find obscene pictures under cover of a watch-case or snuff box. In short, there would often seem to be a general combination of human and infernal efforts to render the juvenile thoughts and affections impure; and not a few parents themselves enter into the horrible league.

On this subject Dr. Dwight remarks; 'The numbers of the poet, the delightful melody of song, the fascination of the chisel, and the spell of the pencil, have been all volunteered in the service of Satan for the moral destruction of unhappy man. To finish this work of malignity the stage has lent all its splendid apparatus of mischief; the shop has been converted into a show-box of temptations; and its owner into a pander of iniquity.' And in another place; 'Genius, in every age, and in every country, has, to a great extent, prostituted its elevated powers for the deplorable purpose of seducing thoughtless minds to *this sin.*' Are these remarks too sweeping? In my own opinion, not at all. Let him, who doubts, take a careful survey of the whole of this dangerous ground.

3. OBSCENE AND IMPROPER SONGS. - The prostitution of the melody of song, mentioned by Dr. Dwight, reminds me of another serious evil. Many persons, and even not a few intelligent parents, seem to think that a loose or immoral song cannot much injure their children, especially if they

express their disapprobation of it afterwards. As if the language of the tongue could give the lie to the language of the heart, already written, and often deeply, in the eye and countenance. For it is notorious that a considerable proportion of parents tolerate songs containing very improper sentiments, and hear them with obvious interest, how much soever they may wish their children to have a better and purer taste. The common 'love songs' are little better than those already mentioned.

It is painful to think what errors on this subject are sometimes tolerated even by decent society. I knew a schoolmaster who did not hesitate to join occasional parties, (embracing, among others, professedly Christian parents,) for the purpose of spending his long winter evenings, in hearing songs from a very immoral individual, not a few of which were adapted to the most corrupt taste, and unfit to be heard in good society. Yet the community in which he taught was deemed a religious community; and the teacher himself prayed in his school, morning and evening! Others I have known to conduct even worse, though perhaps not quite so openly.

I mention these things, not to reproach teachers,—for I think their moral character, in this country, generally, far better than their intellectual,—but as a specimen of perversion in the public sentiment; and also as a hint to all who have the care of the young. Pupils at school, cannot fail to make correct inferences from such facts as the foregoing.

4. DOUBLE ENTENDRES.[15] - By this is meant seemingly *decent speeches, with double meanings.* I mention these because they prevail, in some parts of the country, to a most alarming degree; and because parents seem to regard them as perfectly harmless. Shall I say—to show the extent of the evil—that they are sometimes heard from both parents? Now no serious observer of human life and conduct can doubt that by every species of impure language, whether in the form of hints, innuendoes, double entendres, or plainer speech, impure thoughts are awakened, a licentious imagination inflamed, and licentious purposes formed, which would otherwise never have existed. Of all such things an inspired writer has long ago said—and the language is still applicable;—'Let them not be so much as named among you.'

I have been in families where these loose insinuations, and coarse innuendoes were so common, that the presence of respectable company scarcely operated as a restraint upon the unbridled tongues, even of the parents! Many of these things had been repeated so often, and under such circumstances that the children, at a very early age, perfectly understood their meaning and import. Yet had these very same children asked for direct information, at this time, on the subjects which had been rendered familiar to them thus incidentally, the parents would have startled; and would undoubtedly have repeated to them part of a string of falsehoods, with which they had been in the habit of attempting to 'cover up' these matters; though with the effect, in the end, of rendering the children only so much the more curious and inquisitive.

But this is not all. The filling of the juvenile mind, long before nature brings the body to maturity, with impure imaginations, not only preoccupies the ground which is greatly needed for something else, and fills it with shoots of a noxious growth, but actually induces, if I may so say, a *precocious maturity.* What I mean, is, that there arises a morbid or diseased state of action of the vessels of the sexual system, which paves the way for premature physical developement, and greatly increases the danger of youthful irregularity.

5. EVENING PARTIES. - One prolific source of licentious feeling and action may be found, I think, in evening parties, especially when protracted to a late hour. It has always appeared to me that the injury to health which either directly or indirectly grows out of evening parties, was a sufficient objection to their recurrence, especially when the assembly is crowded, the room greatly heated, or when music and dancing are the accompaniments. Not a few young ladies, who after perspiring freely at the latter exercise, go out into the damp night air, in a thin dress, contract consumption; and both sexes are very much exposed, in this way, to colds, rheumatisms, and fevers.

But the great danger, after all, is to reputation and morals. Think of a group of one hundred young ladies and gentlemen assembling at evening, and under cover of the darkness, joining in conclave, and heating themselves with exercise and refreshments of an exciting nature, such as coffee, tea, wine, &c, and in some parts of our country with diluted distilled spirit; and 'keeping up the steam,' as it is sometimes called, till twelve or one o'clock, and frequently during the greater part of the night. For what kind and degree of *vice*, do not such scenes prepare those who are concerned in them?

Nothing which is here said is intended to be levelled against dancing, in itself considered; but only against such a use, or rather *abuse* of it as is made to inflame and feed impure imaginations and bad passions. On the subject of dancing as an amusement, I have already spoken in another part of the work.

I have often wondered why the strange opinion has come to prevail, especially among the industrious yeomanry of the interior of our country, that it is economical to turn night into day, in this manner. Because they cannot very well spare their sons or apprentices in the daytime, as they suppose, they suffer them to go abroad in the evening, and perhaps to be out all night, when it may justly be questioned whether the loss of energy which they sustain does not result in a loss of effort during one or two subsequent days, at least equal to the waste of a whole afternoon. I am fully convinced, on my own part, that he who should give up to his son or hired laborer an afternoon, would actually lose a less amount of labor, taking the week together, than he who should only give up for this purpose the hours which nature intended should be spent in sleep.

But—I repeat it—the moral evil outweighs all other considerations. It needs not an experience of thirty years, nor even of twenty, to convince even a careless observer that no small number of our youth of both sexes, have, through the influence of late evening parties, gone down to the chambers of drunkenness and debauchery; and, with the young man mentioned by Solomon, descended through them to those of death and hell.

It may be worth while for those sober minded and, otherwise, judicious Christians, who are in the habit of attending fashionable parties at late hours, and taking their 'refreshments,' to consider whether they may not be a means of keeping up, by their example, those more vulgar assemblies, with all their grossness, which I have been describing. Is it not obvious that what the *wine*, and the fruit, and the oysters, are to the more refined and Christian circles, wine and fermented liquors may be to the more blunt sensibilities of body and mind, in youthful circles of another description? But if so, where rests the guilt? Or shall we bless the fountains, while we curse the stream they form?

SECTION III. *Diseases of Licentiousness.* - The importance of this and the foregoing section will be differently estimated by different individuals. They were not inserted, however, without consideration, nor without the approbation of persons who enjoy a large measure of public confidence. The young ought at least to know, briefly, to what a formidable host of maladies secret vice is exposed.

1. *Insanity.* The records of hospitals show that insanity, from solitary indulgence, is common. Tissot, Esquirol, Eberle, and others, give ample testimony on this point. The latter, from a careful examination of the facts, assures us that in Paris the proportion of insane persons whose diseases may be traced to the source in question, is *one* in from *fifty-one* to *fifty-eight*, in the *lower classes*. In the higher classes it is *one* in *twenty-three*. In the insane Hospital of Massachusetts—I have it from authority which I cannot question,—the proportion is at least one in three or four. At present there are about twenty cases of the kind alluded to.

2. *Chorea Sancti Viti*, or *St. Vitus's dance*. This strange disease, in which the muscles of the body are not always at the command of the patient, and in which the head, the arms, the legs, and indeed every part which is made for muscular motion often jerks about in a very singular manner, is sometimes produced in the same way. Insanity and this disease are occasionally combined. I have known one young man in this terrible condition, and have read authentic accounts of others.

3. *Epilepsy.* Epileptic or *falling sickness fits*, as they are sometimes denominated, are another very common scourge of secret vice. How much they are to be dreaded almost every one can judge; for there are few who have not seen those who are afflicted with them. They usually weaken the mind, and sometimes entirely destroy it. I knew one epileptic individual who used to dread them more than death; and would gladly have preferred the latter.

4. *Idiotism.* Epilepsy, as I have already intimated, often runs on to idiotism; but sometimes the miserable young man becomes an idiot, without the intervention of any other obvious disease.

5. *Paralysis* or *Palsy*, is no uncommon punishment of this transgression. There are, however, several forms of this disease. Sometimes, a slight numbness of a single toe or finger is the first symptom of its approach; but at others a whole hand, arm, or leg is affected. In the present case, the first attacks are not very violent, as if to give the offender opportunity to return to the path of rectitude. Few, however, take the hint and return, till the chains of their slavery are riveted, and their health destroyed by this or some other form of disease. I have seen dissipated young men who complained of the numbness of a finger or two and the corresponding portion of the hand and wrist, who probably did not themselves suspect the cause; but I never knew the disorder permanently removed, except by a removal of the cause which produced it.

6. *Apoplexy.* This has occasionally happened; though more rarely.

7. *Blindness*, in some of its forms, especially of that form usually called *gutta serena*, should also be added to our dark catalogue. Indeed a weakness of sight is among the first symptoms that supervene on these occasions.

8. *Hypochondria.* This is as much a disease by itself as the small pox, though many regard it otherwise. The mind is diseased, and the individual has many imaginary sufferings, it is true; but the

imagination would not be thus unnaturally awake, if there were no accompanying disturbance in the bodily functions. Hypochondria, in its more aggravated forms, is a very common result of secret vice.

9. *Phthisis*, or consumption, is still more frequently produced by the cause we are considering, than any other disease I have mentioned. And we know well the history of this disease; that, though slow in its progress, the event is certain. In this climate, it is one of the most destructive scourges of our race. If the ordinary diseases slay their thousands, consumption slays its tens of thousands. Its approach is gradual, and often unsuspected; and the decline to the grave sometimes unattended by any considerable suffering. Is it not madness to expose ourselves to its attacks for the shortlived gratifications of a moment?

There is indeed a peculiar form of this disease which, in the case in question, is more commonly produced than any other. It is called, in the language of physicians, *tabes dorsalis*, or *dorsal* consumption; because it is supposed to arise from the *dorsal* portion of the spinal marrow. This disease sometimes, it is true, attacks young married people, especially where they go *beyond* the bounds which the Author of nature intended; and it is occasionally produced by other causes entirely different; causes, too, which it would be difficult, if not impossible to prevent. Generally, however, it is produced by *solitary vice*.

The most striking symptom of this disease is described as being a 'sensation of ants, crawling from the head down along the spine;' but this sensation is not always felt, for sometimes in its stead there is, rather, a very great weakness of the small part of the back, attended with pain. This is accompanied with emaciation, and occasionally, though not always, with an irregular appetite. Indeed, persons affected with this disease generally have a good appetite. There is usually little fever, or at most only a slight heat and thirst towards evening, with occasional flushings of the face; and still more rarely, profuse perspirations in the latter part of the night. But the latter symptom belongs more properly to common consumption. The sight, as I have already mentioned, grows dim; they have pains in the head and sometimes ringing in the ears, and a loss of memory. Finally, the legs become weak, the kidneys and stomach suffer, and many other difficulties arise which I cannot mention in this work, followed often by an acute fever; and unless the abominable practice which produced all the mischief is abandoned, death follows. But when many of the symptoms which I have mentioned, are really fastened upon an individual, he has sustained an injury which can never be wholly repaired. All he can hope is to prolong his days, and lengthen out his life—often a distressing one. A few well authenticated examples of persons who debased themselves by secret vice, will, I hope, satisfy those who doubt the evils of this practice.

One young man thus expressed his sufferings to his physician. 'My very great debility renders the performance of every motion difficult. That of my legs is often so great, that I can scarcely stand erect; and I fear to leave my chamber. Digestion is so imperfect that the food passes unchanged, three or four hours after it has been taken into the stomach. I am oppressed with phlegm, the presence of which causes pain; and the expectoration, exhaustion. This is a brief history of my miseries. Each day brings with it an increase of all my woes. Nor do I believe that any human creature ever suffered more. Without a special interposition of Divine Providence, I cannot support so painful an existence.'

Another thus writes; 'Were I not restrained by *sentiments* of *religion*,[16] I should ere this have put an end to my existence; which is the more insupportable as it is caused by myself.'

'I cannot walk two hundred paces,' says another 'without resting myself; my feebleness is extreme; I have constant pains in every part of the body, but particularly in the shoulders and chest. My appetite is good, but this is a misfortune, since what I eat causes pains in my stomach, and is vomited up. If I read a page or two, my eyes are filled with tears and become painful:—I often sigh involuntarily.'

A fourth says; 'I rest badly at night, and am much troubled with dreams. The lower part of my back is weak, my eyes are often painful, and my eyelids swelled and red. I have an almost constant cold; and an oppression at the stomach. In short, I had rather be laid in the silent tomb, and encounter that dreadful uncertainty, *hereafter*, than remain in my present unhappy and degraded situation.'

The reader should remember that the persons whose miseries are here described, were generally sufferers from *hypochondria*. They had not advanced to the still more horrid stages of palsy, apoplexy, epilepsy, idiotism, St. Vitus's dance, blindness, or insanity. But they had gone so far, that another step in the same path, might have rendered a return impossible.

The reader will spare me the pain of presenting, in detail, any more of these horrid cases. I write for YOUNG MEN, the strength—the bone, muscle, sinew, and nerve—of our beloved country. I write for those who,—though some of them may have erred—are glad to be advised, and if they deem the advice good, are anxious to follow it. I write, too, in vain, if it be not for young men who will resolve on reformation, when they believe that their present and future happiness is at stake. And, lastly, I have not read correctly the pages in the book of human nature if I do not write for those who can, with God's help, keep every good resolution.

There are a few publications to which those who are awake to the importance of this subject, might safely be directed. One or two will be mentioned presently. It is true that their authors have, in some instances, given us the details of such cases of disease as occur but rarely. Still, what has happened, in this respect, may happen again. And as no moderate drinker of fermented or spirituous liquors can ever know, with certainty, that if he continues his habit, he may not finally arrive at confirmed drunkenness, and the worst diseases which attend it, so no person who departs but once from rectitude in the matter before us, has any assurance that he shall not sooner or later suffer all the evils which they so faithfully describe.

When a young man, who is pursuing an unhappy course of solitary vice, threatened as we have seen by the severest penalties earth or heaven can impose,—begins to perceive a loss or irregularity of his appetite; acute pains in his stomach, especially during digestion, and constant vomitings;—when to this is added a weakness of the lungs, often attended by a dry cough, hoarse weak voice, and hurried or difficult breathing after using considerable exertion, with a general relaxation of the nervous system;—when these appearances, or symptoms, as physicians call them, take place—let him *beware!* for punishment of a severer kind cannot be distant.

I hope I shall have no reader to whom these remarks apply; but should it be otherwise, happy will it be for him if he takes the alarm, and walks not another step in the downward road to certain and terrible retribution. Happiest, however, is he who has never erred from the first; and who reads these pages as he reads of those awful scenes in nature,—the devastations of the lightning, the deluge, the tornado, the earthquake, and the volcano; as things to be lamented, and their horrors if possible mitigated or averted, but with which he has little personal concern.

Sympathizing, however, with his fellow beings—for though *fallen*, they still belong to the same family—should any reader who sees this work, wish to examine the subject still more intimately, I recommend to him a Lecture to Young Men, lately published in Providence. I would also refer him, to Rees' Cyclopedia, art. *Physical Education*.

The article last referred to is so excellent, that I have decided on introducing, in this place, the closing paragraph. The writer had been treating the subject, much in the manner I have done, only at greater length, and had enumerated the diseases to which it leads, at the same time insisting on the importance of informing the young, in a proper manner, of their danger, wherever the urgency of the case required it. After quoting numerous passages of Scripture, which, in speaking of impurity, evidently include this practice, and denouncing it in severe terms, he closes with the following striking remarks.

'There can be no doubt that God has forbidden it by the usual course of providence. Its moral effects, in destroying the purity of the mind, in swallowing up its best affections, and perverting its sensibilities into this depraved channel, are among its most injurious consequences; and are what render it so peculiarly difficult to eradicate the evil. In proportion as the habit strengthens the difficulty of breaking it, of course, increases; and while the tendency of the feelings to this point increases, the vigor of the mind to effect the conquest of the habit gradually lessens.

'We would tell him (the misguided young man) that whatever might be said in newspapers respecting the power of medicine in such cases, nothing could be done without absolute self-control; and that no medicine whatever could retrieve the mischiefs which the want of it had caused: and that the longer the practice was continued, the greater would be the bodily and mental evils it would inevitably occasion.

'We would then advise him to avoid all situations in which he found his propensities excited; and especially, as far as possible, all in which they had been gratified; to check the thoughts and images which excited them; to shun those associates, or at least that conversation, and those books, which have the same effect; to avoid all stimulating food and liquor; to sleep cool on a hard bed; to rise early, and at once; and to go to bed when likely to fall asleep at once; to let his mind be constantly occupied, though not exerted to excess; and to let his bodily powers be actively employed, every day, to a degree which will make a hard bed the place of sound repose.

'Above all, we would urge him to impress his mind (at times when the mere thought of it would not do him harm) with a feeling of horror at the practice; to dwell upon its sinfulness and most injurious effects; and to cultivate, by every possible means, an habitual sense of the constant presence of a holy and heart-searching God, and a lively conviction of the awful effects of his displeasure.'

I should be sorry to leave an impression on any mind that other forms of licentiousness are innocent, or that they entail no evils on the constitution. I have endeavored to strike most forcibly, it is true, at solitary vice; but it was for this plain reason, that few of the young seem to regard it as any crime at all. Some even consider it indispensable to health. This belief I have endeavored to shake; with how much success, eternity only can determine.

Of the guilt of those forms of irregularity, in which *more* than one individual and sex are *necessarily* concerned, many of the young are already apprized. At least they are generally acquainted with the more prominent evils which result from what they call excess. Still if followed in what they deem moderation, and with certain precautions which could be named, not a few are ready to believe, at least in the moment of temptation, that there is no great harm in following their inclinations.

Now in regard to what constitutes excess, every one who is not moved by Christian principle, will of necessity, have his own standard, just as it is in regard to solitary vice, or the use of ardent spirits. And herein consists a part of the guilt. And it is not till this conviction of our constant tendency to establish an incorrect standard for ourselves, and to go, in the end, to the greatest lengths and depths and heights of guilt, can be well established in our minds, that we shall ever be induced to avoid the first steps in that road which may end in destruction; and to take as the only place of safety, the high ground of total abstinence.

But although the young are not wholly destitute of a sense of the evils of what they call excess, and of the shame of what is well known to be its frequent and formidable results,—so far as themselves are concerned,—yet they seem wholly ignorant of any considerable danger short of this. For so far are they from admitting that the force of conscience is weakened by every repeated known and wilful transgression, many think, (as I have already stated) promiscuous intercourse, where no matrimonial rights are invaded, if it be so managed as to exempt the parties immediately concerned from all immediate suffering both moral and physical, can scarcely be called a transgression, at all.

I wish it were practicable to extend these remarks far enough to show, as plain as noon-day light can make it, that every criminal act of this kind—I mean every instance of irregularity—not only produces evil to society generally, in the present generation, but also inflicts evil on those that follow. For to say nothing of those horrid cases where the infants of licentious parents not only inherit vicious dispositions, but ruined bodies—even to a degree, that in some instances excludes a possibility of the child's surviving many days;—there are other forms of disease often entailed on the young which as certainly consign the sufferer to an early grave, though the passage thither may be more tedious and lingering.

How must it wring the heart of a feeling young parent to see his first born child, which for any thing he knows, might have been possessed of a sound and vigorous body, like other children, enter the world with incipient scrofula, diseased joints or bones, and eruptive diseases, in some of their worst forms? Must not the sight sink him to the very dust? And would he not give worlds—had he worlds to give—to reverse those irreversible but inscrutable decrees of Heaven, which visit the sins of parents upon their descendants—'unto the third and fourth generation?'

But how easy is it, by timely reflection, and fixed moral principle, to prevent much of that disease which 'worlds' cannot wholly cure, when it is once inflicted!

I hazard nothing in saying, then—and I might appeal to the whole medical profession to sustain me in my assertion—that no person whose system ever suffers, once, from those forms of disease which approach nearest to the character of special judgments of Heaven on sin or shame, can be sure of ever wholly recovering from their effects on his own person; and what is still worse, can ever be sure of being the parent of a child whose constitution shall be wholly untainted with disease, of one kind or another.

This matter is not often understood by the community generally; especially by the young. I might tell them of the diseased eyesight; the ulcerated—perhaps deformed—nose and ears, and neck; the discoloration, decay, and loss of teeth; the destruction of the palate, and the fearful inroads of disease on many other soft parts of the body; besides the softening and ulceration and decay and eventual destruction of the bones; and to crown all, the awfully offensive breath and perspiration; and I might entreat them to abstain, in the fear of God, from those abuses of the constitution which not unfrequently bring down upon them such severe forms of punishment.

A thorough knowledge of the human system and the laws to which all organized bodies are subjected, would, in this respect, do much in behalf of mankind; for such would be the change of public sentiment, that the sensual could not hold up their heads so boldly, as they now do, in the face of it. Happy for mankind when the vicious shall be obliged, universally, to pass in review before this enlightened tribunal!

Young men ought to study physiology. It is indeed to be regretted that there are so few books on this subject adapted to popular use. But in addition to those recommended at page 346, there are portions of several works which may be read with advantage by the young. Such are some of the more intelligible parts of Richerand's Physiology, as at page 38 of the edition with Dr. Chapman's notes; and of the 'Outlines of Physiology,' and the 'Anatomical Class Book,' two works recently issued in Boston. It must, however, be confessed, that none of these works are sufficiently divested of technicalities, to be well adapted, as a whole, to the general reader. Physiology is one of those fountains at which it is somewhat dangerous to 'taste,' unless we 'drink deep;' on account of the tendency of superficial knowledge to empiricism. Still, I am fully of the opinion that even superficial knowledge, on this long neglected topic, is less dangerous both to the individual and to the community, than entire ignorance.

And after all, the best guides would be PARENTS. When will Heaven confer such favors upon us? When will parents become parents indeed? When will one father or mother in a hundred, exercise the true parental prerogative, and point out to those whom God has given them, as circumstances may from time to time demand, the most dangerous rocks and whirlpools to which, in the voyage of life, they are exposed? When will every thing else be done for the young rather than that which ought never to be left undone?

Say not, young reader, that I am wandering. You may be a father. God grant that if you are, you may also act the parent. Let me beg you to resolve, and if necessary re-resolve. And not only resolve, but act. If you are ready to pronounce me enthusiastic on this subject, let me beg you to suspend your judgment till the responsibilities and the duties and the anxieties of a parent thicken round you.

It is painful to see—every where—the most unquestionable evidence that this department of education is unheeded. Do you ask how the evidence is obtained? I answer by asking you how the physician can discover,—as undoubtedly he can,—the progress of the drinker of spirituous liquors, by his eye, his features, his breath, nay his very perspiration. And do you think that the sons or daughters of sensuality, in any of its forms, and at any of its stages, can escape his observation?

But of what use is his knowledge, if he may not communicate it? What person would endure disclosures of this kind respecting himself or his nearest, perhaps his dearest and most valued friends? No! the physician's lips must be sealed, and his tongue dumb; and the young must go down to their graves, rather than permit him to make any effort to save them, lest offence should be given!

The subject is, however, gaining a hold on the community, for which none of us can be too thankful. I am acquainted with more than one parent, who is a parent indeed; for there is no more reserve on these subjects, than any other. The sons do not hesitate to ask parental counsel and seek parental aid, in every known path of temptation. Heaven grant that such instances may be speedily multiplied. A greater work of reform can scarcely be desired or anticipated.

But I must draw to a close. Oh that the young 'wise,' and that they would 'consider!' 'There is a way which seemeth right unto a man, but the end thereof is death.'

There is, then, but one course for the young. Let them do that which they know to be right, and avoid not only that which they are sure is wrong, but that also of which they have *doubts.* Let them do this, moreover, in the fear and love of God. In the language of a great statesman of the United States to his nephew, a little before his death, let me exhort you, to 'Give up property, *give up every thing—give up even life itself, rather than presume to do an immoral act.*' Let me remind you too, of the declaration of that Wisdom which is Infinite;—'HE THAT SINNETH AGAINST GOD, DESTROYETH HIS OWN SOUL.'

# CHAPTER VIII

SECTION I. *Choice of Friends.* - The importance, to a young man, of a few worthy female friends, has been mentioned in Chapter V. But to him who aspires at the highest possible degree of improvement or usefulness, a select number of confidential friends of his own sex is scarcely less valuable.

Great caution is however necessary in making the selection. "A man is known by the company he keeps," has long since passed into a proverb; so well does it accord with universal experience. And yet many a young man neglects or despises this maxim, till his reputation is absolutely and irretrievably lost.

Lucius was a remarkable instance of this kind. Extremely diffident, he was introduced to a neighborhood where every individual but one was an entire stranger to him; and this person was one whose character was despised. But what is life without associates? Few are wholly destitute of sympathy, even brute animals. Lucius began to be found in the company of the young man I have mentioned; and this too in spite of the faithful and earnest remonstrances of his friends, who foresaw the consequences. But, like too many inexperienced young men, conscious of his own purity of intention, he thought there could surely be no harm in occasional walks and conversations with even a bad man; and who knows, he sometimes used to say, but I may do him good? At any rate, as he was the only person with whom he could hold free conversation on "things that were past," he determined occasionally to associate with him.

But as it is with many a young lady who has set out with the belief that a reformed rake makes the best husband, so it was with Lucius; he found that the work of reforming the vicious was no easy task. Instead of making the smallest approaches to success, he perceived at last, when it was too late, that his familiarity with young Frederick had not only greatly lowered him in the estimation of the people with whom he now resided, but even in the estimation of Frederick himself; who was encouraged to pursue his vicious course, by the consideration that it did not exclude him from the society of those who were universally beloved and respected.

This anecdote shows how cautious we ought to be in the choice of friends. Had Lucius been a minister or reformer by profession, he could have gone among the vicious to reclaim them, with less danger. The Saviour of mankind ate and drank with "publicans and sinners;" but HE was well *known* as going among them to save them, though even he did not wholly escape obloquy.

Few are aware, how much they are the creatures of imitation; and how readily they catch the manners, habits of expression, and even modes of thinking, of those whose company they keep. Let the young remember, then, that it is not from the remarks of others, alone, that they are likely to suffer; but that they are *really* lowered in the scale of excellence, every time they come in unguarded contact with the vicious.

It is of the highest importance to seek for companions those who are not only *intelligent* and *virtuous*, in the common acceptation of the term, but, if it were possible, those who are a little above them, especially in *moral excellence.*

Nor is this so difficult a task as many suppose. There are in every community, a few who would make valuable companions. Not that they are perfect,—for perfection, in the more absolute sense of the term, belongs not to humanity; but their characters are such, that they would greatly improve yours. And remember, that it is by no means indispensable that your circle of intimate friends be very large. Nay, it is not even desirable, in a world like this. You may have many acquaintances, but I should advise you to have but few near friends. If you have one, who is what he should be, you are comparatively happy.

SECTION II. *Rudeness of Manners.* - By rudeness I do not mean mere coarseness or rusticity, for that were more pardonable; but a want of civility. In this sense of the term, I am prepared to censure one practice, which in the section on *Politeness,* was overlooked. I refer to the practice so common with young men in some circumstances and places, of wearing their hats or caps in the house;—a practice which, whenever and wherever it occurs, is decidedly reprehensible.

Most of us have probably seen state legislatures in session with their hats on. This does not look well for the representatives of the most civil communities in the known world; and though I do not pretend that in this respect they fairly represent their constituents, yet I do maintain that the toleration of such a practice implies a dereliction of the public sentiment.

That the practice of uncovering the head, whenever we are in the house, tends to promote health, though true, I do not at this time affirm. It is sufficient for my present purpose, if I succeed in showing that the contrary practice tends to vice and immorality.

Who has not seen the rudeness of a company of men, assembled perhaps in a bar-room—with their hats on; and also witnessed the more decent behavior of another similar group, assembled in similar circumstances, without perceiving at once a connection between the hats and the rudeness of the one company, as well as between the more orderly behavior and the uncovered heads of the other?

To come to individuals. Attend a party or concert—no matter about the name;—I mean some place where it is pardonable, or rather *deemed* pardonable, to wear the hat. Who behave in the most gentle, christian manner,—the few who wear their hats or those who take them off? In a family or school, which are the children that are most civil and well behaved? Is it not those who are most scrupulous, always, to appear within the house with their heads uncovered? Nay, in going out of schools, churches, &c., who are they that put on their hats first, as if it was a work of self-denial to hold them in their hands, or even suffer them to remain in their place till the blessing is pronounced, or till the proper time has arrived for using them?

Once more. In passing through New England or any other part of the United States, entering into the houses of the people, and seeing them just as they are, who has not been struck with the fact that where there is the most of wearing hats and caps in the house, there is generally the most of ill manners, not to say of vicious habits and conduct.

Few are sufficiently aware of the influence of what they often affect to despise as little things. But I have said enough on this point in its proper place. The great difficulty is in carrying the principles there inculcated into the various conditions of life, and properly applying them.

SECTION III. *Self-praise.* - Some persons are such egotists that rather than not be conspicuous, they will even speak *ill* of themselves. This may seem like a contradiction; but it is nevertheless a truth.

Such conduct is explicable in two ways. Self condemnation may be merely an attempt to extort praise from the bystanders, by leading them to deny our statements, or defend our conduct. Or, it may be an attempt to set ourselves off as abounding in self knowledge; a kind of knowledge which is universally admitted to be difficult of attainment. I have heard people condemn their past conduct in no measured terms, who would not have borne a tithe of the same severity of remark from others. Perhaps it is not too much to affirm that persons of this description are often among the vainest, if not the proudest of the community.

In general, it is the best way to say as little about ourselves, our friends, our books, and our circumstances as possible. It is soon enough to speak of ourselves when we are compelled to do it in our own defence.

2862621R00078

Made in the USA
San Bernardino, CA
11 June 2013